THE WILD HOG MURDERS

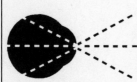

This Large Print Book carries the
Seal of Approval of N.A.V.H.

A DAN RHODES MYSTERY

THE WILD HOG MURDERS

BILL CRIDER

THORNDIKE PRESS

A part of Gale, Cengage Learning

GALE
CENGAGE Learning·

Detroit • New York • San Francisco • New Haven, Conn • Waterville, Maine • London

GALE
CENGAGE Learning™

LIBRARY OF CONGRESS CATALOGING-IN-PUBLICATION DATA

Crider, Bill, 1941–
    The wild hog murders / by Bill Crider.
        p. cm. — (Thorndike Press large print mystery)
    ISBN-13: 978-1-4104-4119-5 (hardcover)
    ISBN-10: 1-4104-4119-9 (hardcover)
    1. Rhodes, Dan (Fictitious character)—Fiction. 2. Sheriffs—Fiction. 3.
Texas—Fiction. 4. Large type books. I. Title.
PS3553.R497W54 2011b
813'.54—dc22   2011031067

Published in 2011 by arrangement with St. Martin's Press, LLC.

Printed in Mexico
2 3 4 5 6 7 15 14 13 12 11

A12005 744365

To Francelle Bettinger
Thanks for the phone call.

CHAPTER 1

Sheriff Dan Rhodes saw the feral hog break from the tree line and streak for the country road, but the driver in front of Rhodes either didn't see the hog or didn't think it posed a problem.

The afternoon sky was dark with clouds, and a light veil of mist gave everything a hazy look. The hog moved fast across the open ground, its trotters a dark blur.

If the hog saw the car, it didn't care. It tore across the open space and ran between two old gray cedar posts where a fence had once been strung. A couple of rusted strands of barbed wire hung from one post, but nothing else remained of the fence.

The hog ran down into the shallow bar ditch without a stumble, up the other side, and right in front of the car.

There was nothing the driver could do at that point. He shouldn't have been driving so fast on a dirt road in the country, but he had a sheriff chasing him, and that had made him imprudent.

Rhodes saw the sudden flash of red brake lights and heard the crash and the loud squeal of the hog all at about the same instant. He was about a quarter mile behind the car, far enough to bring the county's Dodge Charger to a safe stop without having to worry about hitting anything or anybody.

When a Ford Focus collides with a three-hundred-pound hog, there's not much left of the car's front end. It doesn't do the hog much good, either, and neither vehicle nor hog is going far afterward.

That didn't matter to the people in the Ford. The driver didn't plan to stay put. Nor did his passenger. As soon as the air bags deflated, they jumped out of the car.

The driver was smaller than his friend and wore a blue shirt, but that was about all Rhodes could see through the mist. The men staggered for a couple of steps, shook their heads as if to clear them, and looked back at the county car. When they saw Rhodes get out, they took off running in the direction from which the hog had come.

Rhodes had already called for backup, so he left the Dodge Charger and started after them. As soon as he crossed the ditch, he stumbled and almost fell. Feral hogs had rooted up the ground, and the heavy clods of earth were wet from the mist. Rhodes felt like he was running across a field of slippery stones. The men ahead of him were either younger or more agile or both, and they didn't seem to be having as much trouble keeping their balance as Rhodes was.

Rhodes stumbled again, and as he recovered himself he heard the baying of dogs and gunshots from the trees. Then there were more gunshots. It sounded as if a small war had started. The shots were followed by squeals of terror and the low rumble of a hog stampede.

Without hesitation, Rhodes turned around and ran back toward the Charger. He'd had a run-in with wild hogs before, and it hadn't turned out well for him. He didn't intend to have a similar experience, not if he could help it.

He heard more gunshots and more baying. It was earlier than hog hunters usually got started, but the dark clouds and the cool day must have brought them out early. They'd found some hogs, sure enough.

Then the hogs thundered from the trees at Rhodes's back, and Rhodes switched to warp speed, or as near to it as he could come. It didn't help. By the time he reached the fence posts, the hogs were nearly on him. Their snorts and fierce squeals made the hairs stand up on the back of his neck. He could almost feel their hot breath on his calves as he crossed the bar ditch.

When he started down the side of the ditch, he turned his ankle and almost fell. He waved his arms to keep his balance and hobbled as fast as he could up the other side of the ditch. He didn't bother to open the door of the Charger. He threw himself across the hood just as the first of the hogs reached him.

Most of the hogs went around the car, but one of them couldn't push enough of the others aside to avoid it. He ran head-on into the side of the front bumper and bounced off.

The impact caused Rhodes to slide across the hood. He grabbed at the windshield wipers and got hold of one of them, though it didn't do any good. It bent backward and broke as Rhodes slid off the car and landed on his back on the dirt road.

Rhodes fought for breath and finally sucked in some air. He coughed, and that made his ribs hurt.

The car protected him from the straggler hogs, and they surged around both ends of it. The powerful stink of the boars lingered in the air as the hogs fled into the field across the road and on into the trees beyond.

Rhodes sat up and leaned against the door of the Charger. His ribs were okay, just a little sore. He took a couple of deep breaths and then stood up. His ankle was all right if he ignored a minor twinge. He looked across the top of the car. He couldn't see the men he'd been chasing, and he couldn't see the hog hunters who'd fired the shots, either.

If they'd seen the county car, they'd probably decided they didn't want to talk to the sheriff right at that moment. There wasn't any law against hunting feral hogs, but considering the damage caused by the herd they'd chased out into the open, the hunters would probably have departed the scene rather than face any possible consequences.

Rhodes wondered what had happened to the men who'd been in the Focus. They might have taken shelter behind a big tree trunk, and if so, they'd be all right. For all Rhodes knew, they were hiding in the woods, watching Rhodes at that very moment.

On the other hand, they might have been trampled by the hogs. If that was the case, Rhodes couldn't leave them there. He decided he'd have to take a look, but he didn't want to go into the trees alone. He got the radio mic and called Hack Jensen, the dispatcher at the jail.

"Where are you?" Hack wanted to know.

"County Road 165. By the old Leverett place."

Rhodes didn't know who owned the property now, and it didn't matter. It had been in the Leverett family for several generations before all the Leveretts died or moved away. Maybe some distant relative still owned it or maybe it had been sold, but everyone in the county still called it the Leverett place.

"I thought you were on 157," Hack said.

"The guy turned off. I followed him. I haven't had time to update you on my position."

"I'll let Ruth know." Ruth Grady was one of the deputies. "She was headed your way, but she's got to come all the way from Mount Industry, and now she'll have to change her route."

"I'll be waiting," Rhodes said.

"We got the report back on the license plate of that Focus," Hack said. "It was stolen down in Houston a couple of days ago. Don't know why anybody'd steal a car that was ten years old. I'd go for a new one if it was me doin' the stealin'.""

"So I guess you're innocent."

"Wasn't me drivin', was it?"

"He could run faster than you can," Rhodes said. "Besides, you're back in Clearview and the driver's off in the woods somewhere."

"Off in the woods? What happened?"

Hack's curiosity was aroused, but Rhodes wasn't going to satisfy it.

"He got out of the car," Rhodes said.

"Why?"

"Because of the hog."

"Hog? What hog?"

"Never mind," Rhodes said, well aware that his nonanswer would get Hack's goat. "I'll tell you later."

"Tell me what? What's goin' on?"

"You'd better send Alton Boyd, too," Rhodes said. Boyd was the county's animal control officer.

"Send Alton? Why?"

"The hog."

"What hog?"

"Never mind," Rhodes said.

Hack started to sputter, and Rhodes grinned. It was déjà vu all over again.

"Just let Ruth know where I am," Rhodes said, "and send a wrecker."

"Wrecker? What do you need with a

wrecker?"

"I blame the hog."

"What hog, dadgummit?"

"I'll tell you later," Rhodes said.

Hack was still sputtering when Rhodes hooked the mic. He walked down the road to look at the blue Focus. The front end was a mess of shattered plastic, and the right headlight was broken. Rhodes hoped that whoever owned it had good insurance.

Rhodes looked back down the road past the Charger and saw headlights haloed by the mist. In a few seconds Deputy Ruth Grady arrived and parked her car behind the one Rhodes had been driving. He walked back to meet her.

"What's up?" she asked when she got out of the car.

"Car hit a wild hog," Rhodes said. He pointed to the trees. "Driver and passenger are in the woods. I guess we'll have to look for them."

Ruth was short, stout, and smart, a good deputy. "Are they armed?"

"I don't know," Rhodes said. "They might be. We'll have to assume that they are. The car's stolen, and the driver stole some gasoline."

"Let's go have a look, then."

"We'll have to wait for Alton Boyd,"

14

Rhodes said. "He needs to get rid of a dead hog. The Ford hit it."

"I hope he comes before it starts to rain."

"It's not going to rain," Rhodes said, looking down the road at more approaching headlights. "Here comes Alton now. Or the wrecker."

It turned out that it was both of them, one behind the other. The wrecker stopped behind Ruth's car, and Boyd parked his van behind the wrecker.

The wrecker driver was Cal Autry, a tall, pear-shaped young man with two days' growth of beard. He wore a Detroit Tigers baseball cap, overalls, a blue shirt, and work boots, all of which were spotted with dark grease.

"Whatcha got for me, Sheriff?" he asked.

"That Focus," Rhodes said. "We need to get rid of a dead hog first, though."

"That'll be my job," Boyd said. "Let's take a look at him."

Boyd was short and bowlegged as a cowboy. He had strong, broad shoulders and the wizened face of a sage. He was no sage, however, and he had a weakness for cheap cigars, which he chewed rather than smoked. The stub of one jutted out from the right corner of his mouth.

The four of them walked to where the hog

15

lay in the road. Rhodes smelled the hog's powerful stench and thought he saw the animal's left hind leg twitch.

"Is he alive?" Ruth asked.

"Looks like he's breathing," Boyd said.

Rhodes couldn't tell in the dim light, but the hog's sides might have moved slightly.

Boyd looked back at the Ford. "Must've just stunned him when he hit the car. Hogs got thick hides and thicker skulls. What you wanna do about him?"

"We can't just leave him here," Rhodes said. "We need to get him out of the road."

"Leave him there long enough, maybe he'll wake up and walk off," Autry said.

"Maybe he will and maybe he won't," Rhodes said. "If he dies, then we have a problem."

"Buzzards'll take care of it," Boyd said. "Eventually."

"In the meantime," Rhodes said, "there's a dead hog in the middle of the road."

"Yeah," Boyd said. "There's that."

"You're the animal control officer," Rhodes said. "What's the drill? You have a paralyzer dart or anything like that?"

"You must work for a different county if you think paralyzer darts for something this big are in the budget," Boyd said. He eyed the hog. "Besides, a dart won't stick in that sucker, 'less you hit him just in the right spot. Let's make sure he's alive before we do anything else."

He walked over to the hog and nudged it with the toe of his shoe.

The hog, which apparently had been waiting for just that moment, squealed like a set of bad brakes. Boyd jumped straight back, almost knocking Rhodes down. Autry caught Rhodes before he fell, just as the hog lurched to its feet.

It stood on wobbly legs for a second, then lumbered sideways down the road as if it had been drinking someone's corn squeezings. After it had gone about twenty yards, it turned and stared back at Boyd, its eyes glowing almost red in the afternoon mist. It opened and closed its mouth, showing off its yellowed tusks.

Boyd turned to run. Rhodes and Autry jumped for the ditch.

The hog lowered its head, squealed, and charged.

Boyd stepped on his own foot. He fell forward, flat on his face, and the hog ran straight over his back. Without ever slowing down, it slammed head-on into the Focus with a powerful crunching sound that signaled the breaking of the other headlight and the splintering of the fender. The hog squealed again, a high, despairing note. It stood facing the car and rocked from side to side for a moment before falling over on its side and lying still.

"Should've shot it in the head when we had the chance," Autry said as he and Rhodes got to their feet. "Then it'd have been dead for sure."

"I think it's dead now," Ruth said, coming up from the ditch on the other side of the road. She stood well away from the hog, as did the others.

Rhodes helped Boyd to his feet. The animal control officer had lost his cigar, which lay in the road. Boyd didn't pick it up.

"Are you okay?" Rhodes asked.

Boyd felt his ribs and reached around to feel his back. "Might be bruised up a little. Scratched, too."

"What about the hog?" Rhodes asked.

"Put a bullet in his head," Autry said. "That'll settle him."

"No need for that," Ruth said. "I'm sure he's dead this time." She walked over to the hog and put a foot on his side. "He's not breathing."

"That Ford must be tougher than it looks," Boyd said.

"Better get him in your van," Rhodes told him.

"You gonna help?"

"We'll all help." Rhodes looked at Autry. "Right?"

"I'll have to charge the county for my time," Autry said.

"That figures," Rhodes said.

CHAPTER 2

Earlier that day there had been a report from a convenience store where a man had driven off without paying for the gas he'd pumped into a blue Ford Focus. The Focus had been in and out of town over the last couple of months, and the driver had committed at least three other petty crimes.

Rhodes had been driving near the store when the report came over his radio, and he'd spotted the car at an intersection just at the edge of town. As soon as the driver saw the sheriff's cruiser in his rearview mirror, he'd sped off, and Rhodes had taken off after him.

Now the chase had ended with Rhodes helping wrestle the dead body of a stinking feral pig into the back of the county's animal control van.

"I wish you'd look at the tushes on that rascal," Boyd said, looking down at the hog's impressive tusks. "They could open up a fella's belly like a buzz saw."

Rhodes preferred not to think about that and said so.

"What you think got them so stirred up?" Boyd asked.

"Hunters," Rhodes said.

Feral hogs were a big problem in Blacklin County and all over that part of the state. There were well over a million of them roaming around Texas. Some people estimated the number was closer to two million, all of them rooting up wetlands and fields, tearing up cattle feeders, breeding faster than rabbits, and eating everything in sight. Hunting them did very little to reduce their numbers. Some people seemed to enjoy it, however, and at least the hunting got rid of a few of them. Some of the hogs, the younger ones, could be used for meat, but the older ones, like the one that had hit the Ford, were next to worthless.

"Let's load it up," Rhodes said.

Boyd had driven past the hog and backed the van up to it. He got out and opened the van's back doors. Everybody bent down and took hold of one of the hog's legs.

"Heave," Rhodes said, and they lifted the dead animal up. Grunting with the effort, they guided its narrow head into the back of the van.

Everybody shoved, and the hog slid into the van. Boyd slammed the door.

"Sure hate to drive back to town with that thing smellin' like it does," he said.

"That's why they pay you the big bucks," Autry said, wiping his hand on his pants. "Who's going to help me hook up that Focus?"

"I would," Rhodes said, "but I'd have to charge you for my time."

"Ha-ha," Autry said, and he clomped off to do his job.

"Drop it off at the impound lot," Rhodes called to him, "and don't touch anything on the inside."

"I know my job," Autry said.

"What about us?" Ruth asked. "What's our job? Are we going after the men from the Ford?"

"That's why they pay us the big bucks," Rhodes said. "I heard a lot of shooting earlier."

"The hunters are bound to be gone by now, don't you think?"

"Maybe, but there might be some more of those hogs hanging around. We'll need to be careful."

"I'd hate to have to go after anybody in those woods," Boyd said. " 'Specially if they had guns."

22

"All you have to do is get rid of that hog," Rhodes said.

"Thinkin' about what you're gonna do, I'd say the hog don't smell so bad after all."

Boyd got in his van and drove away. Autry already had the Focus up on the wrecker, and he followed Boyd. They'd have to drive about a quarter of a mile before they found a place to turn around and head back to Clearview.

Rhodes and Ruth got their shotguns and flashlights out of the county cars.

"Watch where you walk," Rhodes told the deputy. "The hogs have torn up the field pretty bad."

Rhodes hoped he could make it to the woods without falling. Not that he was eager to get into the woods.

"Didn't you have a problem with some hogs once upon a time?" Ruth asked.

"It was before you came to work with us," Rhodes said, remembering the time he'd spent in the hospital. "It could've been worse."

They walked a little farther, picking their way carefully, and Ruth said, "Did you get a look at the men in the car?"

"Not much of one. I know that one of them was smaller than the other one and had on a blue shirt. That's about it."

"What about the clerk where they stole the gas?"

"I don't think so. He was busy with a customer."

"Security camera?"

"There's one in the store, I'm sure," Rhodes said. "I don't know if they have one for the parking lot."

In fact, he was pretty sure they didn't. Clearview, Texas, wasn't exactly the place to go to see all the latest high-tech surveillance equipment in action.

"So we don't have much to go on," Ruth said.

"We don't," Rhodes said, "but if we run across two men lost in the woods, we can be pretty sure they're the ones we're looking for."

"What about the hunters?"

"They won't be lost, and like you said, they're probably gone. I haven't heard any shooting lately, and I haven't heard anything from the dogs in a good while, either."

Almost as soon as Rhodes spoke, they heard shots, two flat cracks from somewhere in the trees.

"Those weren't rifle shots," Ruth said.

"Handgun," Rhodes said. "Somebody's doing some close-in work."

"On a hog?"

"The dogs could've pulled one down. The hunters could have used a pistol to kill it."

Ruth was skeptical. "You said you hadn't heard the dogs, and neither have I. The hunters are gone. Even if they were here, I don't think they'd be using a pistol."

"We'll just have to see what we find," Rhodes said. "And be careful."

When they entered the woods, the going wasn't any easier. There were lots of oaks and pecan trees, which was to be expected. The hogs looked for mast and rooted up the ground as they fed on it. Rhodes stumbled but put out a hand and caught hold of a tree branch to avoid falling.

"I'm surprised a lot of those hunters don't break their legs," Ruth said while Rhodes steadied himself.

"I think there have been a couple of them in the ER this year," Rhodes said.

"You might be there next."

"I wouldn't be a bit surprised."

They started on their way again, and Ruth said, "Where do you think those shots came from?"

"Straight ahead, more or less. It's hard to be sure, though, in these trees."

The mist was thicker under the trees, and it was darker than it had been in the field. Rhodes remembered some scary animated movie he'd seen when he was a kid. He didn't recall much about it other than tree branches grasping at people in the dark, but grasping trees weren't nearly as dangerous as wild hogs.

Or as people with guns, for that matter.

"Do you hear something?" Ruth asked.

Rhodes stopped to listen. He heard some night noises, a squirrel or a bird in the tree branches, a car on the road a long way off, a screech owl somewhere ahead of them.

"People talking, I mean," Ruth said when he told her.

"No," Rhodes said.

"I was thinking about those pistol shots," Ruth said. "If somebody shot a hog, they'd be hauling it out of here. The dogs would be barking. We'd hear a truck."

Rhodes had thought the same thing.

"We'd better be careful," Ruth said.

"I thought we were being careful."

"You know what I mean."

Rhodes knew, all right, and he planned to take plenty of care, though it was hard to walk through unfamiliar woods without making noise. The only good thing about it was that they hadn't had to use the flashlights yet. The lights would have made them good targets.

"What's that up ahead of us?" Ruth whispered.

"Looks like somebody's sitting there," Rhodes said, and they stood still, trying to make out the person or whatever it was.

Rhodes could see a dark bulk lying still near the trunk of the tree. If it was a man, he wasn't moving. Rhodes moved forward. Ruth moved away from him, and both of them brought up their shotguns.

When they got to within ten or fifteen yards of the figure, it became clear that it was a man. Rhodes called out to him.

"This is the sheriff," he said. "Put your hands behind your head and don't move."

He waited for a couple of seconds, and Ruth said, "Maybe he heard you. He's not moving."

"He's not putting his hands behind his head, either," Rhodes said.

He punched the button that turned on his flashlight and, holding the light well away from himself, trained the beam on the man. His head was at an odd angle, and his open eyes reflected the light.

"I think he's dead," Ruth said.

Rhodes directed the beam at the man's chest, and then he saw the dark stains on the front of a blue shirt.

"It wasn't a hog that we heard being shot,"

Ruth said.

They walked over to the man and shined both flashlights on him. He was the smaller of the two men Rhodes had seen, the one who'd been driving. He hadn't shaved in a day or so, and his clothes looked as if they hadn't been changed for a while.

"This probably explains those pistol shots we heard," Rhodes said. "This is a crime scene now."

"Unless it was an accident," Ruth said.

"Possible. Not likely."

"We can't work the scene very well in this weather," Ruth said.

"We'll do the best we can," Rhodes said. "I'll get started. You go back and radio Hack and tell him to get Duke and Buddy out here to patrol the area. Tell him to put out a bulletin, and tell him to spread the news that there's an armed and dangerous man on the loose out here."

"An armed and dangerous man with no description."

"That's right. I couldn't tell anything about him. Probably average size and weight, and that's all."

"People will love to hear that," Ruth said. "Milton Munday will love it even more."

Milton Munday was the Clearview radio station's muckraking talk show host, and

Rhodes knew Ruth was right. Munday would work himself into a frenzy about a nondescript madman with a gun.

"We have to let people know anyway," Rhodes said.

"I know. I'll talk to Hack."

"Bring the camera back with you."

"I will."

"Don't tell Hack any more than you have to."

"I won't," Ruth said. "Do you think there are any clues lying around here?"

"Not a chance," Rhodes said.

The ground around the tree had been rooted up by hogs, and sticks and leaves lay all over the place. The hunters might or might not have been there, though someone other than the dead man certainly had been. It was just that it was hard to tell where anyone might have walked because the hogs had torn up the ground.

"It would be handy if somebody had dropped a driver's license," Ruth said.

"How many times has that happened?"

"Not many, not around here. But you read all the time about bank robbers who provide their ID if the teller asks them or about some goober who'll show his license to a store clerk he's robbing if the clerk says only adults can rob the place."

"The key phrase in that being 'not around here,' " Rhodes said.

"Sure would make life easier if it did happen." Ruth shined her light on the dead man. "What about him?"

"We'll need to get him out of here," Rhodes said.

"How will we do that?" Ruth asked. "He's bigger than we are."

"Have Hack call the EMTs."

"It won't be easy for them to get back in here."

"We need the justice of the peace, too," Rhodes said. "To declare the man dead."

"The JP won't like having to come out here any more than the EMTs will."

"That's why they pay him the big bucks," Rhodes said.

CHAPTER 3

The JP wasn't happy, but he didn't complain much. He declared the man dead, and the EMTs drove the ambulance to the edge of the woods. They got the dead man out without messing up the scene too much. Rhodes was glad he didn't have to help carry him and then ride in the ambulance over the bumpy field.

Ruth and Rhodes had searched for half an hour or more while waiting for the JP and the EMTs. They hadn't found anything that looked like a clue, which was what they'd expected. A bit more surprising was the fact that Rhodes hadn't found anything on the body other than a few coins, a cell phone, and a pocketknife. The man's wallet was missing.

After the EMTs and the JP were gone, Ruth asked, "Do you think our victim was robbed?"

"Could be," Rhodes said, but he didn't

really believe it.

"Are we going to secure the area?"

"I don't think the hogs will be back," Rhodes said, "and I know the hunters won't."

"What if the killer comes back?"

"Never happens. Why don't you stay on patrol and be sure you drive by places where you can be seen. Let people know we're out and about."

"You think this is connected to all the other trouble we've been having with hogs lately?" Ruth asked.

Rhodes had been wondering about that. "I hope not, but we're in the right area for it."

"Mrs. Chandler's place, you mean."

That was the place, all right. Rhodes had been called out there several times lately, and it hadn't been pleasant.

"You want me to come back and work the crime scene in the morning?" Ruth asked.

"No, I'll do that," Rhodes said. He wanted to look around a lot more of the area, and it was getting too dark to see things. He'd wait until morning, and he had another job for Ruth. "Tomorrow I want you to go over that car we impounded and see if you can find anything that'll help us. Fingerprint it first."

"All right, but didn't you say the car was

stolen?"

Rhodes nodded.

"Well, you know what that means."

Rhodes knew. Fingerprints all over the place, and no telling how many different ones.

"Just do the best you can," he said.

"I will, but it's going to take me a while," Ruth said.

"The county commissioners love to pay overtime," Rhodes said, and they both laughed.

"Sounds good to me," Ruth said.

Rhodes drove back to town and went to the jail to write his reports. He hated to write the one about the damage to the county car. It seemed as if he had more trouble with cars than he should.

He also knew that Hack would be ready for him, but Rhodes didn't give him a chance to get started.

"Any calls I need to worry about?" he asked before Hack could get a word in.

"Just the usual," Hack said.

" 'Less you want to count the steaks," Lawton said.

Lawton was the jailer and Hack's partner in their many attempts to annoy Rhodes, who thought of them as the Abbott and

Costello of Blacklin County, not that he'd ever tell them that. To Rhodes, they even looked like the comedy team, Lawton being short, stout, and round-faced, while Hack was taller and thinner. He had a thin mustache.

Hack was clearly annoyed by Lawton's comment. As the straight man, Hack was supposed to start the routine, which, if things went as usual, would confuse Rhodes as much as "Who's on First." Rhodes knew it would be a mistake to ask what steaks Lawton was talking about, but he did it anyway.

"The ones that got shoplifted over at the HEB," Hack said.

The HEB was Clearview's newest grocery store, and in fact its only grocery store if you didn't count Walmart. Most people living in Clearview didn't even remember the A&P or the Safeway that had flourished many years earlier, much less the smaller mom-and-pop stores that had long since disappeared.

"Somebody shoplifted steaks?" Rhodes asked.

"Rib eyes," Lawton started, but Hack held up a hand. Lawton shut up.

"Rib eyes," Hack said, as if Lawton hadn't spoken. "They had 'em on sale. I don't like

34

'em all that much myself, not as much as I like a good filet. I know people say a rib eye is better 'cause of the fat, but I don't like fat. I like a good filet or the tender side of a T-bone."

"You cook yours well done?" Lawton asked.

"I never do. I like mine about medium or even medium well, but I don't like to cook all the juice out. Some people, now —"

"Hold on," Rhodes said. He knew they were leading him on, taking revenge for his not telling them about the hog, but he couldn't stand it any longer. "Who stole the steaks?"

"Rib eyes," Lawton said.

Rhodes sighed. "Who stole the rib eyes?"

"Some entrepreneur," Hack said.

"That's a pretty big word," Lawton said.

"The sheriff knows what it means. You do know what it means, don't you?"

"I know what it means," Rhodes said. "I don't know what it has to do with stolen rib eyes."

"Well," Hack said, "that's how we caught the guy."

"*We?*" Lawton echoed.

"Okay, that's how Buddy caught him."

"So he's under arrest?"

"Right back there in the cells," Hack said.

35

"Won't be eatin' any rib eye tonight," Lawton said.

"Just tell me what happened," Rhodes said.

"You gonna tell us about the hogs and about that dead man you found?" Hack asked.

"I'll tell you. After I find out about the rib eyes."

"Buddy caught the guy who stole 'em," Hack said.

" 'Caught' ain't the right word, exactly," Lawton said. "He found him, is more like it."

"Found him where?" Rhodes asked.

"Being an entrepreneur," Hack said. "Side of the road not far from the county line."

"He was sellin' rib eyes out of the back of his car," Lawton said. "Had him a little sign and ever'thing. He was askin' a dollar a pound."

"Just about sold 'em all before Buddy found him," Hack said.

Lawton nodded. "It was a real good price."

"Times like this, a fella can't afford to pass up a bargain," Hack said. "Now, about that hog."

Rhodes didn't try to put them off. He told them the whole story.

"So the car's in the impound lot already, and there's one man dead and another one on the run," Hack said. "That about it?"

"That's about it," Rhodes agreed.

"All because some fella stole some gas," Lawton said. "That's just not right."

"There was more to it than the gas," Rhodes said. "There's always more to it when somebody gets shot."

"The fella that got away," Hack said.

"What about him?"

"You think he did it?"

"He's the number one suspect," Rhodes said.

"What about those hunters?" Lawton asked. "I saw this movie once about some fellas that stumbled onto a bunch of hunters. Didn't turn out so good for 'em."

"*Deliverance*?" Hack asked.

"Coulda been. I think a hog was mentioned in that."

"Was a pig. Burt Reynolds sure was good in that one."

"That other guy didn't come out so well," Lawton said. "What was his name?"

"Ned Beatty," Rhodes said.

"That's the one," Lawton said. "Felt sorry for him."

"Good thing you didn't stay out there in those woods all by yourself tonight," Hack

37

said. "What with them hunters roamin' around and all."

Rhodes thought about the gunshots he'd heard just before the hog stampede. He hadn't thought about the shots again because of all the excitement that had come right afterward, but now he did. There'd been too many shots for the hunters to be shooting at the hogs. Something else had been going on. He'd have to remember that tomorrow.

"Nothin' like that movie could happen here," Lawton said.

"I wouldn't count on it," Hack said.

Rhodes let them argue about it while he finished his report. When he was done, he told Hack he was going home.

"You think the deputies'll find the killer tonight?" Hack asked.

"You never can tell."

"No way," Lawton said. "He's in Houston by now. That's where the car came from, remember?"

Rhodes remembered.

"How'd he get to Houston?" Hack asked. "No car. Can't walk that far. Nobody picks up hitchhikers anymore."

"He wouldn't hang around here," Lawton said. "He knows the sheriff'd catch him."

Rhodes had heard enough. He told Hack

he was going home.

"You can call me there if there's an emergency," he said.

"I always do," Hack said.

"Don't I know it," Rhodes said.

When he went through the front door of the house, Rhodes was greeted by Yancey, the Pomeranian, who bounced around like a ball of fluff and yipped as excitedly as if he hadn't seen Rhodes in months.

Rhodes walked on back to the kitchen with Yancey yipping at his heels. Rhodes's wife, Ivy, sat at the kitchen table reading a book, something by a writer named Harlan Coben. Rhodes had never heard of him.

"I wondered when you'd get here," Ivy said, marking her place in the book with a piece of paper and laying it on the table.

"Had some trouble with wild hogs," Rhodes said.

"Not Mrs. Chandler again, I hope."

"No, this was different — and worse."

Rhodes sat across from her and told her the short version of the story. Yancey lay under Rhodes's chair, keeping a wary eye on Sam, the black cat who'd recently come to live with them. Sam liked to lie near the refrigerator, and he didn't like Yancey. He didn't like much of anybody, for that matter, as far as Rhodes could tell. He looked at Yancey with slitted eyes.

"I'm glad you didn't get hurt," Ivy said when Rhodes had finished his story. "Do you want some supper?"

"I could use some," Rhodes said, wondering what Ivy might have cooked up this time. She was trying to help him eat healthy meals, which wasn't easy. For every healthy meal she served, Rhodes sneaked two hamburgers. Or cheeseburgers. His schedule didn't make it easy to follow a diet of any kind unless fast food counted as a diet.

Ivy stood up. She was short and shapely, and to Rhodes she still looked around thirty in spite of the gray in her short hair.

"What are we having?" Rhodes asked.

Ivy smiled. "Meatless meat loaf."

Rhodes thought about that. "Isn't that one of those oxymorons, like 'congressional ethics'?"

Ivy slipped on a pair of oven mitts. "There you go, getting cynical again."

Rhodes wasn't sure if she meant he was being cynical about the alleged meat loaf or about Congress.

"You'll like it," she said, so he figured she'd meant the meat loaf, which she took out of the oven.

"I kept it warm," she said.

Rhodes wondered if that mattered. Ivy put the pan with the meat loaf on a hotpad in the middle of the table, then went to the cabinet for a plate.

Rhodes noticed that some of the loaf was missing.

"Have you already eaten?" he asked.

Ivy put his plate and a glass of water in front of him. "I got hungry."

She laid a fork, knife, and spoon beside the plate and handed Rhodes a napkin.

Rhodes cut a slice of the meat loaf and used his fork to get it on his plate. Ivy set a bowl of mashed potatoes on the table, and Rhodes spooned some of them out. When Ivy sat down, he started to eat.

The meat loaf wasn't bad. Rhodes thought it had a lot of cheese in it, and he liked cheese, especially in cheeseburgers. He thought cheese was probably more fattening than meat, but he didn't mention that to Ivy.

"Are you going back out tonight?" Ivy asked as Rhodes ate.

"I don't think so. The killer's either out of the county or hiding out somewhere. We have a bulletin out on him, but there's no description. It could be anybody."

"So he could be outside right now, knocking on our door, and you wouldn't recognize him."

"That's right," Rhodes said.

He heard Yancey's nails clicking on the floor and glanced over at Sam. The cat had given up watching Yancey and gone to sleep. Yancey was trying to sneak up on him, something he'd never attempted before.

"Have you been feeding Yancey vitamin pills?" Rhodes asked.

Ivy laughed. "He's just curious."

"He's never been curious before."

"I think he's gotten more used to having Sam around. Maybe they'll be friends."

Rhodes almost choked on a mouthful of meat loaf. When he'd managed to swallow it, he had to take a swallow of water before he could talk.

"That'll be the day," he said at last.

Yancey eased along until he was about a yard away from Sam. Sam's eyes popped open, and he bared his fangs. Yancey yipped, turned, and ran. His toenails clicked down the hallway.

"He's headed for the bedroom," Ivy said. "He'll hide in there under the bed all night."

"Just another dust bunny," Rhodes said.

Ivy was indignant, or pretended to be. "I'll have you know there are no dust bunnies under the beds in this house."

"Just kidding," Rhodes said.

He finished eating and wiped his mouth with the napkin.

"I think I'll go check on Speedo," he said.

Speedo was a border collie who lived outside. Rhodes didn't like to come home without paying him at least a quick visit.

"Don't stay long," Ivy said. "It's almost bedtime."

"You think you can sleep with a killer roaming the streets?"

"Haven't you told me more than once that murder's usually an impulsive act and that hardly anybody kills a second time?"

Rhodes was impressed. "I'm not sure if I said that. Maybe you heard it on a TV show."

"You said it, all right, and I believed it. Besides, who said I was planning to sleep?"

Rhodes got up and headed for the kitchen door.

"I'll be right back," he said.

CHAPTER 4

Early the next morning Rhodes went outside to visit with Speedo and make up for the time he hadn't spent with him the previous evening. The wind was from the north, and it had blown the mist away. The sun hadn't risen far enough to take all the chill out of the air. It outlined the low clouds in the east with pink.

Speedo dashed around the yard as if he liked the weather. Yancey, who'd also come out for a visit, bounced after him like a dust mop gone mad. Speedo had his chew toy, and Yancey wanted it. Rhodes sat on the porch and watched them romp.

He didn't really believe what Ivy said he'd told her, that no one ever killed a second time. Some people certainly did. The first murder might be an impulsive or desperate act that would never be repeated, but now and then there was a second murder to cover up the first one. Rhodes hoped that didn't happen this time.

He'd given a lot of thought to the situation at the Chandler place. It was messy. That was the only way to describe it.

It had all started with a pig named Baby.

Or maybe not, Rhodes thought. It had really started when Janice Chandler had moved to Clearview and bought the old Tallent place to open an animal shelter. And not just any animal shelter. She seemed to have a soft spot for swine, and the first animal she'd taken in was Baby, a pet pig that had belonged to a man named Floyd Pearce. Floyd had been up in years, and he couldn't take care of Baby anymore. So he asked Janice if she'd take him off his hands.

That had been the right thing to do. A lot of people would have just turned the pig loose in the woods and let him go feral like so many others, but not Floyd. He was too attached to Baby to do that, and of course Janice was glad to add him to the several other pigs she already had.

The other pigs were already feral. They'd been shot and wounded, or hit by cars, or otherwise put out of commission but not killed. Janice had taken them in. She had pens for them.

The other hogs didn't like Baby. Baby didn't like them. So Baby had crashed out.

45

It would have been better if Baby had never been seen again, but that wasn't the case.

It was a few weeks ago that Hack had gotten the call that sent Rhodes out to see Janice Chandler and her son, Andy. Andy had come to town with his mother, and he helped out around the place.

One thing was for sure, the Chandlers had done things right. The story going around town was that Janice got a big insurance payout when her husband had died. There was a new house on the property, with an asphalt road leading up to it and a circular drive in front. There was a new hog-proof fence along the road up to the house and all along the county road in front. The fence was about three feet high, too high for hogs to climb. It was made of steel wire like a rectangular net with openings too small for hogs to get through, so it worked to keep hogs both in and out.

The Chandlers stood by the gate, waiting for Rhodes. That wasn't all that waited for him. Baby was there, too, or what was left of him.

Rhodes parked the car and got out.

"Who'd do a thing like that?" Andy Chandler said.

Andy was about forty, Rhodes guessed, and about twice as big as his mother. He

46

didn't look much older than she did, as far as Rhodes could tell, but he'd never really gotten a good look at her.

Andy was a couple of inches taller than Rhodes, and Rhodes wasn't a short man. Andy looked as if he could pick up a fully grown hog and carry it around if he wanted to.

"Somebody very sick, that's who," Janice Chandler said.

She looked almost like a child standing by her towering son. She wore an old-fashioned sunbonnet to shade her eyes and overalls over a blue work shirt. Rhodes wondered if she'd bought the overalls in the children's department.

"What are you going to do about it, Sheriff?" she asked.

The *it* to which she referred was the remains of Baby. Or most of the remains. Rhodes could see the tail and hide, which lay over the pig's entrails. He couldn't see the head.

"It's not there," Andy said when Rhodes asked. "The sick SOB who killed Baby must have kept it. God knows why."

"Baby was as gentle as a puppy," Janice said. "Just as friendly, too." She paused to wipe her eyes. "He'd do anything for an apple."

"Somebody didn't like him," Rhodes pointed out.

"Hunters," Andy said. "We've heard them in the woods."

They'd done more than just hear them, or so Rhodes had been told. The rumor was that the Chandlers hunted the hunters. Not with bullets but with shotguns loaded with shells holding rock salt instead of shot. Rock salt wouldn't do much damage unless the shooter was within a yard of whoever he was firing at, but it could sting and scar if it hit bare skin.

So far Rhodes hadn't had any complaints from hunters, who probably thought they could deal with the Chandlers in their own way, so Rhodes didn't know if the rumors were true. If they were, Rhodes figured the Chandlers had more to be worried about than the hunters, who, after all, were using real ammo. It wouldn't be smart for the Chandlers to go after them.

"You haven't bothered the hunters, have you?" Rhodes asked.

Andy stiffened and seemed to get even taller. "What right do they have to kill innocent animals?"

Rhodes didn't think that answered his question. He said, "The hogs aren't exactly innocent."

"They're just doing what comes naturally, and people are slaughtering them."

Rhodes didn't see that he'd get anywhere by arguing, but Andy was just getting started.

"The next thing you know, they'll be hunting them from helicopters. Did you know hunters from other states can arrange to come to Texas just to hunt hogs?"

Ranchers could already hunt hogs from helicopters and had been doing it for years in some parts of the state. It wasn't a sport. It was what Andy had called it, a slaughter. Still, the hogs had to be controlled somehow.

"I don't think anybody came here in a helicopter or from out of state to kill your pig," Rhodes said.

"Maybe not," Andy said, "but somebody killed it — and mutilated it. What are you going to do about it?"

"I'll try to find out who's responsible."

"You'd better do more than try," Janice said.

She didn't tell him what would happen if he didn't, which was just as well, since he hadn't had any luck. There were no clues at all other than the pig parts, and Rhodes could learn nothing from them.

The next call had come a few days later.

Baby was back, or his head was. It was a lot the worse for wear, but Andy said it was Baby, all right. It was in the road by the gate, almost exactly where the other pig parts had been.

"This has to stop," Andy said.

This time his mother wasn't with him. Andy said she just couldn't face the sight of Baby's head lying there like that.

Rhodes started to say that he thought things had already come to a stop because there wasn't anything else of Baby that was missing, but he knew that wouldn't be wise.

"When did you find it?" he asked.

"This morning when I came down to put a letter in the mailbox."

The Chandlers were on one of the rural routes, and a big black mailbox stood on a post near the gate. Andy must have put the letter inside already, because the box was closed and the red flag on the side was up.

"Any idea when it was put here?" Rhodes asked.

"Had to have been last night," Andy told him. "I had to get some stuff from Wal-mart's, and it was dark when I got back. Baby wasn't here then." Andy shook his head. "I'm real disappointed in you, Sheriff. I thought you'd have found the killers before now."

Rhodes wasn't ashamed. He might have found some answers if he'd had anything to go on, but he didn't. He suspected it was hog hunters, but every farmer and rancher in the county hated hogs. Any of them might have decided to have a little fun at the Chandlers' expense.

"Fun" was the right word, too, because whoever had killed Baby had probably thought it would be quite a joke to leave the remains for the Chandlers to find. Rhodes didn't consider it a joke, and the Chandlers certainly didn't, either, but there were those who would.

"It better not happen to any of our other animals," Andy said. "I can't be responsible for what we might do if somebody sick enough to do this tries it again."

It was Andy's final comment that had Rhodes worried now as he watched Yancey snatch up the squeeze toy that Speedo had dropped on the grass. Yancey bounded away, with Speedo in hot pursuit.

Rhodes worried that the Chandlers might decide to load their shotguns with something more lethal than rock salt. Or that even if they didn't, one of the hunters would shoot back.

Then there was the dead man. Not to mention a killer on the loose.

Rhodes sighed, stood up, and called the dogs. Speedo reached him first, and Rhodes gave him a good petting before going back inside with Yancey bouncing along behind.

Ivy was in the kitchen. She'd fed Sam his breakfast of what Rhodes assumed was a delicious blend of turkey and giblets from a foil package. Rhodes was faced with the less appetizing prospect of miniature rectangles of shredded wheat, to be covered with nonfat milk. It was a little like eating hay, but Rhodes knew it was supposed to be good for him.

"Any calls?" he asked, sitting at the table.

"Not a one," Ivy said. She handed him the milk carton. "Did you think the killer might have turned himself in this morning?"

"Too much to hope for," Rhodes said.

He poured the milk on the cereal and watched Yancey edging toward Sam. The cat turned and looked at Yancey. That was all it took. Yancey scooted from the room and down the hall.

"I have to go now," Ivy said. "You be careful today."

"I'm always careful," Rhodes said.

"Right," Ivy said. She leaned over and kissed him on the forehead. "Sometimes I forget how careful you are."

She left, and Rhodes finished the cereal.

Sam looked at him as if hoping Rhodes would give him the milk that was left in the bowl.

"You wouldn't like it," Rhodes said. "Trust me."

He ran water in the bowl, then put it and the spoon in the dishwasher.

"You behave yourself today," he told Sam, but the cat didn't deign to answer. The cat never did.

The crime scene looked hopeless. The churned-up ground didn't take tracks, and no one had helpfully dropped a driver's license. Rhodes scanned the area for more than an hour without turning up a thing.

He had a feeling that Ruth Grady was having the opposite kind of luck in fingerprinting the car. She would be finding more prints than they could possibly sort out. Maybe she'd find something useful in the car itself, but Rhodes didn't think it was likely.

The county had bought a metal detector a few years back, and Rhodes had brought it along. He wasn't going to give up on the scene until he'd tried everything. He slipped on the headphones and turned on the machine.

After another half hour, he was ready to

quit, but he kept going. After ten more minutes, he got a faint signal. It took him a few seconds to zero in on the object, which was hidden under a leaf in a hog track.

A shell casing. Rhodes picked up a convenient nearby stick and stuck it in the casing's opening. He put the casing in a paper bag and set it aside while he searched some more.

Eventually he quit without finding a second. Either the shooter had picked it up or it had eluded him. Well, one was good enough, Rhodes figured. Now all he had to do was find a gun to match it to. It was possible, even likely, that the killer had ditched the gun — in a creek, in a ditch, even somewhere else in the woods. If he hadn't, however, the shell casing might very well prove useful later on.

Rhodes gave up on the crime scene after another half hour and walked back through the woods. He didn't know where the hogs holed up during the daytime, but he was sure they weren't anywhere nearby. Or if they were, they were quiet and well hidden. If there was any solution to the problems they caused, Rhodes didn't know what it was. Live traps didn't work. Hunting didn't work. Rhodes wouldn't be surprised if the whole countryside was overrun by hogs before long, and after that the towns.

He got back to the car and started for the Chandler place. He'd just turned around when a call came through from Hack.

"Mikey Burns has the answer," Hack said.

"The answer to what?" Rhodes asked.

"The hogs."

"He told you that?"

"He just got off the phone."

"What's the answer?" Rhodes immediately regretted asking. He knew Hack wouldn't tell him.

"You'll have to ask him," Hack said.

"He didn't tell you?

"He did, but you oughta hear it from him."

"I can hardly wait," Rhodes said.

Mikey Burns was a county commissioner, and he and Rhodes had a prickly relationship. Burns never seemed to think Rhodes was doing his job as well as it could be done by someone who was smarter and quicker on the uptake, but since Rhodes had won the previous election by a landslide, having run unopposed, Burns was stuck with him.

Burns's most recent great idea was to have the county buy an M-16, the kind of gun that could fire nearly a thousand rounds a minute and take out a tank, that is, if any terrorists in tanks happened to invade Blacklin County, a possibility that Rhodes considered more remote than Burns did. The purchase had fallen through, and Burns hadn't been happy about it.

The county barn where Burns kept his office was a big metal building with long covered sheds in back where the road equipment for Burns's precinct was kept. The office was in the building in front, and it was presided over by Mrs. Wilkie, a woman who'd once had it in mind that she and Rhodes would make a good team. She'd given up on that idea, and she was now pursuing Mikey Burns.

She patted her orange hair and gave Rhodes a cool look when he entered. Rhodes thought about warning her against workplace romance, but he just smiled and asked if Mikey was available.

"*Mr. Burns* is in," she said. "You may go in."

"Thanks," Rhodes said, and he went through the connecting door to Burns's office.

Burns's name was Michael, of course, but everyone called him Mikey. Rhodes had a feeling that Mrs. Wilkie did, too, when no one was around.

Burns stood up at his desk. He wore, as

usual, a bright aloha shirt, this one some-thing in green and yellow with coconuts and palm trees on it.

"Hack tells me you have an answer to the hog problem," Rhodes said.

"I do," Burns said. "Have a seat."

Rhodes sat in one of the two chairs in the office, and Burns settled down behind his desk.

"All right," Rhodes said. "Tell me. What's the answer."

"Robin Hood," Burns said.

CHAPTER 5

Rhodes knew who Robin Hood was. He had no connection to either Errol Flynn or Sherwood Forest.

"Robin Hood?" Rhodes said. "You mean Dr. Qualls?"

Dr. William Qualls was a retired college professor who'd moved to Blacklin County to escape the big-city life, and some of the humidity, that he'd had to put up with in Houston. Qualls bought himself a house in the country, where he'd found himself living near a huge chicken farm that as far as Qualls was concerned had polluted the county's air with its stink for far too long. As a way of protesting what he saw as a lack of concern on the part of county officials, Qualls had begun sticking notes to telephone poles with arrows. He'd even shot an arrow into one of the tires on Burns's prized red Pontiac Solstice.

"Not Qualls," Burns said.

The commissioner's mouth twisted as he spoke the name. The professor had paid his fine after being caught, but he hadn't served ten years in the state pen, which was what Burns had planned for him.

"Who, then?" Rhodes said.

"Bow hunters."

"Bow hunters?"

"That's what I said. Lots of people like to hunt those hogs, but they're not organized, and hunting at night is dangerous. So is hunting with rifles. What we'd do is get the bow hunters organized, send them out in the daytime with a deputy leading them. Or if not a deputy, maybe a graduate of the Citizens' Sheriff's Academy."

Rhodes thought about some of the graduates. Seepy Benton came to mind.

"That might not be such a good idea," Rhodes said.

"Bow hunting? It's a lot safer than hunting with a rifle. The arrows don't carry too far, so nobody's likely to get hurt. How many hogs has that animal control officer of yours trapped this month? Five? Ten?"

Boyd wasn't Rhodes's animal control officer. He worked for the county, but Rhodes knew it wouldn't do him any good to try to correct Burns, who hadn't even given Rhodes a chance to tell him it was the

59

academy grads and not the bow hunting that wasn't such a good idea.

"He averages about twenty a month," Rhodes said. "He has a lot of other things to do."

"I know," Burns said. "That's why we need the bow hunters. A good team of them could hunt down no telling how many hogs in a month. Even if they didn't kill a lot of them, people would at least see that we were trying to do something about the hogs." He paused and looked at Rhodes. "And it's a lot better than bringing in people in helicopters."

"It hasn't come to that yet," Rhodes said. "Have you talked to your constituents about this?"

Burns sat forward in his chair. "What does that mean?"

"It means that Mrs. Chandler's in your precinct. She doesn't like people who hunt hogs. She'd like someone who organized hunts even less."

"I see what you mean," Burns said. He leaned back. "She has a lot of money, too. She might try to get someone to run against me."

"She might even run against you herself," Rhodes said.

"Hah. She wouldn't stand a chance."

"Maybe not, but if someone saw a chance to step in and make it a three-person race . . ."

"I still think bow hunting's a good idea."

"Maybe so," Rhodes said, "but not for my department. We enforce the law. We don't lead hunting parties."

"If the deputies were off duty . . ."

"No," Rhodes said. "Not even then."

"I knew you wouldn't go for it," Burns said. He flicked the front of his shirt with his fingers as if getting rid of a pesky speck of dirt. "You're never receptive to new ideas."

Rhodes knew Burns was thinking about the M-16. He hoped the commissioner didn't want to start that discussion again, though the M-16 would indeed be effective against the hogs as long as you didn't mind all the collateral damage that was certain to ensue.

"You talk to the other commissioners," Rhodes said. "If they want to get some hunting parties together, that's up to them, and to you. Just don't ask my department for help."

"You wouldn't try to stop us?"

"Not if all your hunters have licenses."

"Hogs aren't game animals."

"You need a license to hunt them all the

same," Rhodes said. "You can check with the game warden if you don't believe me."

Burns didn't respond to that, not directly. He said, "Maybe it's not such a good idea after all. I won't take up any more of your time."

Rhodes stood up. Burns apparently hadn't heard about the murder yet, and Rhodes didn't intend to tell him. Burns would find out soon enough, and then he'd berate Rhodes for not having brought in any suspects.

"If I come up with any good ideas about getting rid of the hogs," Rhodes said, "I'll let you know."

"You did all right with the chicken farm," Burns said.

"That wasn't me. That was Qualls."

Through a series of events, including murder, Qualls had found himself the owner of the very farm he'd protested against. He'd taken all the right steps to clean things up, and the air in Blacklin County was the better for it. Not perfect, but better.

"You never like to take credit, do you, Sheriff," Burns said.

Rhodes hadn't thought about it, so he shook his head.

"I know we don't always get along," Burns said, "but sometimes you do good work.

Now get out of here and do some of it."

Rhodes didn't know exactly how to respond, so he just said, "I'll try," and left.

Rhodes's next stop was the jail, where he put the shell casing in the evidence locker.

"You gonna buy you a bow and arrow?" Hack said after Rhodes logged the evidence. "Get you a green outfit with a feather in the cap?"

"I do look a little like Errol Flynn," Rhodes said.

Hack laughed. " 'Bout as much as I do."

He might have carried on with the conversation, but Jennifer Loam came in. She was a reporter for the *Clearview Herald*. Rhodes had often thought she'd move on to some bigger and better newspaper. She had the ability and talent, but now that big-city newspapers were laying off reporters and their daily editions were shrinking to the size of the *Herald,* Jennifer wasn't going anywhere.

"Good morning, Mr. Jensen," she said to Hack. "Good morning, Sheriff."

Rhodes and Hack said, "Good morning," and waited. Rhodes knew what was coming.

"I'd like to get a statement about the murder last night," Jennifer said.

Rhodes knew she checked the reports every morning. He said, "You already know as much as I do."

Loam was blond and had innocent blue eyes. She looked young and harmless, but she was professional and tenacious. She didn't let Rhodes get away with that.

"You were there," she said. "I wasn't. Maybe you have a few more details you'd like to add to the story before I write it down. Or maybe you'd like to reassure people that there's not a murderer running loose in the county ready to cut their throats while they sleep."

Rhodes looked at her, and she grinned.

"That's what the competition is saying," she told him.

"Milton Munday," Rhodes said. He didn't listen to the show. It got his blood pressure up. "It figures."

"What else is he sayin'?" Hack asked.

"Aside from the fact that the sheriff is incompetent, that nobody is safe, and that we should all lock our doors at night?" Jennifer asked.

"Yeah," Hack said. "Aside from that."

"Not much."

Munday thrived on fear, other people's fear, and it worked for him. Rhodes didn't think he'd be a resident of the county for long. Radio, unlike newspapers, wasn't dying, and Munday seemed destined for bigger markets.

"You think he believes any of that?" Hack asked.

Jennifer shrugged. "Who knows? I can give you a little fairness and balance, though, Sheriff. Just give me something to work with."

"We're doing all we can," Rhodes said, "but that's not much. We don't have any suspects, and we don't have anybody in custody."

"That's not exactly comforting."

"Best I can do. The killer could be anywhere by now. Houston. Canada. Mexico."

"So you think he's an illegal immigrant?"

"Munday again?"

"He didn't make any accusations, just mentioned the possibility."

"Look," Rhodes said, "here's what happened."

Jennifer got out her little recorder. She also took notes, and Rhodes went over the whole story with her, step by step. When he'd finished, he said, "There are just too many possibilities for me to settle on any one of them. We have a lot of work to do, but we'll catch the killer if he's still around here. We always get our man."

"You really want me to print that?"

"Maybe not the last part," Rhodes said.

Jennifer looked over her notes. "So the killer could be someone who was with the victim in the car, one of the hog hunters, or someone else who was roaming around in the woods."

"Maybe he shot himself," Hack said.

Rhodes looked at him.

"It could happen," Hack said.

"I'll check with Dr. White later and find out," Rhodes said, but he didn't believe it for a minute. He turned back to Loam. "Don't put that in your story."

"I won't, but Hack's right, you know."

Hack grinned so wide that Rhodes thought he might split his face open.

Loam asked a few more questions and left. Ruth Grady came in almost at once.

"Find anything?" Rhodes asked.

"Plenty of fingerprints," Ruth said. "Enough to keep the IAFIS computers busy for a month or two."

Rhodes had been afraid of that. IAFIS was the FBI's Integrated Automated Fingerprint Identification System, and it was generally pretty fast, but not with single prints and not with as many as they'd be sending.

"Anything that looks like a solid lead?" he asked.

Ruth shook her head. "Not a thing. Oh, there was a lot of stuff in the car, and I've got it bagged and tagged, but most of it was trash. The rest looked like it belonged to the owner and not whoever was driving the car. We can go over it and see if any of it's any use, but I don't think it will be."

Rhodes hadn't expected anything different.

"One more thing," Ruth said.

"A good thing?"

"I don't know. There were some blood spots in the carpet in the trunk. I sent them off for analysis. Eventually we'll get a report."

"It might help us," Rhodes said.

"Or it might not," Ruth said. "I know. But there's some good news, too."

"What's that?"

"Since you said the guy stole some gas, I printed the gas cap and the filler cover. Got some good prints. And I printed the victim. If those prints match . . ."

"We'll know he's the one who stole the gas," Rhodes said. "Now all you have to do is figure out which of the other zillion prints belong to the other passenger."

"Or if any of them do."

"Yeah," Rhodes said. "There's that. Even if they do, what does that prove? Not that

67

he's the killer."

"So what's next?" Ruth asked.

Rhodes was way ahead of her on that one, at least. He already had a list.

"You get the driver's prints into the system. I'll talk to the Chandlers and see what they can tell me about last night, and then I'll check on the autopsy. And why don't you see if you can find out who some of the hog hunters are. We need to find out who was in those woods last night."

"All right," Ruth said. "That should be easy enough. To find out who some of the hunters are, I mean. I'll bet nobody's going to admit being in those woods, though, not if they've listened to Milton Munday."

"You hear his program today?" Hack asked.

"I listened while I worked," Ruth said. "It's always a pleasure."

"I'll bet," Rhodes said.

CHAPTER 6

Blacklin County had no medical examiner, so Rhodes considered himself lucky to have someone like Dr. White, who knew what he was doing, kept good records, and wrote comprehensive reports. He was even certified by the American Board of Pathology, though that wasn't required, either.

Blacklin County didn't have a morgue for Dr. White to work in, but Clyde Ballinger, who owned the largest funeral home for miles around, let White perform autopsies there. He even had a room set aside for it and didn't charge the county a penny. He said he liked being a good citizen.

Ballinger lived alone in a little house in back of the funeral home. The house had once been the servants' quarters for the large mansion that now served another purpose entirely.

When Rhodes went in, Ballinger was sitting at his desk reading a paperback. The funeral director was a short, compact man with black hair and a suit to match. It was a nice suit, and Ballinger had probably bought it in Houston or Dallas. There was no longer a store in Clearview that sold suits.

Maybe that was the reason that Ballinger was one of only two or three men in town who still wore suits to work, Rhodes thought. Even some of the bankers and lawyers didn't wear suits anymore.

The suit might have been unusual for Clearview but not for a funeral director, and there was nothing at all unusual about Ballinger's having a book in his hand. He read a lot. What struck Rhodes as odd was that the book Ballinger held appeared to be brand-new.

"What's up with that?" Rhodes asked, indicating the book.

Ballinger held it up for Rhodes to see. The title was *Baby Moll,* and the cover looked like one that would have been right at home on the books Ballinger used to find in the local garage sales.

"It's what they call the retro look," Ballinger said. "It's a retro *book,* too."

"You're a poet and don't know it," Rhodes said.

Ballinger grinned. "Sure I know it. Anyway, lots of the old stuff's being reprinted

70

now. Good thing, too, since I can't find much in garage sales anymore. People are buying all the old books and trying to sell 'em on eBay, and they bring more than the new ones do. It's a shame if you ask me. Takes all the fun out of it."

"You're still reading, though," Rhodes said.

Ballinger put the book down on his desk. "Why would I quit? Finding the books might not be any fun now, but reading them still is."

Rhodes nodded. "Murder in books is always more fun than the real thing."

"Like the guy you sent here yesterday," Ballinger said. "He was murdered, right?"

"Right."

Ballinger opened a drawer on the side of his desk and brought out Dr. White's report. He handed it to Rhodes and picked up his book.

Rhodes read through the report. He didn't see anything he didn't expect to find. The victim had been in good general health and had died of two gunshot wounds, one of them to his heart. The bullets had been recovered from the body and had been fired from a .38. The bullets were now in a locker in the autopsy room.

The victim's only identifying mark noted

was a large mole on his right shoulder. There were no personal effects except some car keys that had no doubt belonged to the person the car was stolen from. According to the report on the car, it had been stolen a couple of months earlier. The owner had left the keys in it while buying a lottery ticket at a convenience store. The victim must have liked to steal things at convenience stores.

"Any help there?" Ballinger asked when he saw that Rhodes was finished with his reading.

"Not a bit," Rhodes said.

"Milton Munday says you'll never catch the killer," Ballinger told him. "He doesn't like you much."

"He doesn't even know me," Rhodes said.

"You've met him, though, haven't you?"

"Only once, and we didn't talk long."

"He's sure livened up the radio in this little county," Ballinger said. "Nearly everybody in town listens to him."

"Not me," Rhodes said.

"I'll bet the commissioners don't listen, either, or the mayor. Munday does love to criticize the power structure."

"You think I'm part of the power structure?"

"Well, sure. You're the sheriff. We all know

you've single-handedly brought law and order to this small frontier village."

"I didn't think you read Westerns," Rhodes said.

"Now and then I do. Some of those old writers I like wrote Westerns and mysteries, too, but I like those Sage Barton books better."

Rhodes didn't want to talk about Sage Barton, a character created by two women who'd come to Blacklin County to attend a writers' workshop in the small town of Obert. There'd been some trouble at the workshop, and a man had been killed. Rhodes had solved the crime, and the two women had written a novel about a tough, good-looking Texas sheriff they'd called Sage Barton. The book had sold and so had the sequel, and people liked to tease Rhodes by saying that the Barton character was based on him.

Barton's life, however, was considerably more colorful than Rhodes's. Barton had weapons that would make Mikey Burns's dream of an M-16 seem like a paltry thing. He romanced FBI agents in pursuit of terrorist masterminds. He didn't chase criminals in a car, either. Instead, he used the county helicopter, which he piloted himself. Barton made Navy SEALs look like sissies by comparison. He could probably strangle a feral hog with his bare hands.

"I don't read those books," Rhodes said, though it wasn't strictly the truth. He'd scanned them, and Ivy had read both of them and reported to Rhodes on their contents.

"You should give 'em a try," Ballinger said. "You might pick up some pointers."

Rhodes said he didn't think so.

"Well, I do. That Sage Barton has a lot on the ball. You take things too easy."

Rhodes didn't mind the criticism, mainly because he knew Ballinger was joshing him.

"I'm not cut out for the kind of adventures Sage Barton has," Rhodes said.

"I wouldn't say that. Lose a couple pounds, work out a little, you might be just like him."

Rhodes stood up. "I don't have time to work out. Too busy catching crooks."

"Well, good luck with that," Ballinger said.

Rhodes was almost at the Chandler place when Hack came on the radio.

"Mikey Burns is mighty upset with you," Hack said.

"You might not want to broadcast that," Rhodes told him. Quite a few people in town had police band scanners and nothing better to do than listen in.

That didn't bother Hack. "Oh, I expect half the town knows about it already. Seems there were a couple of things you forgot to tell him this morning."

Rhodes hadn't mentioned the damage to the car, but he had a feeling Burns still didn't know about that.

"He's heard about the Milton Munday show," he said.

"He sure has, and he's not happy. I told him you were hot on the trail of the killer, so you couldn't see him. That's the truth, ain't it?"

"Absolutely," Rhodes said.

"You better see him tomorrow, then. You might want to have a talk with Munday, too."

"Or I might not," Rhodes said.

The Chandlers' house sat in the middle of what would have been a green yard in the summer, but the fall weather had already turned most of the grass to brown. Rhodes turned the county car at the open gate and drove through.

Both sides of the short road leading up to the house were fenced with hog wire, so the gate was usually open. The wire glinted in the sun.

Rhodes parked in front of the house and got out. He could smell the hog pens, but they didn't smell nearly as bad as the chicken farm that was located on the opposite side of the county. Or as bad as the farm once had. Qualls had cleaned things up as well as was possible, and Rhodes thought most people were okay with that.

Janice Chandler came around the house from the back. She wore an old-fashioned sunbonnet and a pair of overalls over a red and blue plaid shirt. White cotton work gloves covered her hands.

"Hello, Sheriff," she said. "I thought you might be dropping by."

"Now why would you think that?" Rhodes asked.

"I heard Milton Munday's show this morning."

Rhodes thought she was grinning, but he couldn't tell for sure because the bonnet shadowed her face.

"Why would that make you think I'd be coming by?" he asked.

"From what he said, it sounded like somebody killed a hog hunter," Janice said. "I figured I'd be the first person you'd want to see. I'll tell you right now, though, that I didn't do it."

Munday didn't know as much as he liked

people to think he did, since the dead man hadn't been one of the hog hunters. Or maybe he had been. It hadn't occurred to Rhodes that he might be because he had on a blue shirt, as had the driver of the car, but there were lots of blue shirts in the world.

The dead man had worn slacks and casual shoes, however. No self-respecting hog hunter would be dressed like that.

"What about Andy?" Rhodes asked.

"He didn't kill him, either."

"I'd like to have him tell me that. Is he around?"

"He's working in back. We have a sick goat."

"Have you called the vet?"

Janice waved the question aside. "Andy's taking care of him."

Rhodes didn't want to go around back and pay a visit to the sick goat, but he'd do it if he had to.

"You want to call him," he asked, "or do you want me to go back there?"

"Andy or the goat?"

Rhodes had to grin at the joke. He'd had an English teacher who'd made the same kind of comments, but that had been a long time ago.

"Andy," he said. "I don't need to talk to the goat."

"I'll call Andy, then," Janice said, and she did.

She had a powerful set of lungs, and Rhodes wondered if she'd developed them through years of calling hogs. Rhodes resisted the urge to cover his ears.

A minute or so after being called, Andy came around the house. Like his mother, he wore overalls and a plaid shirt. Rhodes figured they shopped together, probably at Walmart, but Andy wasn't wearing gloves, and he wore a battered and stained straw hat instead of a bonnet.

"Hey, Sheriff," Andy said. "What brings you out here?"

"You don't listen to Milton Munday?"

"Oh," Andy said. "That."

Rhodes noticed that Andy had a red mark on one cheek, the kind of mark that might have been made by a tree branch whipping across it.

"Yes," Rhodes said. "That. I wondered if you two might have heard any shooting at the Leverett place yesterday afternoon."

Andy looked at the ground. Janice said, "We sure did. It spooked some of the animals, so we had to come out and quiet them down."

"You didn't go over to the Leverett place to see what it was all about?"

"Hah. We know what it was all about. Hog hunters. We don't hold with that."

"I know," Rhodes said. "You didn't try to put a stop to it, I guess."

"Those people have guns," Janice said. "We wouldn't stand a chance. Would we, Andy."

"No, ma'am," Andy said. "Not a chance."

"They'd shoot us down like dogs," Janice said. "Or hogs."

"If you had guns yourselves, you'd stand a chance," Rhodes said.

"We don't shoot people, Sheriff," Janice said.

"A little rock salt wouldn't hurt them."

"They might shoot back at somebody using rock salt, and they have something a lot more dangerous."

That was true, but Rhodes thought she was the type to take the risk. He couldn't read her face, however, because of the bonnet, and Andy kept staring at the ground.

"So you didn't even bother to go out and see what the shooting was all about," Rhodes said.

"I told you," Janice said. "They had guns. We hunkered down in the house and minded our own business, like we always do."

"That's the smart thing, all right," Rhodes said.

"You betcha."

Hogs squealed in back of the house.

"Andy," Janice said, "you better go check on Peabody." She looked at Rhodes. "Peabody's the goat."

Andy turned without a word and headed back around the house.

"You have anything else, Sheriff?" Janice asked.

"Not right now," Rhodes told her.

"Then I'd better get back to work."

"You do that," Rhodes said, and she left him there.

Rhodes stood thinking things over for a minute, then got in the county car and left.

Rhodes was on the way to see Mikey Burns when Hack called.

"You need to come by the jail. We got a situation here."

"What kind of situation?" Rhodes asked.

"Just a situation. You comin'?"

"I'm on the way," Rhodes said.

CHAPTER 7

The situation was a man a bit over six feet tall, though he looked taller because the white Hoss Cartwright hat he wore added a full foot to his height. Unlike Hoss's hat, this one had a rattlesnake-skin band. He wore a black shirt, black jeans, a black denim jacket, and black ostrich-skin boots. He looked somehow familiar, but Rhodes couldn't figure out why. He knew he'd never seen the man before. He would have remembered the hat if nothing else.

"Name's Rapinski," the man said. His voice rumbled out of his broad chest. "Hoss Rapinski."

Rhodes resisted the urge to hum the theme from *Bonanza*. He looked at Hack, who rolled his eyes.

"Glad to meet you, Mr. Rapinski," Rhodes said.

Rapinski extended his hand. "Call me Hoss."

Rhodes shook hands with Rapinski. "I have a feeling that's not your real name."

"Eugene don't have quite the same ring."

Rhodes had to agree with him. "What can I do for you?"

"You know who I am?" Rapinski asked.

"You look familiar," Rhodes said.

Rapinski grinned. "You prob'ly seen me on TV."

"You have a TV show?"

"Nope, but I been on the news."

Rhodes looked at Hack again.

"He's a bounty hunter," Hack said.

"Fugitive recovery agent," Rapinski said. His already big chest swelled a little.

"Same thing," Hack said.

"Depends on how you look at it, I guess," Rapinski said. "I've caught a few high-profile fugitives in your state."

Rhodes didn't remember seeing Rapinski on the news, but he nodded anyway.

"ID?" Rhodes asked.

Rapinski got his wallet from his back pocket and showed Rhodes his license.

"You know what the law says about bounty hunters, I guess," Rhodes said.

Rapinski put away his wallet and pulled back the denim jacket to reveal a Glock in a shoulder holster.

"I'm licensed to carry in this state," he

said. "All legal and everything."

"And . . ." Rhodes said.

"And I don't plan to make any arrests here. I know better than that. I'm not a peace officer. That's why I'm here talking to you. I might have to call you in if I locate my principal."

"Who might that be?"

"It might be the Zodiac Killer," Rapinski said. He chuckled at his little joke.

Rhodes didn't chuckle. "Let me rephrase that. Who are you looking for?"

"Name's Gary Baty. Jumped bond a month or so ago in Arkansas. I traced him to Houston, and I think he might be around here now."

"Why do you think that?"

"Confidential sources."

Rhodes let that pass. "What was he accused of?"

"Bank robbery. He was wearing an ankle monitor, but he took it off and then took off himself."

Rhodes thought it over. He thought he might know the man. It seemed unlikely, but it was a possibility.

"Where did it happen?" Rhodes asked.

"The bail jump? Up in Arkansas. The bank robbery was in Little Rock. That's where Baty lived. Would've been smarter to go somewhere else besides the state next door. Like South America."

"Probably so," Rhodes said. "Let's you and me take a ride."

"Where to?"

"Funeral home."

"I'll follow you," Rapinski said. "I don't like riding in cop cars. No offense."

"None taken," Rhodes said.

Rhodes parked in back of the former mansion, and Rapinski parked beside him. It was no surprise to Rhodes that the bounty hunter drove a black Hummer.

"What you got to show me?" Rapinski asked, stepping out of the Hummer. Anyone smaller would have had to climb down with a ladder. Rapinski had no problem at all.

"Just a client," Rhodes said. "Not mine. The funeral home's."

They went inside. Rhodes led Rapinski to Ballinger's office, the one where he met the public. The funeral director sat at a desk the size of a library table. Its smooth glass top was uncluttered. It held only a small notebook and a desk calendar.

Rapinski had to take off his hat to get through the door, revealing a head shaved as clean as an egg.

"Hoss Rapinski, this is Clyde Ballinger,"

Rhodes said.

Ballinger stood up and came around the desk. The two men shook hands, and Ballinger said, "I've seen you on the news."

Rapinski looked at Rhodes and grinned.

"Rapinski might know the man who was brought in last night," Rhodes said.

"You really think so?" Ballinger asked.

"I don't have a clue," Rapinski said. "The sheriff's the one brought me here."

"Well," Ballinger said, "let's take a look."

He led the men to the room where the dead man lay in an open bottom-of-the-line coffin. Rapinski held his hat in front of him with both hands.

"Here he is," Ballinger said.

"You do nice work," Rapinski said after giving the body a quick glance.

"Thanks," Ballinger said, "but I don't do that anymore. I have two very capable assistants, both licensed embalmers."

"Well, he looks real natural," Rapinski said, paying what many people believed to be the highest compliment a funeral director could receive. "That's him, all right. Gary Baty."

"He shouldn't have jumped bail," Rhodes said. "It didn't pay off."

"Not for me, either," Rapinski said, "but at least he's off the streets. What happened to him?"

Rhodes gave him the short version.

"Know who did him in?" Rapinski asked.

"No," Rhodes told him, "but I'll find out."

"You sound like you believe that."

"The Mounties don't have anything on our sheriff," Ballinger said. "He always gets his man."

"So do I," Rapinski said, "and now I got this one. Might not get paid for him, but it's worth a try. He figured to come to a bad end."

"Because he robbed a bank?" Rhodes asked.

"*A* bank? That was just the one he got caught for. The story is that he was behind more than just the one robbery. Not that he was actually in on them but that he planned them. He was a heck of a planner. The jobs he did, he wasn't armed. The others involved guns. Nobody but Gary knows the whole story, though. *Knew* the whole story since Gary's dead now."

"Somebody knew," Rhodes said.

Rapinski nodded. "Sure. The guy who carried out the plans. You think he's the one that killed Gary?"

"I wouldn't know about that," Rhodes said, but he thought about the missing billfold and cell phone, assuming that either one had existed. Maybe Baty's body hadn't been robbed. The killer could have taken the billfold because he thought it might have something in it that would have told who Baty was. He couldn't have known that Rapinski would show up and identify the body the very next day. He'd taken the cell phone, if there was one, because Baty had called him on it. Speculation, sure, but it made sense.

"I know what you're thinking, Sheriff," Rapinski said. "You're thinking there might be a bank robber on the loose in your town and you can cash in if you catch him."

Rhodes hadn't been thinking that at all, but he played along.

"Cash in? How?"

"Publicity. Local TV news, maybe wire service stories. Now, if it was me that caught him, it'd go network, no question."

"Maybe so, but you're a bounty hunter."

Rapinski shook his head. "Fugitive recovery agent."

"Whatever. Anyway, you said it yourself back at the jail. You're not a peace officer. You can't arrest anybody."

"A citizen can make an arrest if he runs into a wanted criminal."

"Not a good idea," Ballinger said. "I saw

87

something about that on *The Andy Griffith Show*."

Rapinski looked at him. Ballinger grinned. Rapinski turned back to Rhodes.

"I won't get in your way, Sheriff, but I might stick around a while."

Rhodes didn't like it, but there wasn't much he could do about it, short of telling Rapinski that the town wasn't big enough for the both of them or that he'd better take the next stage, or Hummer, out of town.

"If whoever killed Baty was the other robber, he doesn't want anybody to know he's here. If he hears you're looking for him, he might kill you, too."

Rapinski laughed. It was a good laugh, big and booming, and entirely out of place in a funeral home. Ballinger gave him a scornful look.

"Sorry about that," Rapinski said to Ballinger. "Couldn't help myself. Your sheriff's a real comedian."

"A regular Larry the Cable Guy," Ballinger said.

"Right," Rhodes said, though he thought of himself more in the smooth Bill Cosby mold.

"Here's something you better think about, Sheriff," Rapinski told him. "If the guy wants to kill whoever's after him, he'd probably think you were more dangerous than I am. You being the kind who always gets his man and all." Rapinski put on his hat and settled it on his head just so. "I'll be seeing you around."

He turned to leave, but his exit was spoiled somewhat because he had to take the hat off again to get through the door.

"Nice fella," Ballinger said when the bounty hunter was gone. He looked at the body in the casket. "You think this Baty is really a bank robber?"

"Rapinski doesn't have any reason to lie," Rhodes said.

"He'd lie just for the fun of it," Ballinger said. "I could tell that by looking at him."

"Not this time. It's too easy to check."

"You and Hack are going to check, then."

"We'd be fools not to," Rhodes said.

Rhodes had a simple weight-control plan. He hardly ever ate lunch. It seemed like he was too busy to stop for even a hamburger at a drive-through. Today, though, he couldn't resist taking the time. He drove out on the highway where all the action in Clearview was now. The downtown area had become little more than a collection of empty buildings and vacant lots, with a few exceptions, like the expansive law offices of

Randy Lawless, whose names were the subject of a good bit of not-so-innocent hilarity in the county.

If the downtown looked like a bombed-out hamlet, however, the area on the highway east of town was booming. There were two new motels, part of a phenomenon that Rhodes didn't quite understand. Every little town in Texas was sprouting motels like mushrooms after a spring rain, and Clearview was no exception. Two more had sprung up on the highway to the north.

The Super Walmart's parking lot had cars in nearly all the parking spaces. The big supermarket down the road swarmed with customers. Nobody who drove by on the highway would ever give a thought to what had happened to the nearly deserted downtown. Only people who'd lived in Clearview for a good while even missed it, Rhodes was sure.

Another place doing plenty of business was the local McDonald's, but Rhodes wasn't interested in a McBurger. Across the highway was a Big Jolly's convenience store. Jolly was Jeff Jolly, and he wasn't big at all. He was short and rotund, but his last name described his disposition well.

It was no wonder he was jolly. He'd started out as a clerk in an early version of the convenience store fifty years earlier. Now he owned six or seven stores of his own, every one of them a gold mine, or so Rhodes had heard.

One reason for their popularity was the hamburgers served at every location. No hot dogs, no deli sandwiches, no wraps. Just burgers, and nothing fancy. You could get cheese added, but that was it. No bacon, no peppers, no sissy sauces. No ketchup or mayo. Mustard only.

Best of all, as far as Rhodes was concerned, was the fact that after the burger was cooked, both sides of the bun were slapped down on the grill and warmed in the grease that remained. Rhodes had feared that when the Bluebonnet Grocery closed, he'd never have a burger wrapped in greasy paper again, and for a while that had been true. Now, Big Jolly had stepped in to save the day.

Rhodes parked in the shade on the side of the store away from the gas pumps and went inside for his burger.

Larry Torrance was the cook, and when Rhodes ordered, Torrance said, "No cheese today, Sheriff?"

"No cheese," Rhodes said. That was how he convinced himself that he was eating healthy. "No tomato, either."

"Tomatoes are good for you," Larry said. He always said that.

"They have evil side effects," Rhodes said, and Larry nodded. It was what Rhodes always said in reply. Larry had never asked what the evil side effects were, which was just as well. Rhodes couldn't have told him.

Torrance put the meat on the grill and pressed it down with a spatula. Rhodes looked around the store while he listened to the sizzle. He didn't see anybody he knew, so he watched a youngster at the soft drink machine fill what appeared to be a gallon container with cola.

"Ready, Sheriff," Torrance said after a while. "Just pay up front."

Rhodes took the bag containing his burger, paid, and left. He didn't want to eat at one of the two small tables in the store, so he drove to the courthouse, where he had an office he seldom used. He bought a Dr Pepper from the machine that no longer dispensed drinks in a glass bottle and went to his office to enjoy the burger.

He soothed the sharp tang of the onion, mustard, and pickles with swallows of Dr Pepper and thought about what he knew and didn't know about Gary Baty's demise.

He knew Baty was dead, but he didn't know who killed him. Had it been hog hunters, the man who'd been in the car with him, or someone else that Rhodes didn't know about?

Baty was a bank robber. That wasn't a real surprise to Rhodes. The economy had been bad for four or five years, and there had been a surge in bank robberies all across the country. What made Baty different was that he had partners and men who'd bought plans from him. Had Baty been with one of those men? If he had, what were they doing in Blacklin County?

If they were planning a job, Rhodes thought, there were only a few possible targets, the two banks in Clearview, the one in Thurston, and the one in Obert. Somehow Rhodes didn't think robbing a bank came into the picture. Otherwise, why kill Baty before the job was done?

Rapinski seemed to believe that the man in the car with Baty had been one of his partners, however, and Rapinski was planning to see if he could catch him. Or that's what he claimed. Rhodes wondered what Rapinski wasn't telling him. He knew he wasn't getting the whole story. Ballinger was right. People like Rapinski never told the truth if they could avoid doing it.

Rhodes finished his hamburger and drank the last of the Dr Pepper. He wadded up the paper bag and tossed it in the trash can. The empty Dr Pepper bottle followed, the plastic making a hollow sound and reminding Rhodes once again how much he missed the glass bottles. There had been a couple of napkins in the bag with the burger, and Rhodes wiped his hands with them before tossing them, too. Then he picked up the phone and called Hack.

Hack answered and said, "Ruth's here," when Rhodes asked. "When you called me from Ballinger's, I got her to come back and do a search on this Baty fella. He got caught on camera robbin' a bank, and the cops caught up with him. He's suspected in a bunch of other cases, but nothin's been proved on those. Believed to've planned a bunch of robberies that he didn't do himself."

"What about the fingerprints?"

Rhodes had wanted Ruth to check on those just in case Rapinski hadn't told the truth about the dead man's identity.

"They're a match," Hack said. "Baty's our victim, all right enough."

"What about Rapinski?"

"He's who he says he is. I've seen him on TV a couple of times myself. That license of his is real."

"All right. Have Ruth call the police and

the FBI office in Little Rock and let them know their fugitive bank robber is in Blacklin County and won't be giving them any more trouble."

"Might get complicated if the FBI's involved."

"I doubt it. They'll be glad to mark him off their list."

"Okay. Anything else?"

"Did Ruth find out anything about the hog hunters?"

"Yeah," Hack said. "She wants to talk to you about that."

"Have her check the motels, see if Baty stayed in any of them."

"She's already done that. He didn't. You comin' in?"

"I'm on the way," Rhodes said.

"They wouldn't talk to me," Ruth said when Rhodes got to the jail.

Rhodes wondered if she'd been taking lessons from Hack and Lawton. "Who wouldn't talk to you?"

"The Eccles cousins," Ruth said. "I know they're the ones who were out hunting hogs last night. I talked to a lot of people, and they all said the same."

Rhodes had dealt with the Eccles cousins before. They lived outside of town on the road to Obert, and they looked more like brothers than cousins. They were gypsy truckers, doing long-haul jobs for whoever would hire them. In between jobs, their hobby seemed to be getting into trouble.

"I'll go talk to them," Rhodes said.

"They won't tell you anything," Ruth said.

"How do you know?"

"Because they said they wouldn't. Let's see, how did they put it. 'You can tell the sheriff that we won't talk to him, either. We don't have to talk to you or him if we don't want to, and we don't want to.'"

"They know something," Rhodes said.

"Maybe so," Ruth said, "but if they do, they're not telling."

"They'll tell me."

"We'll see," Ruth said.

CHAPTER 8

On the way to visit the Eccles boys, Rhodes stopped at the house owned by Seepy Benton, a professor at the local branch of a community college as well as a graduate of the Citizens' Sheriff's Academy. Benton liked to think of himself as an unofficial deputy and ace crime solver, neither of which was true. In this case, however, Rhodes thought that Benton might actually be able to help out.

It was the middle of the afternoon, but Benton was home. He often finished with his teaching and office hours and came home to grade papers in privacy before going back to teach his evening class.

"What can I do for you, Sheriff?" Benton asked when he answered Rhodes's knock on his door. "Have you come up against some heinous crime that needs my special skills?"

Rhodes didn't ask what those skills were.

"Nothing like that. I just stopped by to see how Bruce is doing."

Bruce was a dog that had formerly lived with the Eccles cousins and served as a guard dog. In that capacity he'd once eagerly sought to take a big chunk out of Rhodes's anatomy.

Bruce was part leopard dog, and he had a bad attitude that Rhodes blamed on his owners. Leopard dogs were descended from mastiffs, and they could be dangerous, as Rhodes had discovered.

Bruce also looked to have a bit of wolf in his ancestry, which didn't help matters. Rhodes had taken him away from the cousins and given him to Benton to care for while the cousins were in jail for a short time. Benton hadn't wanted a dog, but he and Bruce had become pals, and Bruce's disposition had improved accordingly. Because the Eccles boys were often gone and had trouble finding someone to take care of Bruce, they'd allowed the dog to stay with Benton.

"Bruce is fine," Benton said. He stepped out of the door. "Let's go around back so you can say hello."

Benton led the way to his backyard, where Rhodes saw the Golden Rectangle that Benton had laid out with gray paving stones.

Benton had tried to explain to Rhodes what the thing was all about, but when he'd mentioned the Fibonacci sequence and started expounding on the math involved, Rhodes had stopped him. There were some things Rhodes felt that he didn't need to know.

Bruce saw Rhodes and wagged his tail. Then he trotted over to sniff Rhodes and assure himself that he knew him. He licked Rhodes's hand, and Rhodes rubbed his head.

"You've done well with him," Rhodes said.

"It's just a matter of treating him humanely and with dignity," Benton said. "We should take care of our animals as well as we take care of ourselves. There's even a passage in Deuteronomy that says we should feed our animals before we eat our own food." He looked at Rhodes. "You have dogs. Do you eat first, or do they?"

"It depends," Rhodes said.

"I know you do the right thing," Benton said. "Which is good. According to the Talmud, a person is measured by how he treats other living creatures."

Rhodes had never met a rabbi, but Benton bore a strong resemblance to what Rhodes thought one would look like, except that he didn't wear a yarmulke. He usually wore a battered old black fedora, though he wasn't wearing it now.

Benton looked at Rhodes again. "I get the feeling that you didn't come here to discuss the Talmud, though."

"Not really," Rhodes said. "I'm sure it's a fascinating topic, but I did have something else in mind. In fact, it has to do with the treatment of animals."

Bruce lost interest in the discussion. He trotted away to examine something he'd seen crawling in the grass. Whatever it was, Rhodes hoped Bruce would treat it humanely.

"What kind of animals?" Benton asked.

"Wild hogs."

"People don't like wild hogs."

"The Chandlers do."

"They're fine folks," Benton said. "I've given them a little advice about caring for animals from time to time. I wasn't talking about them. I should have said that *most* people don't like wild hogs. They hunt them and kill them."

"That's right, and two of the people who do that are Bruce's former owners."

"Lance and Hugh. They like Bruce. They stop to check on him now and then, to make sure I'm doing the right thing by him. They seem happy to let me take care of him."

"Good," Rhodes said. "I'm glad you're their friend. I think you might be able to help me when I pay them a little visit."

"I knew it," Benton said. "You've uncovered an atrocious crime, and you need my detecting skills."

"Not exactly," Rhodes said. "Do you ever listen to Milton Munday?"

"That goober?" Benton asked, giving Rhodes the impression that he was a good judge of character. "You must be kidding."

"I'm not kidding," Rhodes said. "Munday was going on this morning about a man who was killed last night. I think Lance and Hugh might know something about it."

"They might not be exactly civilized," Benton said, "and they don't always treat animals the way they should, but they're not murderers."

"I don't think so, either, but I'm pretty sure they were hunting hogs last night around where the murder happened. They might have seen something that could help me find the killer."

"So you need me to use my incredible powers of persuasion to get them to talk," Benton said. "I can do that."

"Good," Rhodes said. "Let's go see them."

"Just let me get my hat," Benton said.

■ ■ ■ ■

The Eccles cousins lived on up the county road from Benton, off on a little hill. Their double-wide trailer sat on top of the hill, and their two big Chevy Silverados, one red, one black, sat out in front. Not far away was the big Mack tractor rig that the cousins used for hauling. It was painted red and had a sleeper cab in back. The words ECCLES TRUCKING were written on the doors in italic script with silver paint outlined in black.

"Very classy logo," Benton said, when he and Rhodes got out of the county car. "I wonder if they came up with the design all by themselves."

"They probably told Herman Johnson to do whatever he wanted to," Rhodes said. Johnson was a local sign painter with an artistic bent.

"I could do better," Benton said.

The door of the double-wide opened, and Lance and Hugh came outside. They were tall and wide, and they both wore Houston Astros baseball caps over their red hair, which was long enough to stick out all around the bottoms of the caps. They had broad, freckled faces and smiling eyes, but their mouths weren't smiling, and they didn't look happy to see their visitors.

"I told your deputy to tell you we didn't have nothin' to say to you," Hugh said. Rhodes knew it was Hugh because of the gap between his front teeth. Lance's teeth didn't have a gap. "You can just turn on around and go back to town."

"That's no way to talk to an officer of the law," Benton said.

"Hey, Seepy," Hugh said. "What you doin' with the sheriff?"

"Helping out," Benton said. "He tells me you've been hunting hogs."

"That's right," Lance said. "Nothin' wrong with that, is there?"

"Not legally speaking," Benton said. "Morally, it's a different story."

"Morally?" Lance asked, as if he'd never heard the word before.

"The Lord's tender mercies are over all his works," Benton said, "and that includes hogs."

"You might think I don't know," Hugh said, "but that's from the Bible."

Benton looked surprised. "That's right. Psalm 145."

"Here's something else from the Bible," Lance said. "An eye for an eye. I don't know what book it's from, but I know what it means."

"Well?" Benton asked.

"It means those damn hogs are tearin' up the country, ruinin' the crops, ruinin' the land. So we got a right to take retribution on 'em."

Benton looked quite happy. Rhodes could tell he was about to launch into a lengthy lesson from the Talmud to prove Lance wrong, so he thought he'd better put a stop to it. Lance and Hugh weren't the kind to be persuaded by rabbinical reasoning, or at least Rhodes didn't think they were.

"We didn't come here to talk about killing hogs," he said. "This is about something else entirely."

"Doesn't matter," Hugh said. "We're not talking. Right, Lance?"

"That's right," Lance said.

The two men turned and went back into the trailer. The door on a double-wide isn't made for slamming, but they did a pretty good job of it, nevertheless.

"I wasn't much help, was I," Benton said.

"I think it was the psalm that did it," Rhodes said.

"Too much?"

"Yes. It's just as well you didn't get around to quoting Deuteronomy."

"Sometimes I get carried away."

It didn't take long for that to happen, either, Rhodes thought. He said, "It's okay. Maybe they'll give you another chance to use those incredible powers of persuasion of yours. I'll see if they'll come back out."

He left Benton standing by the county car and mounted the little concrete steps in front of the trailer door. There was no doorbell, so he rapped on the door with his knuckles. No reply came from inside, but Rhodes thought he heard something. He strained his ears and caught the faint strains of George Jones singing "He Stopped Loving Her Today." The Eccles boys had good taste. Rhodes knocked again, louder this time.

"They're going out the back door," Benton yelled.

Rhodes turned to him. "What?"

"The back door. I heard the back door."

Rhodes heard something, too. He jumped off the porch and ran along the front of the trailer. Benton was a little ahead of him.

"Go back to the car," Rhodes said, but Benton either didn't hear or didn't care to obey. They turned the corner at the end of the trailer, ran a few more steps, turned the back corner, and stopped. There was nobody there.

That was when Rhodes heard the front

door. *Tricked by two men who probably hadn't even graduated from high school,* Rhodes thought as he turned to run back the other way.

He heard the rumble of the Mack's engine, and by the time he got to the front yard, the big tractor rig was turning toward the dirt road that led up the hill to the double-wide.

Rhodes sprinted for the county car. Benton panted along behind him. Rhodes didn't intend to wait for him. When he reached the car, he opened the door and jumped in, turning the key in the ignition before the door closed. He pulled on his seat belt and put the car in gear just as Benton opened his own door. Rhodes started to pull away, but Benton dragged himself inside and allowed the car's momentum to slam the door shut.

The Mack was running wide open down the hill. It turned the corner at the gate leaning dangerously to the side and took off on the county road, throwing up clods of dirt as it went.

Benton bounced around in the front seat of the Dodge as he struggled with his seat belt. When he finally got it fastened, he was still jostled quite a bit. His hat had slipped down on his forehead, hiding his eyes.

Rhodes was also jostled by the rough road. He struggled to keep the car under control.

"Where are they going?" Benton asked.

Rhodes didn't answer, mainly because he didn't know. He got the radio mic and called Hack. When the dispatcher came on, Rhodes told him the situation.

"What's that county road number?" Hack asked.

Rhodes told him.

"Duke's out that way, not far from Obert," Hack said. "I'll see if I can get you some backup."

Rhodes hooked the mic and concentrated on his driving. He didn't think Duke, the county's newest deputy, would be of much help. The county roads wound around all over the place, one joining another at odd junctions. The Eccles cousins would know them all, Rhodes was sure, and Duke wouldn't know them nearly as well. Rhodes had lived in the county all his life, but even he didn't know all of them.

"You ought to be able to catch a big truck like that," Benton said.

Rhodes hit a bump, and the county car went briefly airborne.

"Or not," Benton said.

"I appreciate your confidence in my driving," Rhodes said as he fought the wheel.

The Mack barreled across a bridge that spanned Pittman Creek and thundered up a hill.

The county car was gaining on them, but the driver turned the truck sharply where there was no real road, just a barbed-wire gate leading into a pasture. The truck tore the wire from its moorings and headed off across the open country, bouncing wildly.

Rhodes didn't even try to follow. He stopped the car and watched.

"Those two are crazy," Benton said.

"Not as crazy as I'd be if I tried to follow them," Rhodes said. "I've already got a new dent in this car. I can't chance tearing up the suspension."

"Do you have any idea where they're going?"

"Nope," Rhodes said. "Once they get over the hill they can go a lot of different directions."

"So you're going to let them get away?"

"I hate to disillusion you," Rhodes said, "but that's about the size of it."

Benton took off his hat and tried to push it into something resembling its proper shape.

"I can live with that," he said.

Rhodes dropped Benton off at his house

and went back to the jail. Nothing unusual was going on around the county, aside from the fleeing cousins.

"Just couple of loose cows," Hack said when Rhodes asked. "Boyd's after 'em. Broken water main shootin' a geyser in the air over at the Kelly place on Pine Street. I called the water department 'bout that. Couple of neighbors arguin' about some trash in the yard. One claims the other put it there. Ruth's on that one."

"Any response to that bulletin you put out last night?" Rhodes asked.

"About the man leavin' the scene of a murder? Not a thing. No reports of any hitchhikers. Nobody called to say they saw him. He's the invisible man."

Not so invisible, Rhodes thought. It would be easy enough to walk back to town from the Leverett place and not be seen after dark.

"I expect ever'body out that way's got their doors locked up tight," Hack said. "No use, though. That fella's long gone, like you said."

"Maybe. The Eccles boys know something about it, though."

"You gonna tell me?"

Rhodes could have drawn it out, but he

didn't bother. He told Hack what had happened.

"That's just like those two," Hack said, "but it might not be what you think it is."

"Why do you say that?"

"They might not want to talk because of somethin' else that happened. You know. The Chandlers."

"You think the Chandlers might have mixed it up with the hunters?"

"I wouldn't be surprised," Hack said. "You could ask 'em."

"I already have. They denied it."

"Too bad you can't ask Lance and Hugh. They might have a different story, if they'd tell it."

"They'll tell it," Rhodes said. "Eventually. Did you get anything more on those bank robberies Baty supposedly planned?"

"Ruth did. She said to tell you there's not any good descriptions of the man who pulled those jobs. Just a big man with a stockin' pulled down over his face. Had on a hoodie when he went in the bank, so nobody could get a good look at him, anyway."

The man in the car with Baty had been big, though that didn't prove anything. It suggested a few ideas, though.

"You heard anything else about our friend

Hoss Rapinski?" Rhodes asked.

"Why would I?"

"He said he was sticking around. Said he wanted to catch himself a killer."

"He's a show-off, all right," Hack said. "He'd love to prove he was smarter than you."

Rhodes gave him a look.

"Not that he'd have a chance of doin' it," Hack said.

"He might if I don't find out some things pretty quickly."

"How you gonna do it?"

"I'm going to hunt some hogs," Rhodes said.

CHAPTER 9

"You must be crazy," Ivy said.

"Probably," Rhodes said, and Yancey yipped in agreement.

"You'll get killed," Ivy said, and Yancey yipped again, as if he was excited at the prospect.

"I don't think so," Rhodes said.

They were in the kitchen, eating dinner, which tonight consisted of some kind of casserole made with cabbage, macaroni, and lots of black pepper. It was good, but Rhodes was glad he'd eaten the hamburger for lunch.

"I know you don't think so," Ivy said, "but that doesn't mean it won't happen. All those men with guns, and the hogs are dangerous, too."

"We probably won't even see any hogs."

"That's another thing," Ivy said. "Who is this *we?* Do you even know any of them?"

After talking to Hack, Rhodes had set out

to find the names of some of the men who'd been in the group with the Eccles cousins the previous night. It had taken him the rest of the afternoon, but he'd found out that one of the men was Arvid Fowler, an electrician and air-conditioner repairman. According to Fowler, he occasionally joined the Eccles cousins on a hunt. He'd been with them at the Leverett place, all right, but he claimed that he hadn't noticed anything out of the ordinary. He told Rhodes he didn't have any idea why the Eccleses would have run away when Rhodes tried to talk to them.

"I know Arvid Fowler," Rhodes told Ivy. "So do you. He fixed the air conditioner for us a couple of years ago."

"Overcharged us, too," Ivy said. "You can't trust a man like that."

"It was on a Sunday," Rhodes pointed out. "He told us he'd have to charge more to come out on a Sunday."

"Well, he shouldn't have. It was an emergency."

"Not for him."

"You're trying to get me off the subject, aren't you," Ivy said.

Rhodes got up and refilled his water glass. "That cabbage sure is hot," he said when he sat back down.

"It's not the cabbage. It's the pepper. Now

stop avoiding the subject."

"What subject?"

"You know what subject."

The dangers of Rhodes's job, though he didn't consider them great, had been a topic of discussion before.

"Don't worry about me," Rhodes said. "I'll be fine. I always am."

"That depends on the definition of 'fine,' " Ivy said.

Rhodes grinned. "I didn't say 'clean.' "

"I know it's your job," Ivy said, ignoring him, "but sometimes I think you take more risks than you really have to."

"Not this time. I promise."

"Not that I could stop you even if you didn't."

"True," Rhodes said, "but you wouldn't try to stop me, would you?"

"Not a chance," Ivy said.

Later that night, Rhodes wished she'd tried.

Arvid Fowler was a wiry man about five and a half feet tall. He had a face like a wise monkey and wore rimless glasses. He had a big pistol strapped around his skinny waist. Rhodes judged it to be a .357 Magnum.

"Reason we go to the Leverett place," Fowler said in answer to a question from

Rhodes, "is that nobody knows for sure who owns it. We don't do any trespassin', and we just go where we're invited, or where the land's open like out there."

"Some people don't like it that you come here," Rhodes said.

They were standing by Fowler's old red pickup, which was parked on the side of the road not far from where the Ford Focus had stopped the previous day.

"If they don't, ain't nothin' they can do about it," Fowler said.

"You were parked on a different road last night," Rhodes said.

"Other side of the woods, yeah," Fowler said. "Thought we'd come in from this side tonight."

It was just about dark. Fowler had told Rhodes that the other hunters would be arriving soon.

"Any reason why you decided to make the change to this side of the woods?" Rhodes asked.

Fowler shrugged. "Just seemed like the thing to do."

Rhodes didn't think that was the truth, but he didn't push it. He figured he'd find out more when some of the other hunters arrived.

"Here comes somebody now," Fowler

said. "I don't think I know that truck, though."

It wasn't a truck, Rhodes saw as it came to a stop behind the county car. It was a Hummer. Hoss Rapinski got out, put on his hat, and joined them.

"Fancy meeting you here, Sheriff," the bounty hunter said. "Who's your friend?"

"This is Arvid Fowler," Rhodes said. "Arvid, meet Hoss Rapinski. He's a bounty hunter."

"Fugitive recovery agent," Rapinski said.

He and Arvid shook hands.

"I seen you on TV," Arvid said. "You're the one brought in Slick Tomlin."

"That's right," Hoss said. He looked at Rhodes. "The law couldn't find him, but I did."

"What do you think you'll find out here?" Rhodes asked.

"Don't know," Rapinski said. "I asked around town and found out this was where the murder happened." He took off his hat and fingered the brim. "I like to look at the scene of the crime and talk to the witnesses."

"Now just a minute," Fowler said. "Ain't nobody a witness to anything. We're just here to hunt hogs."

"I meant witnesses to the hog hunting,"

116

Rapinski said. "That's all."

Before Fowler could question him, a pickup pulled to a stop behind the Hummer. Rhodes heard dogs barking.

"That's Winston," Fowler said. "He brings the dogs."

Len Winston got out of his truck, and Fowler went to help him with the dogs.

"You ever hunted hogs?" Rapinski asked Rhodes.

"Nope. Might be interesting, though."

"Come on, Sheriff, you don't care about any hogs. I know you're looking for witnesses, same as I am."

"Witnesses to hog hunting?"

Rapinski put his hat back on and didn't answer. Another pickup arrived. A man named Ed Garver got out and helped Fowler and Winston with the dogs. Rhodes walked over to see what they were doing. Rapinski followed him.

"Body armor," Fowler said when Rhodes asked. "Kevlar, just like the bulletproof vests you lawmen wear."

"You think somebody's going to shoot at the dogs?" Rapinski asked.

"Hogs' tusks are worse than bein' shot," Winston said. "Who're you?"

Rhodes introduced Rapinski to Winston and Garver.

"Don't know as we need any more people," Garver said.

Garver worked as a plumber for a man named Trey Allison, and he was nearly as big as Rapinski. Like Fowler, he had a pistol, which Rhodes was sure was a .38. He wasn't as impressed by the bounty hunter as Fowler had been.

"We won't get in the way," Rhodes said. "Mainly we'd like to hear about last night."

"I already told 'em we didn't see anything or hear anything," Fowler said.

"What about Lance and Hugh?" Rhodes asked. "You think they'll be here?"

"Doubt it," Fowler said. "If they were comin', they'd be here already."

He explained to Winston and Garver what had happened between Rhodes and the Eccles cousins.

"Those two are about half crazy," Winston said. "I don't know why they'd run off like that. Do you, Ed?"

"Nope," Garver said. "They got nothin' to hide, far as I know."

It was dark now. The dogs whined and strained at their leashes, eager to be off on the chase. Winston had trouble holding them back. The dogs were tan with dark muzzles.

"What kind of dogs are those?" Rapinski asked.

"Black Mouth Curs," Winston said. "Won't no other kind of dog will do for huntin'. Coons, hogs, you name it."

"They run quiet," Fowler said. "Don't start to bay till they got 'em a hog."

"Strong, too," Garver said. "Not afraid of anything. They'll stand at a hog's head till you get there with the gun, no matter how big and mean that sucker is."

"You must have had one bayed up last night," Rhodes said. "I heard the dogs."

"Sure," Fowler said. "That's the way it was."

"What happened to the hog?"

"He got away. We left. That was it."

Rhodes wasn't convinced, but Garver changed the subject.

"Harvest moon tonight," he said, looking across the field. "Ought to be able to see pretty well without lights."

"Yep," Fowler said. "Let's go."

"Before we do," Rhodes said, "just tell me some more about what happened last night. You know there's more to it than hog hunting. I heard all the shooting."

"Don't know nothin' about that," Fowler said. "You can stay here if you want to, but we're goin'. Right, boys?"

"Right," Winston and Garver said together. "Can we leave, Sheriff?"

"Don't let me stop you," Rhodes said.

"Hold the dogs," Winston said to Garver, handing him the leashes. "I got to get my gun."

He went to the cab of his pickup and brought out a .30-30 rifle.

"I'm ready now," he said, and Fowler jogged down into the bar ditch and out into the field on the other side. Winston and Garver followed. The dogs were so eager it was as if they were dragging the big plumber behind them.

"Well," Rapinski said to Rhodes, "did you learn anything?"

"Not a thing," Rhodes said.

"You going with them?"

"I guess so," Rhodes said.

"Let's go, then," Rapinski said.

He and Rhodes moved down into the ditch. They were almost to the woods when Rapinski spoke again.

"That Garver's a big guy. You know him?"

"I've heard he does good work," Rhodes said.

"Been around here long?"

"Couple of years. Came up here from Galveston before Hurricane Ike blew in and decided he liked this part of Texas. No hurricanes."

"Seems like he'd have had a lot of work if he'd gone back home after the storm. Took 'em a while to rebuild. He could've made a lot of money."

"I'm sure he does all right here," Rhodes said. "Everybody needs a plumber now and then."

"I guess so," Rapinski said.

They walked in silence for a while, careful to avoid twisting an ankle on the dirt clods. The shadows cast by the bright orange moon made walking across the field even more treacherous than usual. Rhodes still felt an occasional twinge from last night's adventure, and it was hard for Rapinski to walk in his expensive boots. They looked good, but they weren't made for hog hunts.

"How'd you happen to wind up here tonight?" Rhodes asked, hoping for a more definitive answer than the one he'd gotten before. "It took me a long time to find out the hunters would be here again."

"Confidential sources," Rapinski said.

"You seem to have a lot of those."

"Just part of the job," Rapinski said.

He might have said more, but they had reached the woods. The three hunters weren't far ahead of them. Rhodes heard Fowler say, "Let 'em loose."

121

"There they go," Garver said. "Old Joe's got a scent already. Look at him run."

"Sarah's right behind him," Winston said. "We better see if we can keep up."

Rhodes remembered the stampede and hoped it wouldn't happen again. So far he hadn't heard any shooting, so maybe it wouldn't.

"Let's see if we can catch up," he said.

"Won't be a problem for me," Rapinski said, and he took off at a run that Rhodes wouldn't have thought possible in those fancy boots.

Rhodes followed as fast as he could.

Chapter 10

Trying to run through the woods at night, no matter how bright the moon, wasn't as easy as it looked in movies, Rhodes thought. He'd often wondered how those horses managed not to slam into a tree every eight or ten paces. If he'd been riding, the horse would've had a concussion before it had gone a block into the woods.

Rhodes couldn't see Rapinski or the others, but he could hear them. He couldn't hear the dogs, however. They were running as quietly as he'd been told.

Then he did hear them, baying loudly in the distance. He picked up the pace a little, dodging tree limbs attached to the trees and jumping over fallen ones. He hadn't gone far before he saw lights, and then he came out of the trees into a little clearing.

The dogs had a hog backed up against a deadfall. The men stood well back. Rapinski wasn't there, and Rhodes figured he'd gotten lost along the way.

The men were silent as they moved around, playing their flashlights on the hog, trying to get a shot at him as the dogs danced around him. They weren't baying now. They growled and snarled, lips pulled back, teeth bared as they held the hog at bay.

The hog grunted and lunged at them, ripping upward with his three-inch tusks, tusks that could take the stomach out of a man, much less a dog. The armor was a good idea.

Rhodes didn't know how much this hog weighed, but he figured it to be close to two hundred pounds, maybe a little more. Its neck and shoulders were overlaid with fat and muscle that could stop a bullet from a small-caliber gun, but the pistols and rifle the hunters carried would be enough to stop it if they could get in a shot.

Rhodes understood the necessity for keeping down the hog population. He knew that the hogs were destructive and caused thousands of dollars of damage to farms and crops at a time when nobody could afford the losses. There was never a time when people could afford losses like that.

He knew that the hogs could never be trapped or killed out of existence, and he suspected that when the end of the world finally came, whether it was by fire or ice, the cockroaches and the hogs would be left behind to fight it out for supremacy.

Yet when he saw the desperation and fear in the little black eyes of the hog, Rhodes couldn't help but feel a bit of the same kind of sympathy that the Chandlers must have felt for the animals. Even if the hunters killed ten or twenty a night, they couldn't make a dent in the population, so why bother?

Rhodes even knew the answer to that: Every little bit helps. Hunting and trapping combined would at least do something toward keeping the number of hogs smaller, if not eliminating them. It didn't make him feel a lot better about what he was seeing.

"I'm gonna see if I can go around and come in from behind him," Garver said. "Don't shoot me."

He moved away with his flashlight. Rhodes lost sight of him and turned back to see what Fowler and Winston would do. They said nothing but kept their lights trained on the hog.

The hog and dogs were getting tired, but that didn't reduce the level of their savagery. The dogs backed up a bit, however, and that gave Winston a clear shot with his rifle.

The crack of sound didn't frighten the

dogs. It didn't scare the hog, either. The animal dropped, kicked out with one of its back trotters, and lay still.

It was quiet in the clearing after the rifle shot. A bit of smoke drifted through the moonlight, and Rhodes smelled gunpowder. The dogs walked over to the hog and sniffed it, then backed off. They were no longer interested now that it was dead.

"Got 'im," Winston said.

He handed his rifle to Fowler and leashed the dogs.

"We goin' after another one?" Winston asked.

"Night's young," Fowler said. "Where's Garver?"

Winston looked around. "S'posed to be comin' in from behind."

"Here I am," Garver said, coming along out of the darkness. "I couldn't get back there, but it looks like you got it. Let the dogs loose, and we'll get another one."

"Any of you seen Rapinski?" Rhodes asked.

"Nope," Garver said. "We got enough to do, keepin' up with dogs and hogs. Let's run 'em."

"Did the Eccles boys run with you last night?" Rhodes asked, hoping to catch them off guard.

"They come now and then. Don't remember about last night," Winston said, and he released the dogs.

The dogs sniffed the air and ran off around the deadfall.

Without another word to Rhodes, the men followed them.

Rhodes had seen enough. He wasn't going to get anything more out of the hunters, and he didn't want to watch another kill, even one as clean as what he'd just witnessed.

When Rhodes turned to leave, he realized that he didn't quite know where he was or how he'd gotten there. He'd assumed the hunters would lead him out of the woods, but they were off chasing hogs, and he was alone. In the daylight, that wouldn't have been a problem, but at night everything looked different and strange.

He tried to remember something he'd heard about how to tell the direction in the woods. He should have paid more attention in Cub Scouts. Moss on the north side of trees? Maybe that worked in some parts of the world, but Rhodes wasn't sure moss even grew on trees in Texas. Besides, it might have been the south side of trees it was supposed to grow on. Or east. Or west.

Moss wasn't going to be any help.

Rhodes looked around. He thought he recognized a tree or two, so he started back. He hadn't gone far before he knew he hadn't recognized anything at all. He should have noted the moon's position in the sky when he started, but it probably wouldn't have helped him.

He stood quietly and looked around, admitting to himself that he was lost, as lost as the people or animals in that animated movie he'd thought of last night. Any minute now, the wind would start blowing, the limbs of the trees would turn into arms, and he'd be grabbed.

He heard the dogs bay. They'd found another hog, and Rhodes knew he could follow the sound and find the hunters again. He thought that was the wisest course, so he turned back. He came to the deadfall and skirted around it. He wasn't quite sure of the direction of the baying, but he wouldn't be far off if he kept going. He must not have been taking exactly the same path that the hunters had taken, however, because there was something there in front of him that he was pretty sure they hadn't seen. If they had, they'd have stopped hunting hogs and gone to look for Rhodes.

It was Hoss Rapinski. He lay sprawled out

on the ground. His hat was about ten feet away. There wasn't any doubt that he was dead.

Rhodes was on his way to find the hunters when he ran into the Chandlers. Both of them carried shotguns.

"Well, well," Rhodes said.

"What's that supposed to mean?" Andy asked.

"Nothing," Rhodes said. "Just an exclamation of wonder."

"Huh?"

"Don't let him bother you, Andy," Janice said. "We have a perfect right to be here."

"That depends on why you're here," Rhodes said. "You have any guns besides the ones I can see there?"

"Why?" Janice asked.

"For one thing, it wouldn't be a good idea if you were out here to cause trouble."

"Trouble?" Andy asked. "Us?"

"Shooting at hunters with rock salt is one thing," Rhodes said. "Killing a man is something else."

"I don't have any idea what you're talking about," Janice said.

"Me, neither," Andy said. "We're here to hunt squirrels."

Rhodes didn't believe a word of it. People

who ran a shelter for animals didn't hunt anything, much less harmless little squirrels.

"There's a dead man over there," Rhodes said. He pointed. "About fifty yards from where we're standing."

"A dead man?" Andy didn't sound surprised.

"Who?" Janice asked.

"Eugene Rapinski," Rhodes said. "Better known as Hoss."

"The bounty hunter?" Andy asked. "I've seen him on TV."

Something in the man's tone seemed false to Rhodes, as if Andy was hiding something.

"Not in person?" Rhodes asked.

"Why would I see a bounty hunter?" Andy asked. "I doubt he's interested in saving animals."

"We'd better leave now," Janice said. "If there's really a dead man here, we'll just be in the way."

"Stick around for a while," Rhodes said. "I have a few questions to ask you."

Janice sighed, but she didn't try to leave. Neither did Andy. Rhodes got to work.

After that, there was a lot of confusion. When he finally had time to look for them, Rhodes couldn't find the hunters. They seemed to have given up on the hogs and left the woods. The hog they'd killed was also gone, so they'd managed to haul it away. There were no tire tracks, so Rhodes thought they must have rigged a sling and carried it on a pole.

Thanks to directions from the Chandlers, the JP and EMTs managed to get to the body. The JP declared that Rapinski was dead. Rhodes could see that the bounty hunter had been shot in the chest, pretty much the way Baty had been. If he'd been a betting man, Rhodes would have wagered that the same gun had killed them both.

After the EMTs had left with the body, Rhodes sent the Chandlers home. They'd answered his questions, but they had refused to let him look at their shotguns. Janice said they'd have been glad to let him, however, if he had a warrant.

"Do you have a warrant, Sheriff?" she'd asked, as nice as could be.

She knew he didn't, and Rhodes didn't push it. Andy insisted that they were just out hunting for squirrels and that he'd never seen Rapinski before except on television, but Rhodes didn't believe him on either count. They were stubborn in their insistence, so he sent them home.

Rhodes had gone over the scene and found only one thing of interest. Feathers.

They weren't the feathers of some bird that hung out in the woods, Rhodes was sure of that. He thought they were down feathers that had formerly stuffed a hunting vest or jacket, one that could have been wrapped around a pistol to silence it.

So now Rhodes had another body on his hands, this one of a semicelebrity, and he didn't have much of a clue as to who had killed him or why.

Rhodes didn't want to think about what Milton Munday would say on his radio show in the morning.

For that matter, he didn't much want to hear what Ivy would have to say when he got home, either.

So he went to the jail to write up his report.

"Gonna be a lot of publicity on this one," Hack said after Rhodes told him the story. "You know what Rapinski said about TV? Well, he's gonna be on TV, all right. Just not the way he expected."

"Milton Munday's bad enough," Rhodes said. "I don't need TV."

"Gonna get it, though," Lawton said. "You're lucky. This is the kind of case Sage Barton would love."

"I'm not Sage Barton," Rhodes said.

"Maybe not, but you're the closest thing we have in Blacklin County," Hack said. "Old Sage, he'd call in an air strike on those woods and kill all the hogs and flush out the killer at the same time."

"Might wipe out all the trees, too," Lawton said, "but you got to break a few eggs if you want an omelet."

"I never did like omelets," Hack said. "Scrambled eggs are okay, though."

"It's just a way of talkin'," Lawton said. "I coulda said scrambled eggs just as easy, but I thought an omelet was classier."

"You wouldn't know classy if it bit you on the butt," Hack said.

Lawton didn't even bother to reply.

"Classy or not," Hack said after a few seconds, "you'd have some sausage to go with 'em if those hogs were all killed in the air strike. How about it, Sage?" He grinned. "I mean, Sheriff."

"No air strikes," Rhodes said.

"Dang," Lawton said. "I sure do like fresh-cooked sausage."

"An air strike would mess up the crime scene."

"Those hogs've messed it up already, I bet," Hack said, "and the only clue you got is those feathers you mentioned, right?"

"That's all," Rhodes said.

"On *CSI* they'd have those analyzed for you in about fifteen minutes," Lawton said. "Tell you what kind of duck they came from, where he spent the winter, and what he had for breakfast."

"Tell you the brand of vest, too," Hack said. "Or jacket or whatever they came from. Tell you where it was bought, what size it was, and what kind of aftershave the guy who wore it was wearin'."

"Maybe I could send the feathers to them," Rhodes said, "instead of the state crime lab."

"Wouldn't be much difference, would it?" Hack asked.

"Just that the time would be about a month before you got a report sayin' they were duck feathers," Lawton said.

"That's all it would tell us, too," Rhodes said. "I think *CSI* is a science fiction show."

"Too bad, because ever'body will expect you to come up with something on those murders," Hack said. "The commissioners won't be happy, and Milton Munday's gonna go for your throat."

Rhodes didn't need Hack to tell him that.

"I'm going home," he said. "I don't think I'll listen to Milton Munday tomorrow."

"You never listen to him," Hack said.

"Right, and I'm not going to start now."

134

"Might be a good time to."

"There's never a good time for that," Rhodes said.

The first thing Ivy said when Rhodes got home and explained things was "I told you so."

Yancey yipped and jumped around Rhodes's ankles as if to emphasize her comment.

"Told me what?" Rhodes said.

"That you were crazy. You might have gotten killed out there tonight."

"Not me," Rhodes said. "I'm not ugly enough to be mistaken for a hog."

"That's probably what that bounty hunter thought, too."

"I have a feeling that wasn't an accident."

"That's what I mean," Ivy said. "You're crazy."

"You're probably right," Rhodes said.

CHAPTER 11

The first call Rhodes got the next morning was from Mikey Burns, who, unlike Rhodes, had listened to Milton Munday's radio show. Burns wanted to see Rhodes at the precinct barn as soon as he could get there.

Rhodes wanted to talk to Arvid Fowler and to get the autopsy report on Rapinski, but he went by to see Burns first. Mrs. Wilkie didn't bother to respond to Rhodes's "Good morning." She just waved him on into Burns's office.

Today Burns wore a bright red aloha shirt with small white flowers on it. The flowers looked like magnolia blossoms to Rhodes, but he wasn't sure that there were magnolia trees in Hawaii. He decided that it didn't really matter.

"What's going on in this county?" Burns asked, without even offering Rhodes a seat.

Rhodes sat down anyway.

"Lots of things are going on," he said

when he was comfortable, or as comfortable as he was going to get. "Did you have anything particular in mind?"

"You know what I'm talking about. The Murder Epidemic."

Rhodes could hear the capital letters at the beginnings of the words.

"Milton Munday?" he asked.

"That's what he's calling it," Burns said. "The Murder Epidemic. The county's getting a bad name, Rhodes."

"I didn't kill anybody," Rhodes said. "So I'm not responsible."

"That's not what Munday says. You're the law here, and it's up to you to prevent murders."

Burns probably didn't know how ridiculous he sounded. It was next to impossible to prevent a murder. First, you had to know who was going to be killed, and that was the easy part. It wouldn't do any good to explain that to Burns, so Rhodes didn't even try.

"What does Munday know about the law?" Rhodes asked instead.

"He knows that all citizens deserve freedom from fear, that's what he knows."

"What's he afraid of?"

"What anybody in the county would be afraid of. Getting murdered."

"Nobody from this county's been murdered. Both victims were from somewhere else. I don't think the murders are connected to this county."

Burns didn't believe it. "You can't be sure of that."

"Maybe not sure, but close enough."

"You mean you know what's going on?"

Rhodes shook his head. "I wouldn't say that. I have some ideas. That's about all."

"What kind of ideas?"

"I can't talk about them," Rhodes said. "They're confidential."

Burns smiled. It wasn't pleasant. "Which means you don't really have any."

"It means they're confidential." Rhodes stood up. "I need to get out and check on a few things. I'll let you know when there's been any progress."

"There had better be some progress, and soon. You might not be lucky enough to run unopposed in the next election."

Rhodes wondered if Burns had his eyes on the sheriff's job. If he did, more power to him. Rhodes wasn't considering retirement, but if someone else got elected, Rhodes would step down gracefully. The next election was a long way off, however, and a lot could happen in that time.

"I wouldn't mind having an opponent,"

Rhodes said. "It would make things interesting."

"I wonder who Milton Munday would
endorse," Burns said.

"Maybe he'll run," Rhodes said, "since he
knows so much about the law."

Burns looked thoughtful. "That might not
be a bad idea," he said.

Jennifer Loam was waiting for Rhodes when
he came out of the building.

"How'd you know I was here?" Rhodes
asked.

"We reporters have ways," Jennifer told
him. "You're lucky I'm the only one here. I
think there are a couple of people from
some TV station in Dallas at the jail."

"Thanks for the warning. I won't go back
there for a while."

"You won't need to. Hack and Lawton are
getting the camera time."

"And loving it," Rhodes said.

"Sure. Who wouldn't?"

"Me," Rhodes said.

"Yes, but you're crazy."

"People keep telling me that."

"Speaking of telling things, what about
this latest murder?"

Rhodes went over things for her, though

she'd already gotten all he knew from his report.

Jennifer got it all down in her notebook and on her recorder. "Do you want me to say that the killer will be brought to swift justice?"

"You can say that," Rhodes told her, "but it might not happen."

"I have faith in you," Jennifer said.

Rhodes looked back at the building he'd just left. "You might be the only one," he said.

Rhodes spotted Arvid Fowler's pickup parked in front of a house on the outskirts of town. Fowler was in the garage, replacing a couple of faulty breakers in the electrical panel in the garage.

"Dangerous job," Rhodes said, walking into the garage.

"Wouldn't be too bad if this place wasn't so crowded," Fowler said.

Today he wore a tool belt around his waist instead of a pistol, and Rhodes preferred it that way. He took off his Tractor Supply Company cap and wiped his forehead with the back of his arm while Rhodes looked around the garage. It was full of boxes, stacks of plastic flowerpots, an old chest of drawers that needed refinishing, two rusty bicycles, and a few other odds and ends. There was no room for the two cars that were parked out on the driveway.

"Not a fire hazard," Fowler said. "Just a mess. So you can't be here to arrest the owner."

"I wanted to talk to you about last night," Rhodes said.

"Yeah, well, you shouldn't have run off like that. We'd have seen to it that you got back to your car all right. The second hog got clean away from us, and when we went back to get the first one, you were gone."

"You must not listen to Milton Munday," Rhodes said.

"Who?"

"Milton Munday. He's the talk show guy on KCLR."

"I don't listen to that station. They never play any music. Nobody else does, either, these days, just stuff they *call* music. Country music's not country, mostly, and rap's not music at all. I don't like to listen to somebody like Munday run his mouth. What makes him think he knows so much, anyway?"

Rhodes couldn't answer that one.

"He's a smart aleck, if you ask me," Fowler said. "So since I don't like any of the music, and since I don't like Munday, I don't listen to anything."

Rhodes thought that was a sensible attitude, but he wanted to turn the conversation back to the hog hunters.

"You all stayed together last night after you left me?" he asked.

"That's right," Fowler said. "We were all chasing the dogs."

"When did you come back for the hog you killed?"

"It wasn't long after we left it. We hauled it off, and Garver took it to Starkey's today to get it dressed out."

Starkey was a retired butcher who dressed hogs and deer and didn't charge too much.

"We'd have done it ourselves," Fowler said, "but we have jobs."

Rhodes wouldn't have done it himself even if he'd killed the hog. That kind of work was entirely too messy. Which reminded Rhodes of the Chandlers' pet hog, Baby. He mentioned the incident to Fowler.

"I heard about it when it happened," Fowler said. "I don't know who'd do a thing like that, except maybe Starkey, and he wouldn't have any reason to."

"The Chandlers think maybe hog hunters had something to do with it."

"Not anybody I know," Fowler said. "Not my bunch, for sure, and that's the truth."

"The thing of it is," Rhodes said, "we've had two murders out in those woods on the nights when you and your friends have been hunting there. When I went to see the Eccles cousins about it, they ran off so they wouldn't have to talk to me, and you and the others say that nothing unusual happened. That's a little hard to believe."

"I can see that it might be," Fowler said, not meeting Rhodes's eyes, "but that's the way it is."

Rhodes didn't let it drop. "Besides the murders, there was a lot of shooting out there the night before last, and it didn't have anything to do with hogs except that it stampeded them. It just doesn't seem likely that with all that going on, you didn't notice a thing."

Fowler looked at the panel and then at the brand-new breaker he held in one hand.

"Likely or not, that's the way it is. I'd like to help you out if I could, Sheriff, but I got a job to do here, and I'm getting paid by the hour. The Fremonts wouldn't like it if I spent all my time talking, even if it's to the Law."

Rhodes thanked him and left, more suspicious than ever. He still wanted the autopsy report, and after he got that, he'd go by and see if the Eccles boys had come back home.

This time, he wouldn't take Seepy Benton along. He didn't know if he could survive without Benton's detecting skills, but he was willing to give it a try.

The autopsy report didn't tell Rhodes much that he didn't know other than giving descriptions of tattoos from various parts of Rapinski's anatomy.

"Los Muertos," Rhodes said.

"The dead men," Clyde Ballinger said, looking at Rhodes over the top of the book he was reading. *The Corpse Wore Pasties.* "I don't know much Spanish, but I know enough to translate that."

"It's also the name of a motorcycle gang," Rhodes said, "or it used to be. The gang broke up four or five years ago, and only a few of the members are left."

Ballinger put down the book. "I didn't know you were an expert on motorcycle gangs."

"I'm an expert on that one," Rhodes said. "I thought Rapinski looked familiar."

"You knew him?"

"Somebody who looks like him," Rhodes said.

Ballinger picked up his book, said, "Oh," and started reading again.

"Why don't I ever get cases like that?"

Rhodes asked.

"Like what?" Ballinger asked.

"Never mind," Rhodes said.

He finished going over the autopsy report. The important thing was that Rapinski had been killed with one shot from a .38. Now Rhodes would have to get Ruth to check the bullet to see if it was a match for the ones taken from Baty. Blacklin County might not have much of a crime lab, but it had the facilities for that kind of work, and Ruth was trained for it.

Ballinger put down his book again. "You think what's left of the motorcycle gang will come to town looking for revenge?"

"Just two of them," Rhodes said.

CHAPTER 12

Rhodes didn't have the facilities of *CSI* at his disposal. He didn't have an investigative team, either, though he could have called in the state police if he'd thought he needed them. He didn't want to do that. His experience had been that calling anybody in on a case was apt to create more problems than it solved. The people who were called often got the idea that the case had been handed over to them and that the investigation was now theirs to run as they saw fit. Rhodes liked to have a hand in things, and being shut out made him uncomfortable and unhappy. He didn't think of himself as a control freak, but maybe he was.

Rhodes was sure that Mikey Burns would do things differently. He'd call in the state police in a New York minute if it had been up to him. Luckily, it wasn't up to him, so Rhodes would go his own way, asking questions, mulling over the answers and seeing what he could see. Sooner or later, he'd find what he was looking for. He always had. Most of the time, anyway.

This time, however, things were likely to be complicated by the attention focused on the crimes by the TV station that had sent its reporters and by Milton Munday.

Rhodes could count on Jennifer Loam to report things fairly, but Munday wasn't a reporter. He was a man out to make a name for himself in a small radio market before jumping to a bigger station. Or maybe *returning* to a bigger station. Rhodes hadn't thought about it before, but it seemed odd for someone like Munday simply to show up in a small town like Clearview and land a radio talk show job. Rhodes wondered where Munday had come from and what his plans were. It might be a good idea to ask him, and Rhodes decided he'd do that later. One more thing to add to his list.

Rhodes drove up the little hill to the double-wide shared by the Eccles cousins. Their big Mack tractor was parked in the yard, and so was one of their pickups, the red one, but the cousins weren't in the trailer. Or if they were, they weren't answering the door.

They might have gone off somewhere in the missing pickup, or they might be somewhere else on the property. It was a nice enough day, not much breeze, not many clouds, a little warm for that time of year. If Rhodes had owned some property and if there'd been a place to fish on it, he might have decided to see if he could catch something for the frying pan. The Eccles boys had a place to fish, a little stock tank that wasn't too far away. He could drive there if he didn't mind bouncing around a little in the car.

Rhodes had once had a little confrontation with Lance and Hugh, not to mention Bruce, at the tank, so he knew the way. The confrontation had been about an alligator that the cousins claimed they didn't own. Everything had turned out all right, but Rhodes would just as soon not go through anything like it again.

The bouncing wasn't so bad, and Rhodes found the tank without any trouble. A low dam ran around about half the tank, and weeds grew all over it. Many of them were still green. Weeds had a way of surviving even through the winter. The black pickup was parked near the dam, but there was no sign of either Hugh or Lance.

Rhodes parked the county car next to the pickup and got out and closed the car door quietly. He could hear someone talking on the other side of the dam, so he walked up to the top of it. Down below and a little to his right, Lance and Hugh sat on the ground. Each of them held a long cane fishing pole in one hand and a bottle of beer in the other. Beside Hugh was a cheap white foam cooler with the top off. A couple of empty beer bottles lay near the cooler.

The surface of the water was free of most of the dark green algae that had covered it the last time Rhodes had seen it, though some of the green goo still floated around the edges. There was none in the water in front of Hugh and Lance, who had pulled it up onto the bank so they could drop their lines in the cleared spot. Their red fishing corks bobbed about ten feet from the shore.

"I wish we'd gone hunting with the fellas last night," Hugh said. "They got a pretty good hog, I heard."

"Not worth it," Lance said. "Not with another dead man out there."

"Let's talk about that dead man," Rhodes said.

"Damn," Hugh said, looking around. "You sure are sneaky, Sheriff. Don't you ever give up?"

"Not often," Rhodes said.

He walked down the side of the dam and stood near the cousins.

"Want a beer, Sheriff?" Lance asked, gesturing toward the cooler with his bottle. "Take two. They're small."

"No, thanks."

"Well, sit yourself down then, and be quiet. We don't want to scare the fish."

"What fish?"

"The fish we're gonna catch," Hugh said. "Sooner or later."

"Let's talk about the dead men while we're waiting," Rhodes said.

"We don't know nothin' about that," Lance said.

"You were just talking about them."

"Yeah, well, we heard somethin' or other on that Milton Munday about them. It's nothin' to do with us."

"Now why don't I believe that?" Rhodes asked.

" 'Cause you're a hard man to convince," Lance said. "Ain't that the truth, Hugh."

Hugh nodded. "You got that right, Lance."

Hugh took a swallow of his beer, draining the bottle. He put the bottle on the ground and got another one out of the cooler. After he twisted off the cap, he took a drink.

"Boy, that's good for what ails you. You sure you don't want one, Sheriff?"

"I'm sure, and I'm tired of fooling with you two. You know something about what happened in those woods the other night, and I want to know what it is."

"You callin' us liars?" Hugh asked.

"I guess I am," Rhodes said.

"That hurts my feelings," Lance said.

"Mine, too," Hugh said.

The cousins stood up and laid their poles down on the bank, leaving the corks in the water. Hugh drank some beer. Lance just looked at Rhodes.

"Two against one," Lance said, "and we got beer bottles. Not good odds, Sheriff."

"Unless he's got a gun," Hugh said. "You got a gun, Sheriff?"

"I have a gun," Rhodes said, and he did. The problem with that was that the little Kel-Tec .32 automatic was in an ankle holster, and there was no way Rhodes could get to it before the Eccles boys got to him. Not that it mattered. Rhodes didn't intend to shoot them anyway.

"I don't see no gun," Hugh said.

"I don't think he's got one," Lance said. "Let's get him, Hugh."

"You'd better think about the last time you tried me," Rhodes said. "If I remember rightly, the two of you wound up in jail."

"Yeah," Lance said, "but that was then, and this is now. We got you at a disadvantage."

"You've had too many beers," Rhodes said. "It's impaired your judgment."

"Hah," Lance said. "We ain't impaired."

He took a step toward Rhodes. So did Hugh. Both men switched their grips on their beers so that they held the bottles by their narrow necks.

Rhodes stood his ground, looking from one cousin to the other. He didn't look at their hands or their feet. Hands and feet could fool you, and Rhodes knew their eyes were the key to whatever they'd do.

"You might not get off as easy this time," Rhodes said. "Randy Lawless won't want to help you."

"He's a lawyer," Hugh said. "He'll help whoever pays him."

He took another step. So did Lance, who flicked a look at his cousin.

That was the cue for Rhodes to move. He didn't back up. He stepped forward and kicked Hugh in the chest.

Hugh yelled, dropped his beer bottle, and staggered backward. Rhodes's momentum almost carried him past Lance, but he was able to grab hold of Lance's shirt and steady himself.

Lance was no longer interested in Rhodes. He turned his head to look at Hugh, who stumbled off the bank and splashed on his back in the water.

Rhodes kept his hold on Lance's shirt, planted his feet, and slung Lance after his cousin.

Lance's arms windmilled, and he lurched into the tank, landing practically on top of Hugh.

Rhodes walked down to the edge of the water.

"You're scaring the fish," he said.

Lance rolled off Hugh and stood up. His cap had come off, and water streamed from his red hair. Hugh lay where he was, coughing and spluttering, his head occasionally sinking under the water. His cap had stayed on.

"Hugh can't swim," Lance said.

"The water can't be more than a foot deep there," Rhodes said.

"He don't know that," Lance said. "He's panicking. You better help him."

"You do it," Rhodes said.

"I ain't the one put him there," Lance said.

He stepped out onto the bank, grabbing hold of a small bush to help his balance.

Hugh continued to splutter and sink and rise and splutter.

Lance watched, his wet clothing sticking to him.

"Gonna drown if you don't get him out," he said.

Rhodes was beginning to think Lance was right, and it was clear that he had no intention of helping his cousin. Rhodes leaned down.

"Take my hand," he said to Hugh. "I'll help you up."

Almost as soon as he said it, Rhodes knew he'd made a rookie mistake. He knew it even before he felt Lance's shoe make contact with his rear end, and he thought about it as the kick launched him out over the water.

Or, more accurately, over Hugh, who hadn't been in any danger of drowning at all and who was waiting for Rhodes with open arms.

Rhodes barely had time to think about what he was going to do, but he knew he couldn't let Hugh wrap him up in a bear hug. Hugh might not drown him, but whatever happened wouldn't be pleasant. So Rhodes doubled his arm and speared Hugh's chest as he struck him.

The combination of the elbow punch and Rhodes's weight was enough to drive Hugh under the surface again, and this time he wasn't faking when he sucked in water and rolled like a big catfish.

Rhodes didn't want to think about big cat-fish. He'd had a close encounter with one of those, too, and it had been a scary experience. He pushed himself away from Hugh, but he'd made another rookie blunder. He'd forgotten about Lance, who landed on his back like a bag of sand and pushed him under the water and down into the slick mud beneath.

Lance straddled Rhodes and held him under, and he made his own mistake. He'd tried to get hold of Rhodes's arms, but he'd missed them. He should have pushed Rhodes's head in the mud. That would have ended things quickly.

Since his head was free, Rhodes raised his torso from the mud and broke the surface. He took a deep breath, threw both arms up and back, and grabbed hold of Lance's shirt. Then he lunged forward and pulled.

Lance came down under the water on top of Rhodes. Rhodes kept him there, hoping that he could hold his breath longer than Lance could.

He could. In only seconds, Lance was thrashing around as if he might be drowning. Rhodes thought it would serve him right if he did drown, but the county couldn't afford all the lawsuits. So Rhodes let him go.

Lance untangled himself and shoved away from Rhodes. He tried to stand up, but Rhodes grabbed his legs and pulled him back down.

"You leave Lance alone," Hugh said, snatching a handful of Rhodes's thinning hair and dragging him backward.

Rhodes took hold of Hugh's arm and jerked him forward. Hugh let go of Rhodes's hair and landed facedown in the water beside his cousin.

Rhodes stood up. Water poured off him, and he was covered with mud and algae.

If some Hollywood director ever cast a remake of *Creature from the Black Lagoon*, Rhodes knew he'd be a natural for the title role, and he wouldn't even need a rubber costume.

Hugh and Lance pummeled the water and each other as they tried to get some air. Rhodes knew they'd have things sorted out after a while, so he pulled his feet out of the mud and stepped out onto the bank.

It took a minute or so, but Lance and Hugh finally managed to stop roiling the water. They caught hold of each other and stood up with some mutual assistance. They didn't look any better than Rhodes did, but that was small comfort.

Rhodes peeled some of the algae off his

shirt. He tossed it in the water and said, "Come on out now, one at a time. You first, Hugh."

"I don't want to," Hugh said.

"Me, neither," Lance said.

Rhodes flicked some more algae into the water. "I didn't want to do this," he said.

"Do what?" Hugh asked.

Rhodes didn't answer. He leaned down and pulled up his right pants leg. The little .32 was still there in the holster. Rhodes unstrapped it and took it out.

"That thing's mighty small," Lance said.

"Mine's bigger than yours," Rhodes said.

"I ain't even got one."

"My point exactly."

Hugh wasn't impressed. "Prob'ly won't even shoot after the soakin' it got."

Rhodes thought Hugh could be right. On the other hand, he could be wrong. Only one way to find out. Rhodes picked up one of the empty beer bottles and tossed it into the water.

"You couldn't hit that even if that little gun would shoot," Lance said.

Rhodes made sure the pistol barrel was free of mud. It was, so he aimed at the bottle and pulled the trigger. The pistol cracked, and the bottle shattered. The pieces sank under the water.

Lance and Hugh looked at the spot where the bottle had been. Then they looked at Rhodes.

"You're scaring the fish," Hugh said.

CHAPTER 13

"Land sakes alive," Hack said when Lance and Hugh entered the jail, followed by Rhodes. That was pretty strong language from Hack, who liked to pretend he was never surprised by anything that happened around the place.

"Looks like Davy Jones's boys from one of them pirate movies," Lawton said. "I forget which one, though."

"Never mind the movie references," Rhodes said. "I need to book these two and get them in a cell."

"What you need to get them is a shower," Hack said.

"That, too, but it can wait until they're booked."

"What're you gonna charge 'em with?" Lawton asked. "Criminal mud-slingin'?"

Rhodes didn't answer. He booked the cousins and let Lawton take over while he went home for a shower of his own.

Yancey didn't recognize him. He ran and hid under the bed as soon as Rhodes came through the door. Rhodes thought that was a good place for him.

Rhodes went into the bathroom, stripped off his wet, muddy clothes, cleaned up his shoes, and took a hot shower. When he was clean and dry, he dressed in fresh clothes and a dry pair of shoes. He clipped his badge on his belt and took the dirty clothes to the washer. He set the soaked shoes out on the porch, where he hoped Ivy wouldn't notice them. It was just as well Ivy wasn't home. She would have laughed too much.

While the clothes washed, Rhodes cleaned the .32. Then he had a sandwich made with the cold remains of the meatless meat loaf. He put some low-fat Miracle Whip on one slice of the bread. The sandwich wasn't bad. It wasn't a cheeseburger, but it was better than nothing.

When he'd eaten the sandwich, Rhodes put the clothes in the dryer and thought about the Eccles cousins. Whatever they'd seen, they didn't want to talk about it, and they were willing to go to jail instead. Part of the problem, Rhodes was sure, was their natural antipathy to the law and its representatives, especially Rhodes. The cousins had a healthy lack of respect for authority, but that wasn't all of it, and he was going to find out the rest.

By the time the clothes had dried, Yancey had come out from under the bed. He jumped up and down and yipped with excitement to show Rhodes how glad he was that Rhodes hadn't turned out to be some mud-covered stranger intent on slaughtering small, helpless dogs.

Rhodes patted him and told him to go pester Sam, who had slept the whole time. Yancey either didn't hear or didn't choose to obey.

"I have work to do," Rhodes said. "You behave while I'm gone."

Yancey yipped in reply, and Rhodes took the clothes out of the dryer and put them away, with Yancey's assistance. After that was done, he left to return to the jail. When he got there, Lawton told him that the Eccles cousins were cleaned up and sharing a cell.

Lawton sounded a bit sullen, and then Rhodes noticed that both Hack and Lawton were pouting as if they were the ones who'd been arrested. It dawned on Rhodes that he hadn't asked them about their interview with the television reporter.

"By the way," Rhodes said, "I just wanted to tell the two of you that I know you did the department proud this morning when you answered that TV fella's questions. What channel was he from, anyhow?"

The two men brightened considerably.

"It was one of the Dallas channels," Hack said. "Hoss was pretty well known up there. They wanted to hear all about how he was killed."

"We didn't know anything," Lawton said, "but that never stopped us before."

Truer words were never spoken, Rhodes thought.

"Funny thing, though," Hack said. "They left before Lawton and I even finished tellin' 'em all we didn't know."

Rhodes wondered how long it had taken the reporter to get frustrated with the way the two men answered his questions. He'd have to be an exceptionally patient man to last more than ten minutes.

"I'm looking forward to seeing you on the news tonight," Rhodes said. "I hope the commissioners are watching. They love it when the county looks good on TV."

"They'll be plenty happy, then," Lawton said.

"Now, then," Hack said. "We've told you about the TV fellas. You gonna tell us what happened with Lance and Hugh?"

Rhodes knew the dispatcher's curiosity

must have been driving him crazy.

"Maybe," Rhodes said.

"Maybe?" Hack asked.

"I'll tell you if you'll give me a straight answer about what's been going on while I've been out serving the good people of the county. I'm talking about crime, not TV reporters."

"Deal," Hack said.

Lawton looked a little put out, but he didn't say anything.

"You first," Rhodes said.

"Loose cows out near Milsby. Boyd's takin' care of that. Two possums in a house on Oak Street. Boyd got that taken care of, too. Got a couple more complaints about that badge charity that's callin' people."

They hadn't had any complaints about the badge charity for a few days. Someone was calling the county's residents and asking for donations to help the sheriff's department buy better, more up-to-date equipment. The caller also said that some of the money would be put into a fund to provide medical care for those "who risked their lives to keep the county safe for decent people to live in." As far as Rhodes knew, none of the money had ever been given to the county or to the sheriff's department.

"We oughta do something about those

calls," Lawton said.

"We will," Rhodes said, "but not today. Murder comes first."

"We know that," Hack said. "So what about Hugh and Lance?"

Rhodes gave them a quick version of what had happened.

"Well, you might've got dirty, but you got the best of 'em," Hack said.

"That's one way to look at it," Rhodes said. "Now I need to talk to them."

"They're a surly pair," Lawton said. "Might not have much to say."

"We'll see," Rhodes said.

Rhodes looked at the cousins through the bars of their cell. Dressed in the natty orange jumpsuits provided by the county, they lay in their bunks and seemed right at home. Rhodes wasn't surprised. It wasn't the first time they'd occupied the very same cell.

"I think we've had this conversation before," Rhodes said.

Neither cousin looked his way. Hugh said, "Which conversation is that?"

"The one where you go ahead and tell me what I wanted to know before you caused me so much trouble."

"I think I remember that," Lance said.

164

"Yeah," Hugh said. "I think I do, too."

"It's gonna be different this time, though," Lance said.

"Yeah," Hugh said.

"You can have a lawyer present if you want one," Rhodes said.

"That ain't it," Lance said.

"How's it going to be different, then?" Rhodes asked.

Lance sat up and swung his feet to the floor. He had to lean over to keep his head from hitting the top bunk.

"You remember what we said about the lawyer back at the tank?" he asked.

"Randy Lawless? You said he'd help whoever paid him."

"That's right. You're pretty good, Sheriff. Not ever'body woulda remembered that. No wonder you're the law in Blacklin County."

"What does that have to do with our conversation?"

"Well, it occurred to me and Hugh that we can't pay him."

Hugh sat up and slid down to sit beside Lance on the lower bunk.

"It's this damn economy," Hugh said. "It sucks."

"It sure does," Lance said. "We ain't had us a good long haul in a month."

"More like two," Hugh said.

Lance nodded. "More like two. And when we ain't haulin', we ain't bringin' the dough. So we can't afford to hire Randy Lawless."

"Even if he cut his rates, we couldn't afford it," Hugh said.

"Too bad," Rhodes said. "You know how sorry I am about that. 'Course, the court will appoint you a lawyer if you can't afford one."

"We appreciate that, Sheriff," Lance said. "We really do. Ain't that right, Hugh."

"It sure is," Hugh said.

Sometimes Rhodes thought the whole world had joined up with Hack and Lawton in a conspiracy against him.

"There must be a point to all this talk," he said.

"Oh, there's a point, all right," Lance said.

"Get to it, then," Rhodes said.

"You sure are touchy," Hugh said. "It's not like we really did anything to you. Nothing more'n a good Babtist preacher would do if he was babtizin' you in a creek."

"I think that's debatable," Rhodes said. "Now like I said, get to the point."

"The point is that we don't want a lawyer," Lance said.

"That's right," Hugh said. "We did use our phone call, though."

Rhodes had a feeling he wasn't going to like the answer to his next question. "Who did you call?"

"Milton Munday," Lance said.

Milton Munday had several things going for him. He was big and not bad-looking, about thirty, with black hair cut so that it looked to Rhodes as if someone had messed it up. Rhodes thought it looked weird, but it seemed to work for Munday.

Looks didn't matter on radio, however. It was Munday's voice that sold him on the air. It was deep and rich and resonant. There was no trace of a Texas accent or an accent of any kind.

Munday was good with inflections and dramatic pauses, too. He could read the menu from a fast-food restaurant and make it sound like a pronouncement on a par with the Declaration of Independence.

At the moment, he wasn't reading a menu or anything else. He was regaling Hack with the reasons why he needed to talk to the Eccles cousins. He was so eloquent that a lesser man than Hack would have forced Lawton to hand over the keys to the cell and release the cousins into Munday's custody for a trip to Mexico.

Munday was so wrapped up in his rhetoric

that he hadn't seen Rhodes return from the cellblock. Rhodes listened to him talk for a while before breaking in on his monologue.

"Can I help you?" he asked.

Munday looked away from Hack. "Who are you?"

"I'm the sheriff," Rhodes told him.

Munday gave him the once-over. "You don't look like a sheriff."

Rhodes tapped his badge. "I'm not required to wear a uniform."

"Nice for you," Munday said.

"I like it," Rhodes said. "Now, can I help you?"

"I want to visit two of my listeners who I understand you have in custody. Lance and Hugh Eccles."

"Why would you want to see them?"

"They say they have some material for me, something I can use on my radio show."

"Your radio show," Rhodes said.

"That's right. Have you heard it?"

"Not often."

"You don't like it?"

"Let's just say I'm not a regular listener and leave it at that."

Munday shrugged. "I have the right to say what I want to. Some people might not like it."

Rhodes knew he wasn't the only one who

didn't particularly like Munday's approach. Munday had attacked just about everybody in the county. In his short time in Clearview, Munday had managed to get under the skin of several commissioners, the mayor, the Clearview Chamber of Commerce, the city council, the city manager, the fire chief, the superintendent of schools, two principals, and several business owners.

Rhodes figured that in some of the cases, the criticism might have been justified, but Munday's scathing commentary went over the line too often.

Not that Munday restricted himself to local topics. He'd also attacked both houses of Congress, the president, the United Nations, and several European leaders.

"You know what?" Munday asked.

Rhodes played along. "I'm not sure. You tell me."

"I don't care if nobody likes me. They don't have to listen if they don't want to. Somebody likes me, though. I have as many advertisers as I can work into the show, and I've doubled the station's audience since I've been in town."

"I'm happy for you," Rhodes said.

"That's nice of you. Now how about letting me have a visit with the Eccles cousins."

Rhodes hadn't been able to get the cousins

to tell him what they wanted to talk to Munday about. He had a feeling they wouldn't tell Munday anything they wouldn't tell him about the hog hunting, however, so they would probably launch into a tale of woe about police brutality. In a way, Rhodes hoped they would.

"Those two aren't known for their truthfulness," he said.

Munday smiled. "I'll have to be the judge of that, I'm afraid."

"All right, then. Lawton, take Lance and Hugh to the visitor's room. Then come back and get Mr. Munday."

Lawton left the room, jangling his keys.

"The visit won't be supervised," Rhodes said, "but I'll be right outside the door if you need me."

Munday straightened, and for a second Rhodes thought he might be going to flex his muscles. He didn't, though.

"I'm not afraid, Sheriff," he said.

"Just a matter of liability," Rhodes said. "You sure you don't just want to listen in?"

"I wouldn't do that."

"Probably got the room wired, right?"

Hack laughed. "Look around, Mr. Munday. Does this place look like it could be wired?"

"You have a point," Munday said, as Lawton came back into the room.

"You can follow me," Lawton said.

Munday did just that. When he was gone, Hack said to Rhodes, "You gonna monitor them?"

"Lawton can wait outside the door. Lance and Hugh won't try anything."

"What you think they'll tell him?"

"That I jumped them and tried to drown them."

"I wish he coulda seen you when you brought 'em in. You think he'll believe 'em?"

"I don't think it matters whether he believes them or not. It won't matter to him. I don't think he believes half the stuff he says on that show of his."

"He'll try to make you look bad," Hack said.

Rhodes grinned. "Let him. Half the town seems to think I'm Sage Barton. If Munday tells Hugh and Lance's version of what happened, most everybody who hears it will think I'm even more like Sage than ever."

"You don't think there'll be trouble?"

"Not a bit," Rhodes said. "Munday doesn't know the Eccleses, but most people around here do. Those two don't have the best reputation for truth-telling, and they've caused trouble more than once. People will be glad I did whatever they say I did. The ones who don't think I'm Sage Barton will know it's an exaggeration, and the ones who think I am will believe I'm a tough guy."

"So it'll all work out," Hack said.

"Sure it will," Rhodes told him. He just wished he believed it.

CHAPTER 14

Munday left the jail with a satisfied smile. Rhodes figured Munday had a good story for his program tomorrow, and he didn't have to bother checking to see if it was true because he wasn't a reporter. Munday claimed that he was an entertainer and that entertainers didn't have to worry about accuracy. Accuracy wasn't the point.

Just what the point was, other than to get an audience, Rhodes wasn't sure, but whatever it was, it worked. Munday was right about one thing: He had a lot of listeners.

"You think he'll bond the Eccleses out?" Hack asked when the door closed behind Munday.

"Not a chance," Rhodes said.

"I'll bet they asked him, though."

Rhodes had had the same thought. "The judge hasn't even set the bail yet."

"Don't matter," Lawton said, coming in after returning the cousins to their cell.

"They'd ask him anyway. It's just the way they are."

"I think I'll talk to them one more time," Rhodes said. "Maybe they'll feel more like talking now that they've had their meeting with Munday."

"You really think so?" Hack asked.

"No," Rhodes said, "but I'm going to give it a try, anyway."

He went back to the cellblock and found the cousins sitting on the bottom bunk with expectant looks, as if they had been waiting for him.

"You gonna listen to Munday's show tomorrow, Sheriff?" Lance asked. "Gonna be a good 'un."

"I don't have time to listen," Rhodes said.

"Gonna miss some good stuff," Hugh said, elbowing Lance and grinning.

"Munday's not going to bond you out," Rhodes said, "if that's what you're hoping. We might be able to work a deal, though."

Hugh quit grinning. "What kind of deal?"

"You tell me what I want to know, and I'll see about dropping the charges against you."

"We got nothin' to tell," Hugh said. "Right, Lance?"

"Right," Lance said. "Whatever you think we saw, we didn't see it."

"It's about my bedtime," Hugh said, and

174

he climbed into the upper bunk and lay down.

It was still daylight outside, but that didn't seem to bother the cousins.

" 'Night, Lance," Hugh said.

" 'Night," Lance said, and he lay down, too.

" 'Night, John Boy," Rhodes said.

"Who the hell is John Boy?" Lance asked.

Rhodes was already on the way out of the cellblock.

"You wouldn't know him," he said.

Ruth was telling Hack about a defaced traffic sign when Rhodes returned.

"Spin tires on pavement?" Hack said. "That one's nearly as old as I am."

"Ain't *nothin'* that old," Lawton said.

"You can't talk. You're older than I am."

"Ain't *nobody* older than you are."

"You listen here," Hack said, but Rhodes cut him off.

"Both of you hold on. How bad is the stop sign, Ruth?"

"Bad enough that it needs to be replaced," Ruth said. "Either that or they need to paint over the words somebody put on it. They're pretty small, so it should be easy enough."

"I'll call the city maintenance crew," Hack said, forgetting about his discussion with

Lawton. "They'll take care of it."

Hack turned to the phone, and Ruth asked Rhodes if there was anything new on the murders. He told her about Lance and Hugh and their meeting with Milton Munday.

"I'm going to listen to him tomorrow," Ruth said. "It'll be great."

"That's what Hugh and Lance said. Right now, though, I want you to see what you can find out about Ed Garver. Do a background check, and call Trey Allison at his plumbing business and see what he has to say."

"You think Garver had something to do with the killings?"

"I just think we need to run a check on him. Rapinski mentioned him last night, and now Rapinski's dead."

Garver had also disappeared during the hunt at the time when Rapinski was killed, but Rhodes wasn't ready to tell anyone that.

"Worth checking out, all right," Ruth said. "I'll get on it."

"The maintenance crew's on the way to replace the stop sign," Hack said, hanging up the phone. "They'll take in the old one and repaint it."

Rhodes hadn't written out his arrest report on Lance and Hugh, so he sat down at his desk to get started. He hadn't gotten far when the phone rang.

Hack answered, listened, thanked someone, and hung up.

"You're not gonna believe this," Hack said.

"Try me," Rhodes said.

"That was Miz Wilkie."

"Uh-oh," Rhodes said. "What does Mikey Burns want now?"

"It's not Mikey."

"What is it then?"

"Motorsickles," Hack said. "She heard 'em buzz by the commissioner's barn and went outside. She says it's some people we know."

"I was afraid of that," Rhodes said.

"How come?"

"Rapinski," Rhodes said. "If you were a biker and people didn't call you Rapinski, they might give you a nickname."

"Rapper," Hack said.

"That would be my guess. I thought Rapinski looked like someone I knew. It was Rapper. They might be cousins like the Eccleses, or they might even be brothers."

"You think he's here to run his own investigation? Unofficial as it might be."

"I wouldn't be surprised."

Rapper wasn't the kind of person to waste any time on mourning. He'd prefer revenge, and it wouldn't matter much to him who he took it out on. He might even blame Rhodes for Rapinski's death.

"You'd think he'd have learned his lesson," Hack said.

"Some people are hard to convince," Rhodes said.

He and Rapper had met on more than one occasion when Rapper had decided to engage in criminal enterprises in Blacklin County. He'd tried selling and manufacturing drugs, and he'd even tried a little moonshining. He never came out the winner in his encounters with Rhodes, but he never quit trying. He'd lost a finger and part of an ear and suffered various other injuries, but so far he'd managed to avoid arrest. This time he might not be so lucky.

"That Rapper never learns," Lawton said. "Is Nellie with him?"

Nellie always rode with Rapper. He was thinner and older, and he reminded Rhodes of some hapless movie sidekick from the days of B Westerns. Fuzzy St. John, maybe, or Fuzzy Knight. One of the Fuzzies, anyway.

"Wait till Munday hears about this," Hack said. "What was that movie with Marlon Brando?"

"*The Wild One*," Rhodes said.

"That's the one. Munday'll work this up into somethin' like that, for sure."

"Who's going to tell him about Rapper?"

"Not me," Lawton said, looking as pious as he could.

"Not me, either," Hack said. "You don't think we'd talk to that goober, do you?"

"He'll find out easy enough," Lawton said. "Rapper's trouble, any way you slice him."

"Sheriff's sliced him a couple of times, all right," Hack said.

"I haven't sliced anybody," Rhodes said.

"Stuck a hay hook in his leg, though," Lawton said. "Shot off his ear. That's bad enough."

"Never mind that," Rhodes said. "See if you can get Arvid Fowler on the phone."

"Yes, sir, Sheriff," Hack said.

He looked in the phone book and then dialed a number. After waiting a while, he took a pencil and scratched on a pad. Then he hung up.

"He's not at his place. Must be out workin'. His answerin' machine has his cell phone number on it, so I wrote it down. You want me to try it?"

"Go ahead," Rhodes said.

This time Hack got Fowler and told him the sheriff wanted to have a word with him. Rhodes picked up the phone on his desk and punched 2. When Fowler came on the line, Rhodes asked if he and the other men were going out to hunt hogs that night.

"We might," Fowler said. "Why?"

"I think you ought to stay home for a while," Rhodes said. "It's getting dangerous out in the woods."

"You got a point," Fowler said. "That's why we're going to a different place next time. Whenever that is."

Rhodes wasn't sure how much Rapper knew about the hog hunts, or even if he knew anything about them. However, Lawton was right about how easy it would be for him to find out. The biker had plenty of sources of information in the county. A number of people lived a sort of off-the-grid life out in the country, and Rapper was bound to know some of them. Some of the ones he knew would also know about the hunts and where the hunters would be.

"Anywhere you go might be too dangerous," Rhodes said.

Fowler was skeptical. "What're you trying to tell me, Sheriff?"

"That there might be someone who's not interested so much in finding out who killed those two men as he is in getting a little revenge. It won't matter to him who he gets it from, either."

"You got somebody specific in mind?"

"You wouldn't know him," Rhodes said. "He rides a motorcycle."

"I know a few folks like that."

"Name's Rapper," Rhodes said.

Fowler was quiet for a couple of seconds. "Don't know him. He from around here?"

"Not exactly," Rhodes said. "He's been here before, though."

"Well, he won't bother me and the boys. We're not scared of real hogs, and we're not scared of anybody who rides a metal one."

"Maybe you should be."

"You don't worry about us, Sheriff. We got guns. We can take care of ourselves."

"That's what Rapinski thought."

"Don't try to scare me, Sheriff."

"All right," Rhodes said. "Just tell me where you'll be tonight."

"Out around Milsby. The old Carroll place."

Rhodes knew where that was. In fact, it wasn't far from where Mrs. Wilkie lived, and that wasn't good. Rapper and Nellie often stayed out in that area.

"You be careful," Rhodes said. "Watch your back."

"I always do," Fowler said and hung up. So did Rhodes.

"You think he's gonna be careful?" Hack asked.

"Not for a minute," Rhodes said.

Rhodes went home, and as soon as he walked in the door, Ivy said, "All right, what happened?"

Yancey charged in from somewhere, his toenails clicking on the hardwood. He jumped up and down at Rhodes's feet, yipping in such excitement that he might not have seen Rhodes for several years instead of just hours. Rhodes wondered if the dog had ratted him out.

"What happened?" Rhodes asked.

Ivy looked around, then turned back to Rhodes. "I never noticed that echo in here before."

Rhodes grinned. "I didn't mean to repeat the question. I just wanted to know what you were talking about."

"You know what I'm talking about, all right. There's mud on the bathroom floor."

"Oh," Rhodes said. He thought he'd cleaned up, but he must have missed a spot or two. He'd have to be more careful.

"Your towel's wet, and someone's been using the washer," Ivy said, "and I smell gun oil."

"Have you ever thought about joining the

sheriff's department?" Rhodes asked. "I could make you an investigator."

"I'd be good at it, too, but you haven't answered the question."

"I got wet," Rhodes said. He looked down at Yancey, who was still excited. "Muddy, too."

"Are you going to tell me about it?"

"Sure. Let's go in the kitchen. I could use a drink."

They went into the kitchen, and Rhodes got a Dr Pepper from the refrigerator. He ordered the soft drinks from Dublin, Texas, on the Internet. Dr Pepper made with real sugar. The real thing. Rhodes wasn't big on alcohol, but he did love Dr Pepper.

He popped the can and went to the table. Ivy was already sitting there. Sam watched from his usual spot by the refrigerator, his yellow eyes alert. Yancey looked in from the doorway, not sure whether to risk coming in when the cat was so wide-awake.

Rhodes held up the can before he sat down. "You want one?"

"I don't think so. I just want to hear the story."

Rhodes sat down and told her. She laughed now and then, and when he was finished, she said, "I've decided I don't want to be an investigator. I've got something better in mind."

"What's that?" Rhodes asked.

"I want to be the department videographer. I'll follow you around with a video camera. We'll get rich selling things to that TV show that has the funny videos."

"I'm not so sure about that," Rhodes said. "The county would probably demand a cut since I'm an employee. They might even take all the money and leave us with none."

"You'd be famous, though."

"I'm already famous. Milton Munday talks about me all the time. And then there's Sage Barton."

Ivy laughed. "Just wait till they make the Sage Barton movie. You'll be on *Entertainment Tonight,* and everybody will want your autograph."

"How do you know people don't already want my autograph?"

"I just know. Don't worry, though. Your time will come."

Rhodes wasn't worried. He didn't want to be a celebrity. He was happy with things just the way they were.

"I have to go out again right before dark," he said.

"That's only about half an hour. What's going on now?"

"Another hog hunt."

Ivy sighed. "I guess it wouldn't do any good to tell you to be careful."

"You know me," Rhodes said.

"I know you, all right," Ivy said. She reached across the table to touch Rhodes's hand. "That's what worries me."

CHAPTER 15

The old Carroll place was now owned by someone who lived in Houston, or maybe it was Dallas. Rhodes could never remember where he lived or who he was. People in the cities were driving up the property values in the county by buying land, but they seldom visited after they'd bought it.

Whoever the owner was, he didn't like the fact that feral hogs were tearing up his property, and he'd given Arvid Fowler and his friends permission to hunt on the land anytime they wanted to. At least that was what Fowler told Rhodes when he was asked.

"Guy's name is Brown," Fowler said as he helped Winston with the dogs. Garver hadn't shown up yet. "I think he'd even pay us a bounty on the hogs if we asked him to, but we hunt 'em for the sport and the meat, not for money."

They were parked off the county road on

a sandy trail leading to the woods that covered a good bit of the property. About fifty yards away on their left was a little cabin that Brown must use when he came to take a look at his land. Rhodes saw that an electric line ran to the cabin, and there was a water well with a pump shed in back.

Garver arrived about that time and joined them. The dogs were leashed and ready to go, and the men were all armed, Fowler and Garver with their pistols, Winston with his rifle.

"You aren't worried after what happened to Rapinski?" Rhodes asked them.

"That's got nothing to do with us," Winston said. "Neither does that other fella. We're sorry about 'em and all that, but what happened to them was just a coincidence. Nothing to do with us."

"The Eccles cousins are in jail," Rhodes said, changing tactics. "Did you know that?"

"Nope," Fowler said. "They get in trouble a lot, though. What'd they do now?"

"Assaulted an officer," Rhodes said. "Namely me. Now why do you think they'd do a thing like that?"

None of the men would meet his eyes. Winston looked at the dogs. Fowler looked at the early-rising moon. Garver looked at the ground.

"Something happened in those woods the other night," Rhodes said. "A man was killed. His name was Baty. He wasn't from around here, and maybe none of you knew him. Or maybe you did."

Rhodes looked at Garver, who didn't look up.

"Maybe none of you knew Rapinski, either," Rhodes continued, "but he's dead, too. Both of them dead, both of them out in the woods near you when it happened. Something stampeded those hogs the other night. That's enough to make a man wonder."

"Just a coincidence," Winston said again. The dogs pulled him a step or two toward the woods. "That's all it is, and you oughtn't make it to be anything else. Those hogs stampede all the time, so that's no surprise. Right now, my dogs want to hunt. Are you gonna go with us, or are we gonna stand here talking all night?"

Rhodes gave up. "Let's go," he said.

The walking was easier on Brown's land. The hogs hadn't messed it up as much as they had at the Leverett place. The trees grew a little closer together in the woods, too. That would make the hunting a little trickier, Rhodes thought, but he didn't mention it. He just hoped that hogs were all they had to worry about.

They reached the woods without incident, and Rhodes started to relax a little. Once they were in the trees, Rapper wouldn't be able to find them, even if he knew they were somewhere on the property. That didn't rule out vandalism to the cars, however. Rhodes wished he'd thought of that sooner.

Then he heard the motorcycles. Their unmistakable roar sounded closer than Rhodes would have thought they could've gotten without betraying their presence. He turned around and saw two single headlights bouncing down the road.

The others didn't notice or didn't care. They didn't know how much trouble they were in. When the motorcycles got closer, Winston looked back and said, "What the hell?"

"Trouble," Rhodes said. "I warned Arvid. Didn't he tell you?"

"He didn't tell me a damn thing," Garver said. "Can't speak for Winston."

Winston looked at Arvid. "Didn't tell me anything, either. What's the deal?"

"The men on those motorcycles don't know you," Rhodes said, "You don't know them, either, but you can bet they don't like you. They have it in for whoever killed that

189

man last night."

"Wasn't us that killed him, dammit," Winston said.

"I don't think that matters," Rhodes told him.

"We're the ones with the guns," Garver said.

"I'd be surprised if they didn't have guns, too," Rhodes said. "I'd just as soon not get into a shooting war. We don't need anybody else to get killed."

"Especially not me," Winston said, looking over his shoulder.

The motorcycles turned off the road and came through the open gate.

"Hell," Fowler said, "let's quit all this talking and get ourselves in the trees. They won't follow us in there."

Rhodes thought Fowler was being overly optimistic, but the motorcycles were nearly on them now. They either had to stand their ground or move into the woods.

Winston didn't waste any more time. He let the dogs pull him on into the trees at a brisk jog, and the others followed him. So did Rhodes.

Arvid seemed to know where he was going, and Rhodes thought he could make out a faint trail in the jiggling beam of Fowler's flashlight. Maybe they'd avoid trouble after all.

Rhodes stopped to listen. He could hear the throbbing sound of motorcycles idling. Rapper and Nellie must have decided not to try crashing through the trees. They probably didn't want to damage their machines. Rhodes ran to catch up with the hunters.

The dogs barked and lunged against the leashes.

"They got a scent," Winston said.

"Let 'em go," Fowler said, and Winston unhooked the leashes. The dogs ran on ahead.

Motorcycles roared.

"They're coming in the trees," someone yelled. Rhodes wasn't sure who it was.

"Let's make 'em sorry they tangled with us," Fowler said from nearby. "Take cover and give 'em hell!"

"No shooting," Rhodes said.

"To hell with that," Fowler said. "It's self-defense, Sheriff."

"Nobody's tried to hurt you yet," Rhodes said.

"Preemptive strike." Fowler's flashlight went dark. "Can't take any chances."

Rhodes saw the other two flashlights blink off. He wished he had a plan to stop what was about to happen, but he couldn't think of anything that might even come close to working.

At least the motorcycles had slowed down to a near crawl. Rapper and Nellie were having a hard time getting through the trees. Rhodes hoped they'd just turn around and leave, though he didn't think that was likely. Rapper wouldn't give up that easily.

The thrumming of the engines stopped.

"There are men with guns here!" Rhodes yelled. "Go on home, Rapper. I'll find out who killed Hoss."

Nobody answered.

"You know I will," Rhodes said, hoping that Rapper was listening. "I can do it legally, and I'll put whoever did it in jail for a long time."

The dogs barked. They were either on the trail or had a hog cornered. Rhodes couldn't tell. He thought he heard someone moving around in the brush, but if he did, he didn't know who it was. It could have been anybody.

He felt a chill, and he thought again of that old movie where the trees had grasping arms. Only this time he didn't think it was the trees that would be grasping. Rapper and Nellie were more likely to be the culprits.

Rhodes wasn't much of a woodsman. He

had trouble moving quietly in the trees, and he thought Rapper would have the same problem. It was hard to say about Nellie. He was sneakier than he appeared to be. Rhodes looked around. He was behind a big tree, or maybe he was in front of it, depending on which direction someone might be coming from. He bent down and got the .32 from the ankle holster.

As he was straightening, he heard the sound of a blow and a muffled cry. Branches rattled, and something fell to the ground. It didn't take much imagination to think it must have been a body, but Rhodes didn't know whose. Not Fowler's. Fowler wasn't far away, in a clump of brush that hadn't moved.

The moon was bright, but while some light made its way through the thick limbs overhead, Rhodes couldn't make out much other than shades of light and darkness among the shadows. He stood still and listened.

If he'd been a real woodsman, he could have heard footsteps on the leaves. Or the snapping of a twig. As it was, he didn't really hear anything other than the frantic barking of the dogs. He wondered how long the dogs could hold a big hog in position before the hog got tired of being barked at and decided to attack. The Kevlar vests might not be enough to save the dogs if the hog got rough.

The barking became more shrill. One of the dogs howled.

"Dammit to hell!" Winston said.

He broke cover about twenty yards from where Rhodes stood and ran in the direction of the dogs. A dark figure stepped out behind him and swung what looked like a tree limb, though it might have been a baseball bat. It caught Winston in the back of the head. He dropped his rifle and dived forward, arms outstretched. When he landed, he skidded along the ground on his face. By the time he stopped skidding, the dark figure was gone.

The dogs howled louder, but they didn't sound hurt. They sounded like they were on the run. Maybe the tables had turned and the hog was now chasing them. Or hogs. Rhodes hoped there was only one.

The sound of the chase was drowned out by the noise of the motorcycles starting up. Rapper and Nellie gunned the engines and made the exhausts rumble like an earthquake.

Fowler's .357 blasted. Rhodes saw the muzzle flash twice from the brush, and then the motorcycles were on their way out of the woods.

"Hold off, Arvid," Rhodes said. "You want to spend the next fifty years in prison?"

"I want to get those bastards," Fowler said. "I think they killed Winston and Garver."

"I don't think so, but we need to check on them. Put the pistol away."

Rhodes came around the tree and headed for Fowler's hiding place without waiting for an answer. He hadn't gone more than a couple of steps before the dogs broke out of the trees and flashed by him like a couple of low-flying jet planes.

The hog wasn't far behind them. It thundered out of the brush, snorting and kicking up dirt as it ran, looking to Rhodes as big as a bear, though it probably wasn't as big as the one the hunters had killed the previous night.

Rhodes dived behind a tree just as Fowler started blasting away. The big pistol rattled the leaves with its roar.

Rhodes couldn't tell if the hog had been hit, but the shooting was enough to turn its attention to Fowler instead of the dogs. It skidded to a stop and stood shaking its head from side to side.

Long ago Rhodes had been in a similar situation, and the hog had plowed into him, putting him in the hospital for longer than he liked to think about. The .32 would be useless against the hog, but Rhodes knew he'd use it if he had to. Maybe he'd get in a lucky shot.

He didn't have to worry about it, however, because the hog charged the bushes where Fowler was hidden.

Fowler panicked. Instead of shooting, he ran out of the cover and dodged through the trees. Maybe he was out of bullets. Rhodes hadn't counted.

The hog wasn't far behind Fowler, and it proved to be as nimble as the man when it came to dodging the trees.

Rhodes chased after the hog, not that he had a plan. He just thought he ought to try to help Fowler, even if he didn't know how he was going to do it.

He should have stayed where he was. The hog heard him trampling along behind it and spun around, planting its trotters and lowering its head. Its tusks glinted in the moonlight, and to Rhodes they seemed to be about twelve inches long.

Rhodes didn't stand there to admire them, however. Wishing he'd worn his Kevlar vest like the dogs had, he turned and ran. He was getting chased by feral hogs way too often lately. It was good exercise but not the kind he enjoyed.

Not far ahead of him was a pecan tree with a limb that was just a bit higher than his head. When he got to it, he grabbed hold of the limb and swung his legs up. The hog ran right under him.

If Rhodes had been Sage Barton, he'd have pulled himself up, thrown a leg over the limb, and sat there laughing at the hog.

Unfortunately, Rhodes wasn't Sage Barton, and there was little chance he could perform the necessary acrobatics. Hanging on to the limb with his right hand, he made a quick turn.

So did the hog, who seemed to be puzzled by Rhodes's sudden disappearance. Rhodes grabbed the limb with his left hand again and reached out with his feet to the trunk of the tree.

It was about eighteen inches too far away. Rhodes moved hand over hand until he could reach the trunk. He risked a look at the hog, which was looking at him but not moving.

On his next try, Rhodes's foot touched the trunk. He thought he could step up it and hook his leg over the limb. It might have worked if his hands hadn't slipped.

Rhodes fell and landed flat on his back. His breath went out of him with a whoosh.

He struggled to suck in some air. Even if someone had offered him a million dollars to get up, he wouldn't have been able to move.

The hog grunted and huffed somewhere nearby. Rhodes figured it would rip him to shreds with those twelve-inch tusks.

It didn't happen, though, because the dogs came back. They announced their presence with barking, and the hog broke for the brush. The dogs went after him.

Rhodes lay where he was, waiting until he could breathe freely again. It took a couple of minutes. Then he stood up, glad that he was able to do it and not worried about how he'd feel the next day.

He took a couple of steps. Nothing seemed to be broken, and he didn't even hurt that much. He would later, he knew, but he couldn't worry about that now. He went to look for Winston and Garver.

Garver lay where he'd fallen, near a clump of what Rhodes was certain was poison ivy. It made him itch just to look at it, and he was careful to avoid touching it. He felt Garver's neck. The pulse was strong and even, so Garver would probably be all right. Rhodes left him there and looked around for Winston, who was sitting up, leaning against the trunk of a tree.

Rhodes went over to him and located the flashlight that Winston had dropped. Rhodes turned the light on and asked Winston how he felt.

"How do you think I feel?" Winston asked in return. "Like the back of my head's been bashed in." He put his fingers behind him and touched his hair. "I'm bleeding back there."

Rhodes held up a couple of fingers and asked Winston how many there were.

"Two. I feel like I'm a little out of it, but I can tell that much."

"You might not have a concussion," Rhodes said, "but then again you might. I'll call the EMTs and get them out here. Garver's going to need them, too. More than you."

Winston didn't argue.

Rhodes hated cell phones, so he didn't carry one often. He'd brought one along this time, just in case, and he used it to make the call. After that was done, he asked Winston if he'd seen Fowler.

"Nope. What happened to him?"

"The hog chased him."

Winston started to laugh, then stopped and put his hand to his head. "He might still be running, then."

"He might be," Rhodes said. "Unless somebody caught him."

Chapter 16

Nobody had caught Fowler, and he came back before the EMTs arrived. By that time Garver was sitting up and talking. He seemed fine, except for the big knot on the back of his head, but Rhodes insisted that he and Winston sit where they were until they got some medical attention. Fowler went off to see if he could bring back the dogs.

The EMTs came, and they ragged on Rhodes a while for having called them out three nights in a row.

"We're gonna charge extra for going into the woods from now on," one of them said. His name was Charlie, and he'd been on all three calls.

"The county would be glad to pay it," Rhodes told him, and Charlie laughed at the ridiculousness of that idea.

After Winston and Garver were taken away to be checked at the hospital, Fowler came back with the dogs. They'd lost the hog or gotten tired of chasing him. Rhodes didn't know which and didn't care. He and Fowler took them to Fowler's pickup and transferred the carriers to it.

"I'll take 'em home, but what about Winston and Garver's vehicles?" Fowler asked.

"I can call the wrecker," Rhodes said, "or Winston and Garver can pick them up tomorrow."

"You think they'll be all right out here tonight?"

"I can't vouch for that," Rhodes said.

"I guess we'll just have to take the chance. These dogs are all I can handle." Fowler looked at Rhodes. "I think I've about had my fill of hog hunting for a while."

"I expect Garver and Winston feel the same way."

"Probably do. I'm sorry I messed up tonight. I was scared. You're not gonna arrest me, are you?"

"I thought about it. You might have killed somebody. Didn't you even think about that?"

"I wasn't shooting to hit 'em," Fowler said. "Just to scare 'em."

That would make as good a defense as any if Rhodes pressed charges. He wouldn't waste his time doing that, though. It would probably all come to nothing in the end. Still, it wouldn't hurt to let Fowler worry about it for a little while longer.

"I'll think it over," Rhodes said. "I'll be in touch tomorrow if I decide to do anything."

"Yeah," Fowler said. "All right. I wasn't trying to shoot anybody, though. Just put a scare in 'em."

"I hear you," Rhodes said.

That didn't mean he believed it, though.

Rhodes stayed around for a few minutes after Fowler left, just in case Rapper and Nellie decided to come back.

They had to have been the two men on the motorcycles. It could have been someone else, sure, but what were the odds? Rhodes didn't think coincidence could extend that far, and he didn't know of any other motorcycles connected with the murders.

The question now was whether Rapper figured he'd had his revenge or if something more was to come. Knowing Rapper as he did, Rhodes would have bet on the something more.

Rhodes thought of another question, too. Had Garver and Winston been singled out? After those two were down, Rapper and Nellie had scooted without even trying to find Fowler and Rhodes.

It was possible that they figured they'd pushed their luck far enough already, but it was also possible that they'd taken care of the ones they'd come after. Rhodes needed to find out what Ruth Grady had learned about Garver when she checked his background.

What he needed more than that, however, was something to tie the two killings together. Even more importantly, he needed to find out what had happened on the night Baty was killed. It wouldn't hurt to find a motive for Baty's killing. That might be the clue Rhodes was looking for, the thread that would stitch everything together.

Rhodes was sure that sooner or later he'd catch hold of the thread. He just hoped it was sooner.

The night was cool and quiet. The big harvest moon was high in the sky, and the thin clouds threw dark shadows on the silvery ground. Rhodes heard nothing that sounded like motorcycles, so he got in the county car and headed for home.

He hadn't gone more than a quarter of a mile down the county road when he *did* hear something that sounded like motorcycles. He looked in the rearview mirror and saw two headlights. They were coming up on him fast.

Rhodes couldn't outrun them because the motorcycles were a lot more maneuverable on the curving road. He wondered what Rapper and Nellie had in mind.

He found out all too soon. Both bikes roared up beside him, one behind the other, and started edging him toward the ditch on his left.

The riders wore helmets with the visors pulled down, but there was no doubt that Nellie and Rapper were under the helmets. Their builds were the giveaway: Rapper short and potbellied, Nellie thinner and taller.

Rhodes had two choices. He could try nudging them back, or he could go into the ditch.

If he nudged them back, he might cause them to flip over.

If he went into the ditch, he was the one likely to flip over.

He had air bags and a seat belt. Nellie and Rapper weren't protected, but they were the ones who'd picked the fight. He was an officer of the law, and they weren't. It was a tough choice. He'd have to think about it.

They pulled closer to the car, and both men kicked out with their booted right feet and struck the side of the car. Rhodes eased over a little bit more to the left.

He slowed down. So did the riders. He wondered what they'd do if he stopped. What *could* they do? Run? Stand and fight him?

He decided he'd find out. He put his foot on the brake, and the car slowed.

Rapper and Nellie slowed, too. They kicked the car even harder, and Rhodes knew they were denting it. What with the dent the hog had made in it and the missing windshield wiper blade, he was running up quite a repair bill for the county. Mikey Burns would feel like it was coming out of his own pocket, too, but Rhodes wasn't worried about him at the moment.

Rhodes had come almost to a stop. The kicking was continuous and so hard it was shaking the car. Stopping wasn't such a great idea, but something else occurred to Rhodes. He was going slow enough for it to work if he was careful.

He pushed the accelerator to the floor. The car's tires spun on the dirt. Then they caught, and the car jumped forward. Nellie and Rapper kept pace, but Rhodes fooled them. He didn't stick to the road. Instead, he turned into the ditch.

He bumped along for a short distance with two tires in the ditch and two on the road. Then when he thought the time was right, he moved all the way down into the ditch. The car slashed through weeds that were as high as the hood. They slapped the car and stained the paint as Rhodes mowed them down.

Rapper followed Rhodes into the ditch. Nellie was right behind him. That was a mistake, as Rapper discovered when Rhodes slammed on the brakes.

The county car slid along on the weeds for a few feet after Rhodes applied the brakes, but Rapper slid faster, and his bike struck the car's rear bumper. The bike went over on its side, with Rapper under it.

Nellie had been going more slowly and was able to come to a stop. Rhodes jumped out of the car while Rapper was crawling out from under his bike. He didn't try to right it. He yowled with what must have been pain and hobbled over to Nellie. Nellie dragged him onto the back of his bike and took off.

Rhodes stood and watched them go. He could add himself to the number of people Rapper blamed for his brother's death, though Rhodes had been pretty sure already that he was on the list.

He left the bike where it was and went back to the jail.

"Did you see the six o'clock news?" Hack asked when Rhodes walked in.

"Shoot, I missed it," Rhodes said.

"How about the ten o'clock?"

Rhodes had lost track of time. He looked at the big round clock on the wall. It was nearly eleven.

"Missed that, too," he said. "I've been busy. How are the Eccleses?"

"Fine as frog hair," Hack said. "I sure wish you could've seen the news, though. Lawton and I looked pretty good for a couple of old men. Ain't that right, Lawton?"

"Sure is," Lawton said. "You had Ivy record the news, I guess."

"I forgot to tell her," Rhodes said.

Hack and Lawton both looked disappointed.

"What you been up to that's so important you missed the news?" Hack asked.

Rhodes felt guilty, so he didn't make them badger him for the report. He told it straight.

"You think Rapper's hurt bad?" Hack asked when Rhodes was finished.

"Not bad enough. That reminds me. Call Autry's wrecker service and have him go out there and pick up Rapper's motorcycle. If Duke's out on patrol, have him see what he can turn up from his informants about Rapper, and if he doesn't get anything, put Buddy on it tomorrow."

Hack picked up the phone to call the wrecker service, and Rhodes sat at his desk to look over the report about Garver that Ruth had left him. It made for interesting reading. Especially as it seemed that Ed Garver had been dead for thirty-five years.

The emergency room at the Clearview hospital wasn't crowded, but Rhodes didn't find Garver and Winston there. They'd been treated and released, so Rhodes drove to Garver's house.

Garver wasn't home. Rhodes didn't find that suspicious in itself. He might have gone after his pickup. Winston might have gone after his, too. They'd have gotten Fowler to take them, Rhodes thought, but he didn't waste any time going by Fowler's house to check. He drove back to the Carroll place to see if anyone was there.

Cal Autry was loading up Rapper's motorcycle when Rhodes went past, and Rhodes gave him a beep from the car horn. Autry didn't acknowledge it. He was busy, so Rhodes didn't hold it against him.

Rhodes got to the Carroll place. Fowler and the others were there, but they were just about to leave. Rhodes parked the cruiser astraddle the road so they couldn't get past it and got out.

"What the hell, Sheriff," Fowler said, getting out of his pickup.

"I need to talk to Garver," Rhodes told him.

"Well, I'm not him. You want to move so I can get by?"

Garver and Winston got out of their own pickups and stood listening. Rhodes thought it would be just as well for Winston and Fowler to leave. He might find out more from Garver if he talked to him alone.

"You and Winston can go," Rhodes said. "Garver, you need to stay here."

He got in the car and pulled it off the narrow road. Fowler and Winston drove by him. Rhodes sat in the car until he saw their taillights on the road back to Clearview. Then he got out and walked over to where Garver waited for him.

"What's the problem, Sheriff?" the plumber asked.

"I just found out that you're dead," Rhodes said. "I'm not used to dealing with zombies."

Garver didn't laugh. "I don't know what

you're talking about. I'm not dead. I'm standing right here in front of you."

The moon gilded Garver's pickup and threw its shadow on the ground. The air was cooler than it had been, and Rhodes wished he'd brought his jacket.

"You might be here," Rhodes said, "but Edward Alvin Garver's not. That Ed Garver's dead, but that's who you're supposed to be. Since you're not, the question is, who are you?"

Garver, or whoever he was, looked off back down the road to town. He probably wished he was on it.

"I'm Edward Alvin Garver. I have my ID here if you want to see it."

"I don't doubt you have some ID," Rhodes said. "It might even look real. It might even *be* real, but it won't prove to me that you're Garver. Now come on and tell me who you are. I'm getting cold standing out here, and I'd be just as happy to question you at the jail. Maybe happier."

"You can put me in jail if you want to. I'm Ed Garver, and that's all there is to it."

Rhodes couldn't really think of a good reason to put Garver in jail. It was possible he was telling the truth. Maybe Ruth had made some kind of mistake, as unlikely as that seemed to Rhodes. Or there could be two Ed Garvers with the same birth date. That didn't explain how Ruth had over-looked one of them, and Rhodes didn't believe she had. Still, his suspicion that the Ed Garver standing in front of him was really someone else, someone who'd stolen the real Garver's identity, wasn't enough grounds for an arrest.

"I don't really have any reason to arrest you yet," Rhodes said. "Are you sure you want to go to the jail?"

"Maybe not. Let me ask you something. If I'm not under arrest, I don't have to answer any questions, do I?"

"No. You don't have to."

"I don't have to talk to you if I don't want to, do I?"

"That's right," Rhodes said.

"Well," Garver said, "I don't want to. My head hurts, and I'm going home now."

He turned and got into his pickup. When he started it, Rhodes stepped aside. The headlights brightened the road. Then Garver drove past, and all Rhodes could do was let him leave.

Rhodes thought about following him, but he didn't think Garver planned to run. He might be wrong, but he'd play it that way and see what happened. Whatever Garver did, things didn't look good for him.

Rhodes smiled. He was still thinking of the man as Garver, but that wasn't his name. Rhodes wondered what his name really was.

He had a feeling he'd find out soon enough.

CHAPTER 17

Rhodes knew he should resist, but he couldn't help himself. The next morning he turned on the little radio/CD player combo that sat on the kitchen counter and tuned in Milton Munday. A commercial was playing. Naturally.

"What is that?" Ivy asked when she came into the kitchen.

Rhodes often wondered how she managed to look so good even before she put her makeup on.

"It's a commercial for Big Jolly's hamburgers," he said.

"You know that's not what I meant. Are you listening to Milton Munday?"

Rhodes admitted that he was. "I thought I'd see what he's saying about me today."

"It's not always about you," Ivy said.

"Maybe not, but I'll bet you a dollar that it is this time."

"It's a bet."

They stood by the counter and waited through another commercial, this one for Walker's Feed and Seed. Then Munday was on the air.

"Yes, folks," he said in his rich, mellow voice, "it's true. This town, our fair city, is being terrorized by violent bikers. I've already told you about last night's vicious attack on some of your friends and fellow citizens, and now I'd like to ask you a question. What do you think our sheriff will do about it? The phone lines are open. Call in and let us hear from you."

"You win," Ivy said. "Too bad I don't have a dollar."

"I'll stay right here until you get one out of your purse," Rhodes said.

He was only half-listening to Munday now, but the broadcaster's voice sounded a bit odd to him. It was almost as if Munday were scared of the bikers.

"I don't think I have a dollar in my purse, either," Ivy said. "I'll make a deal with you."

Rhodes was suspicious of Ivy's deals. Somehow he never came out the winner.

"What kind of deal?" he said.

"I'll fix you sausage and eggs for breakfast."

Sausage and eggs? Rhodes hadn't even known there was any sausage in the house.

"That sounds fair," he said.

"Good. I haven't cooked breakfast in a while," Ivy said. "It'll be a treat for both of us."

"Is it spicy sausage?" Rhodes asked, hoping the answer would be yes.

"It's spicy, all right. I made it myself."

Uh-oh. "You made it yourself?"

"It's a special recipe."

Rhodes didn't think Ivy had the equipment to make sausage, no matter how special the recipe was.

"What kind of recipe?" he asked.

"It's vegetarian sausage. It's good. You'll like it."

Rhodes looked over at Sam, lying by the refrigerator. The cat opened its eyes as if it felt Rhodes's gaze. It yawned.

"How do you know it's good?" Rhodes asked.

"I just know. You go out and visit Speedo." Ivy switched off the radio. "I'm tired of listening to that."

Rhodes was tired of it, too. He hadn't paid any attention to the man who called in to say he didn't think Rhodes could handle the bikers, much less solve the murders that Munday said "held the town in the grip of terror, wondering who would be the next to die." Well, not much attention. He wondered

216

if Munday had mentioned the Eccleses. If he hadn't, they'd be sadly disappointed. The biker gang, all two of them, would be a better topic for discussion, Rhodes figured.

He headed for the back door while Ivy got out the frying pan. Yancey heard him and came bounding out from wherever he'd been hiding and zipped out into the yard as soon as the door was opened wide enough for him to squeeze through.

It was cold but not frosty cold. Speedo came out of his Styrofoam igloo, shook off some of the straw bedding that clung to him, and charged Yancey. As usual the dogs seemed invigorated by the cool weather. Rhodes stood on the steps and watched them take turns chasing each other around the yard.

Brown leaves from the pecan trees lay all around on the grass, but Rhodes didn't plan to rake them. They'd make good fertilizer when they rotted, and until then they'd protect the lawn from the cold. Or so Rhodes told himself.

After a while, Rhodes whistled up Yancey, and the two of them went back inside. Speedo went back into his igloo for a nap.

Rhodes smelled the sausage. He had to admit it smelled good, though not a whole lot like real sausage. He got out a plate and utensils, then poured a glass of water while Ivy scrambled the eggs. When she served them up with the sausage, he put some picante sauce on them and dug in.

"Not bad," he said after he'd tried the sausage.

"I knew you'd like it," Ivy said, laying a couple of pieces of toast on his plate.

"You didn't fix any for yourself," Rhodes said.

"I need to get dressed. You go ahead and eat."

Rhodes didn't need any further encouragement. He started to ask Ivy to turn the radio on before she went out of the kitchen, but he decided not to. Why subject himself to the aggravation?

Yancey lay under the chair where Rhodes sat and eyed Sam. Sam slept curled into a black ball and didn't move. Rhodes could hardly tell he was breathing.

After he'd finished eating, Rhodes rinsed off the plate and put it into the dishwasher along with his glass, knife, and fork.

"That's my housework for the day," he told Yancey, but by then, like Sam, the dog was asleep.

When Rhodes entered the jail, Hack and Lawton were ready for him.

"You hear Milton Munday's show today?" Hack asked.

"About two minutes of it," Rhodes said. "He's worried about motorcycle gangs. Did he mention our customers?"

"Lance and Hugh? Not a word. I guess he forgot 'em."

"He's really worried about those bikers. You'd think they came here to get him, almost."

Rhodes wondered why Munday would be worried. Surely he didn't know Rapper and Nellie. Or maybe he did. It occurred to Rhodes that he didn't know much about Munday. When it came right down to it, he didn't know *anything* about Munday.

"Lance and Hugh were a little upset when I told 'em Munday didn't mention them," Lawton said.

"Isn't he still on the air?" Rhodes asked.

"Yeah," Hack said, "but he's all about the bikers today. You'd think the Hell's Angels were in town. I told you it'd be like this."

"You did," Rhodes said. "I give you all the credit. Did Duke turn up anything on Rapper?"

"Nope. Buddy's on it today, though."

Before Rhodes could respond to that, Ruth Grady came in, and Rhodes asked her about the report on Garver.

"No mistakes," she said. "Edward Alvin Garver is our man. Or isn't our man."

Rhodes hadn't mentioned any of this to Hack or Lawton, and they were immediately curious.

"What's all that about?" Hack asked.

Ruth explained it.

"Well, he's a good plumber, whoever he is," Hack said. "I know that for sure and certain. He fixed Miz McGee's sink faucet when it went bad on her, and he didn't overcharge her for it, either."

Rhodes didn't think that information was relevant. He and Ruth sat down and went over the report again.

The real Edwin Alvin Garver had been born in Arkansas thirty-five years previously. He'd died not long afterward, never having left the hospital, and was buried just outside Fayetteville.

"What do you think?" Rhodes asked.

"That our plumber friend, no pun intended, got hold of this Ed Garver's birth certificate," Ruth said. "After he had that, he got the rest of the identification he needed and ditched his own identity. He started his life over again."

"Too easy to get a birth certificate in Arkansas," Hack said. "They oughta toughen up."

"It doesn't take much doing to get a birth certificate in Texas, either," Rhodes said. "All you need is a valid driver's license and a valid credit card. Those can be arranged without a birth certificate if you know the right people."

"Or the wrong ones," Lawton said.

"Right or wrong, why would a man do something like that?" Hack asked.

"Lots of reasons," Ruth said. "Too many to count."

"Garver claimed he came here from Galveston to get away from all the damage Hurricane Ike did," Rhodes said. "I wonder if that's true."

"It makes a good story," Ruth said, "but my guess is he's from Arkansas."

"So was Baty," Rhodes said. "That's where some of the bank robberies were."

"You think we ought to talk to Garver?" Ruth asked.

"If he'll talk." Rhodes told her about his previous conversation with Garver. "He might not even be in town anymore."

"You can arrest him now," Ruth said. "Identity theft's a crime, and we have enough right here to justify holding him."

"Let's go see if we can find him, then," Rhodes said.

■ ■ ■ ■

Garver had bought a nice little house when he moved to Clearview, and now Rhodes wondered where his money had come from, plumbing or bank robbery.

The house was in one of the newer additions to the town, out on the north side, not too far from the high school. The grass was brown, but so was everyone's in Clearview at that time of year. It had been trimmed and edged around the walk and driveway. Did killers take good care of their lawns? Rhodes had never thought about it before. Garver's pickup wasn't in the driveway, but it might be in the garage, which was closed.

Rhodes parked at the curb. Ruth parked behind him, and they both got out.

"Probably at work," Rhodes said.

"If he hasn't skipped the county," Ruth said.

They went up the walk, and Rhodes rang the bell. Nobody answered, not that Rhodes had expected anyone.

"You go ahead and do your patrol," he told Ruth. "I'll go by Allison's Plumbing Company and see if Garver's there."

Ruth left, and Rhodes stood looking at the house for a while, thinking about

Garver. Maybe this was all some kind of mix-up, and Garver would be in the clear. Rhodes hoped that was all there was to it and that today Garver would be willing to talk.

He doubted that would be the case, however.

Allison's Plumbing Company had been around ever since Rhodes was a boy. Trey Allison's father, George Allison Jr., had owned it then, and still had an interest in it, though he was now too old to do much work and seldom showed up even to look things over. George Allison III, whom everybody called Trey, was fully in charge.

Trey was little, short, and wiry, the better to crawl around in tunnels under houses or to move around in attics, Rhodes thought. He had curly gray hair that he covered with a black-and-white-striped engineer's cap, as if he were about to board a train and take off for a rail trip to the West.

"Hey, Sheriff," he said when Rhodes walked into the shop. "Am I under arrest?"

Allison sat on a wooden stool behind a high wooden counter covered with all kinds of couplings and fittings and short lengths of pipe. Behind Allison was a wall of shelves with more of the same kinds of things.

Rhodes supposed everything there was useful for something, but he didn't have any idea what that something might be.

"Not you," Rhodes said. "I'm looking for Ed Garver."

Allison jumped down off the stool. Rhodes could see only his head and the engineer's cap as Allison walked around the counter.

"What's Ed been up to?" Allison asked when he was in front of the counter. He seemed nervous. "I hope it's nothing serious, because he's on a job that's pretty complicated."

"What kind of job is that?" Rhodes asked.

"Stopped-up pipe."

"That doesn't sound so bad."

"Usually it's not," Allison said, "but this pipe's stopped up because it collapsed. It's that old clay pipe they used a long time ago, so there's no telling what problems might crop up later on if it's left there. We're replacing all the pipes under the house and in the yard, all the way to the street. Lot of digging and tunneling."

"I hope you have somebody who can finish it if Ed's not available. Did he show up for work today?"

Rhodes half-expected the answer to be no, but Allison said, "Sure. He's always here. Never been late, never missed a day of work.

Best man I have on the payroll. I hope he's not in any real trouble."

"I just want to talk to him," Rhodes said, wondering why Allison was overselling Garver. "For now."

Allison took off his engineer's cap, twisted it up, and stuck it in the back pocket of his jeans. "Look, Sheriff, whatever you think he did, I'll bet he didn't do it. He's steady, and he's reliable. I'd sure hate to lose him."

"Where did you say he was working?"

"The old Prickett house. You know where it is?"

Rhodes knew. Dan Prickett had owned a radio shop and record store fifty or sixty years ago, and it must have been a pretty good business because he'd built a big house on the outskirts of town. He was long dead, and his family was gone. Someone else owned the house now.

"I'll go on out there and talk to Garver," Rhodes said. "Best he doesn't know I'm coming."

Allison looked shocked. "You know me, Sheriff. I wouldn't call him or anything."

"I'm sure you wouldn't, but I thought I'd mention it just in case."

Allison took out his cap, straightened it out, and pulled it onto his head. "You can trust me, Sheriff. I sure hope Ed's in the clear, though."

"Clear of what?"

"Whatever it is you're going to talk to him about. That's all. I don't think he'd do anything bad."

"That's what I plan to find out," Rhodes said.

The Prickett place was built of stone and had been kept up pretty well over the years, but it didn't look so good now, what with a tunnel dug all the way from the house to the curb, with dirt piled on the side. Under a big oak tree there was another huge pile of dirt that Rhodes assumed had come from beneath the house. He could see the edges of a blue tarp sticking out around the bottom of the pile.

Garver's pickup was parked at the curb, and so was another, larger pickup with a pipe rack on one side and all sorts of metal storage cabinets built into the bed with covered cubbyholes on the sides. Rhodes didn't know who might be driving that one.

He stopped behind Garver's pickup and got out. He could hear a radio playing loud country music, or what passed for it these days. The sound was coming from the back of the house, so Rhodes walked around there to see who he could find.

He didn't find anyone, but he did find the radio. It sat on a box near a square hole about three feet deep. From the hole a tunnel ran beneath the foundation of the house. A lawn chair wasn't far away from the hole, so Rhodes sat in it to wait. He wasn't sure how long he could take the loud music, but at least it wasn't Milton Munday.

Rhodes had been seated only a couple of minutes when someone slithered out from under the foundation. His clothes were covered in mud and so was most of his face, but Rhodes could see that he wasn't Garver.

The man didn't notice Rhodes sitting in the chair. He pulled a red cloth out of his back pocket and started to wipe his hands and face.

While he was doing that, Garver dragged himself out onto the lawn and stood up. Rhodes was surprised to see him. Even though the pickup had been out front, Rhodes couldn't believe that Garver was still in town.

Garver saw Rhodes at once. He was as muddy as the other man, but he had a wide white cloth tied around his head. Or it had been white before it got muddy. Garver frowned and walked over to Rhodes.

"How's the head?" Rhodes asked when Garver reached him. He had to raise his voice to be heard over the music.

"It's okay. I got the bandage covered up. I told you I didn't want to talk to you."

Rhodes stood up. "I know you did. That was when you had a choice. Now you don't have one. We can prove you aren't Edward Alvin Garver, and all the fake ID in the world won't change that. Clean yourself up a little, and we'll go down to the jail."

Garver tensed and took a deep breath. Rhodes thought he was going to yell or make a break for it. Instead, Garver let the breath out slowly and relaxed.

"Can I take my truck?" he asked.

"Sure. I'll follow you."

"Right."

Garver walked over to the other man, who was now watching them with obvious curiosity. The two talked for a second. Then Garver started for the front of the house without a word to Rhodes. Rhodes followed him. He could feel the other plumber watching him, but he didn't look back.

When Garver got in his pickup, he opened the door and got a towel. After he'd cleaned himself off a bit, he threw the towel back in the pickup and brought out a cell phone. Rhodes saw him punch in some numbers. Garver waited for a few seconds and then started talking. Rhodes couldn't hear him,

228

thanks to the music that still played. It probably didn't bother the owner of the house, who would have checked into a motel that had good plumbing, but Rhodes wondered if the neighbors minded it. He wouldn't be surprised if they'd called in a complaint to the sheriff's department.

Garver talked for quite a while. Rhodes got in the county car and waited, making a little bet with himself about who Garver was calling.

Rhodes didn't mind waiting. Garver wasn't going anywhere because Rhodes had parked close to the pickup's bumper. The plumber couldn't pull out without Rhodes moving.

Finally Garver stopped talking and started the pickup. Rhodes started the county car and backed up so Garver could leave. Then he followed Garver to the jail.

Just as they got there, a shiny black Infiniti pulled up to park. Rhodes didn't have to see the driver to know that it was Randy Lawless. Garver had called a lawyer, and not just any lawyer. Lawless was the best in the county, the man Hugh and Lance couldn't afford to hire this time.

Rhodes had won his bet with himself.

CHAPTER 18

Randy Lawless wore a blue sports coat, gray pants, and an open-necked white shirt. His black shoes were polished to a shine.

"Hey, Sheriff," he said, coming up as Rhodes got out of the county car. "I see you've arrested one of my clients."

"And a recent one at that," Rhodes said, "if you're talking about Ed Garver, or whoever's in that pickup over there. Although he's not under arrest. Yet."

"Good, good," Lawless said. "Maybe we can keep it that way. I'll be sitting in with him when you question him."

Rhodes had been hoping for a friendly chat, and if Garver had been as innocent as he claimed to be, that was what they'd have had. Having Lawless around changed things. It meant that Garver was almost certainly guilty of something, but Rhodes wasn't sure exactly what. It could be the murders, the stolen identity, or something else. Or all of the above.

"Let's go on inside, then," Rhodes said, "and see what happens."

"I'll just talk to my client first," Lawless said. "If you don't mind."

"Far be it from me to stand between a man and his making a living," Rhodes said. "I'll wait for you in the jail."

Lawless went over to talk to Garver. Rhodes watched them for a couple of seconds. Garver talked and Lawless shook his head. Rhodes wasn't learning a thing, so he went on inside.

Hack and Lawton looked up.

"Jennifer Loam called," Hack said. "She wanted to know what progress you were making on those killings. I told her you were busy investigating."

"That was the truth, too," Rhodes said. He looked at Lawton. "Is the interview room ready?"

"Sure is. It's always ready. You want to talk to Lance and Hugh in there?"

"No, Ed Garver. He's outside, but he'll be coming in shortly. Randy Lawless will be with him."

"Oh, boy," Hack said.

"My sentiments exactly," Rhodes said.

"You think Randy knows anything about Garver?"

"I think they just met in person out in the parking lot. They met on the phone about five minutes before that."

"So Randy's as much in the dark as we are."

"Garver's probably filling him in right now," Rhodes said.

"I bet it's a good story," Lawton said. "I bet Garver's a bank robber. What d'you think, Hack?"

"You already took the easy answer," Hack said. "You always take the easy answer."

"That's 'cause I'm quick-witted and speak up first."

"Quick-witted? I guess that's close. I'd say you were about half right."

Lawton's face got red. "You better watch how you talk about me."

"I'm just sayin'."

"I'll show you who's just sayin'."

Lawton started toward Hack's desk, but the dispatcher was saved from whatever Lawton had planned by the entrance of Garver and his lawyer.

"We're ready to talk to you, Sheriff," Lawless said. "Lead the way."

Rhodes looked at Hack and Lawton, who had already calmed down. They were doing their best to look as if nothing had happened.

"Just follow me," Rhodes said to Garver and Lawless, and he led them to the interview room, which was furnished with an old table and four wooden folding chairs. Rhodes pulled one of the chairs up to the table and sat down. Lawless and Garver sat opposite him.

A digital recorder sat in the middle of the table, and Rhodes turned it on.

"Now, then," Lawless said. He nodded at the recorder. "Before we start serious talking, I want to know if you're planning to charge my client. If you're not, he doesn't have to answer any questions."

"Let's hear what he has to say," Rhodes said. "Maybe he'd like to talk. What about it, Ed?"

Rhodes used the name sarcastically, to see if it got a rise out of Garver.

It didn't, but it did get a mild response. "I have something to talk about, I guess."

"You know the consequences," Lawless said.

"Yeah. You told me already."

Lawless shrugged. "It's your choice, then."

"Yeah. Okay. Here's the deal, Sheriff. I'm not really Ed Garver."

"We'd already established that," Rhodes said, not surprised in the least. "So who are you?"

"I'm William Dale Dalton."

"Fine. Who's William Dale Dalton?"

"Me."

Rhodes looked at Lawless. Lawless just grinned.

"That's not exactly what I meant," Rhodes said. "Let's try it this way. Why have you been posing as Ed Garver?"

"Because I got scared."

It was just as Rhodes suspected. He was never going to get a straight answer from anyone ever again. He was, however, going to keep trying.

"Scared of what?" he asked.

"Scared of my wife."

Rhodes didn't know what answer he'd been expecting, but that wasn't it.

"Your wife?"

"Sheila. That's her name. Sheila Dalton. Well, Sheila Herndon Dalton, if you want the whole thing. She was a Herndon before she married me. I should've known better than to marry a Herndon, to tell you the truth. They're all of them crazy. I wasn't so much scared of her as of her brothers."

"I don't think I'm following you," Rhodes said.

"It's like this, Sheriff. Sheila and I got along real good before we got married, but after we lived together a few years, it turned out that we got on each other's nerves. You know how it is."

Rhodes didn't know how it was, not precisely. He thought that couples learned to accept any little flaws they saw in each other and kept on going, maybe loving each other more because of the flaws. If it didn't work out, though, there was always divorce.

"How bad was it?" Rhodes asked.

Garver, or Dalton as Rhodes thought of him now, put his arms on the table and leaned forward. "Bad. Real bad. She cussed me all the time, and she claimed I was running around with Marilyn Hendricks. I wasn't, but after a while I wished I was. Marilyn's kinda cute, and she doesn't cuss, at least as far as I know."

"That's all?" Rhodes asked.

"No, I could've stood the cussing and the accusing. She hit me, too."

Rhodes looked at Dalton. He wasn't a big man, but he wasn't small, either.

"Sheila's a big woman, Sheriff," Dalton said. "Arms like this." He held up his hands and described a circle the size of a dinner plate. "She's mean, too, mean as a snake."

"You could have tried counseling," Rhodes said. "Or even gotten a divorce."

"You don't know her brothers," Dalton said. "They blamed me for the trouble.

She's their little sister, and they're even bigger and meaner than she is." Dalton paused. "Well, meaner, anyway."

"So you left," Rhodes said.

"So I left. I looked around on the Internet and found out how to get somebody else's name, and I did it. I don't know what else you think I did, but that's the only thing."

"Where did you leave from?" Rhodes asked. "I don't think you mentioned that."

"Ozark," Dalton said. "Ozark, Arkansas."

"Satisfied, Sheriff?" Lawless asked. "He's guilty of running away, but it's not a big deal. I think we can work something out, don't you?"

"Not right now," Rhodes said. "He still hasn't told me the main thing I need to know."

"There's more?"

"Just one thing," Rhodes said. "You were hunting hogs on the Leverett place two nights ago. I know you were there, and I know something happened that nobody's talking about. I want to know what it was."

Dalton looked at Lawless. The attorney said, "You don't have to tell him."

"That's right," Rhodes said. "You don't have to tell me, but you should."

"You're not threatening my client, are you, Sheriff?" Lawless asked.

"Me? I never threaten people," Rhodes said. "I'm just saying that he should tell me. He's admitted a criminal act, and I thought he might want to mitigate it by telling me something I need to know."

"What criminal act would that be, Sheriff?"

"I don't have a copy of the Penal Code right here with me," Rhodes said, "but it's an offense if somebody uses the identity of a deceased person without legal authorization."

"That's true enough," Lawless said, "but you left out the part about intent to defraud. Can you prove that Mr. Garver, uh, Dalton, had that intent?"

"I'd say he was defrauding his wife, his employer, and even me, but I don't have to prove it. That's up to the courts. I'm sure you can mount a fine defense for him if he's got the money to pay you."

"I don't want to get into a court fight," Dalton said. "That way those Herndon brothers will find me for sure."

Dalton had lived in Clearview as Garver for a couple of years. Rhodes doubted that the Herndons were still looking for him, if they ever had been. Rhodes hadn't entirely bought the story.

"We might be able to avoid any court

fight," Rhodes said. "If you tell me what happened out there that night."

Dalton didn't say anything. He didn't look at his attorney, either. He just stared at the table in front of him.

"What my client's done doesn't qualify as a felony," Lawless said. "He didn't defraud anybody for gain. He wouldn't have to do jail time."

"We'll see," Rhodes said. "It would still be better if he'd talk to me."

Dalton looked up. "I promised I wouldn't say anything to anybody. You might think I don't know you got Hugh and Lance in jail here because they wouldn't tell you, but I know, all right."

"It's no secret they're here," Rhodes said, "but it's not because they wouldn't tell me what I wanted to know. It's because they assaulted me."

"Well, they just did that because you tried to make 'em talk."

Rhodes didn't respond to that. He leaned back in his chair and waited. Sooner or later, somebody was going to tell him. Rhodes thought it would be Dalton.

"What happens if I don't tell you?"

"Nothing much," Rhodes said. "Unless you've been cheating the tax man. The IRS doesn't like it when that happens."

"I'm no crook. I told Mr. Allison the whole story. He knows who I am, and I'm paying taxes as Dalton."

That explained why Trey had been so nervous, Rhodes thought.

"Well, at least the IRS won't be after you, but whether you talk or not, you're not going to be Ed Garver anymore. Do people call you William or Bill?"

"Neither one. Willie's what I used to go by. Willie Dalton."

Rhodes excused himself and left the room. He went out to where Hack was and told him to get Ruth on the radio.

"Have her check on William Dale Dalton, a.k.a. Willie Dalton, from Ozark, Arkansas. See what she can come up with."

"Okay. Anything else?"

"That's it. I'll check with you later."

Rhodes left Hack and went back to the interview room. Lawless and Dalton were talking, but they stopped when he came in.

Rhodes went to his chair and sat down. "Okay, Dalton, your days as Garver are over, no matter what. Maybe we can work a deal if you talk, though. Keep things out of the paper, so the Herndon brothers won't read about you. You can start using your real name and stay right here in Clearview after you settle up for your crime. The

Herndon brothers will never know where you are."

"You can't be sure they won't. They're sneaky."

"I can't be sure, but I'd bet on it."

Dalton sat quietly for a while. Finally he said, "Okay, I'll tell you what happened. You might not want to hear this, Mr. Lawless."

"Are there more crimes involved?"

"Could be."

Lawless settled back in his chair. "I'll stick around, then."

"Tell me what happened, Dalton," Rhodes said.

"Well," Dalton said, "it was like this . . ."

CHAPTER 19

The hunters had met about dark the way they always did, according to Dalton. Nothing was different at the start, not that anybody noticed, but then they ran up on a whole mess of hogs that they hadn't expected.

"Usually they're up and stirring around by sundown," Dalton said, "but this bunch was still holed up, and we sort of stumbled on 'em. Even the dogs were surprised. I don't know what the deal was. It was like they were fed and happy and didn't need to go off and root around."

That was unusual enough in itself, but what happened next was the really bad part, and the confusing part as well. Dalton still hadn't quite figured it all out.

"That's when the shooting started," he said, but he didn't know who was doing the shooting.

"All I know is, the bullets ricocheted all

around us, the bark flew off the trees, the dead limbs fell all over the place. We thought somebody was trying to kill us. The hogs thought somebody was trying to kill them, too, I guess, 'cause they jumped up squealing and snorting and took off at a dead run."

Rhodes knew about that part.

"Nobody got hit, though," Dalton said. "We were lucky, or maybe whoever was doing the shooting was aiming at something else. That's the whole story, Sheriff."

Rhodes didn't think so. If that had been the story, it wouldn't have been a secret, and every one of the hog hunters would have marched right to the jail to file a complaint against the unknown shooter. Or shooters.

"There must be a little more to it, Dalton," Rhodes said. "You might as well tell me the rest."

Dalton didn't have any more to say. "That's it, Sheriff. That's all I know."

"No, Dalton, that's not all you know. With what you've told me, I can probably get Hugh and Lance to fill me in on the rest, but it would be easier if you did it."

Dalton looked at Lawless.

"You're on your own," Lawless said. "I told you not to talk, but you didn't listen." He relented a little. "You still don't have to talk if you don't want to."

"Hell, he's right," Dalton said. "Somebody else'll tell him now if I don't. I sure hate it that the others will know I ratted 'em out, though."

"I won't tell them," Rhodes said.

"They'll figure it out."

"Maybe not. Go ahead and tell me."

Dalton slumped down in the chair. "Somebody shot back."

Now they were finally getting to it. Rhodes had suspected something like that because even as he'd fled the stampeding hogs, he'd been sure he'd heard more than one gun.

"Who shot back?" he asked.

"All I know is, it wasn't me," Dalton said. "It might have been one person or it might have been two. I was ducking and covering, and I didn't pay any attention."

Rhodes wasn't sure he believed that. Last night, Fowler hadn't hesitated to shoot at Rapper and Nellie, and the others had been ready to do the same. Rhodes figured Fowler might have fired the first shot the other time, too. He'd have to ask him about that.

"So after it was over," Rhodes said to Dalton, "you all agreed not to talk about it?"

"That's right. It didn't last long, and we got out of there as soon as we could. We didn't think anybody was hurt, so there was no harm done. We just wanted to get away from those woods in case somebody came back after us."

"And you didn't see who it was."

"We didn't see anybody, and we didn't know why they started shooting at us. We were scared, Sheriff. Wouldn't you have been scared?"

Just running from the hogs had been scary enough for Rhodes, without any shooting involved.

"Nobody was hit?" he asked.

"That's what I said. We were all fine, and we didn't see who was shooting. I guess they got away, too."

Rhodes wondered what had happened to the shooter, or shooters. What had they been doing there, and why had they started shooting? What did they have to do with the murder of Baty, if anything?

Dalton didn't seem able to answer those questions, but Rhodes didn't trust him. He'd lied about who he was for years, so who was to say he wasn't lying now?

There was something else that worried Rhodes, too, so he asked about it. "You all left the woods together? Nobody stayed behind?"

"We wanted out of there," Dalton said.

"Who'd stick around and maybe get shot? Not me."

What if he had, though? What if he'd been the one who killed Baty? The bank robberies had been in Arkansas, and that's where Dalton came from. A coincidence, maybe, but one that deserved a little consideration.

Hoss Rapinski was yet another consideration. Dalton had disappeared into the trees, and Hoss had been killed. A second coincidence?

Rhodes wondered about Rapinski, too. He was a bounty hunter, true. Everybody seemed to know that, but what if he'd been more than a bounty hunter? What if he'd been a licensed private investigator? Or even an unlicensed one? Could he have been in Blacklin County for more than one reason? Could he have been hired by the Herndons to find Dalton?

It bothered Rhodes that whoever had been shooting at the hunters had gotten away without being seen, and it bothered him even more that Baty's killer had done the same.

If Dalton had killed Baty, what had happened to the man who jumped out of Baty's car? Had he run from all the shooting and disappeared? Why hadn't anyone seen him?

Those were all questions that had been

bothering Rhodes, and he would have liked to find the answers. He had a feeling Dalton either didn't know them or wouldn't tell.

"You're sure you didn't see who was shooting at you?" Rhodes asked.

"I'm sure," Dalton said.

"The Chandlers are rumored to do that kind of thing."

"Might've been them. I wouldn't know. I told you, I was too scared to worry about who it was."

"You know why they don't like hog hunters?"

"Animal lovers," Dalton said. "Got that farm and all. Had some trouble about a pig, so I heard."

"And of course you wouldn't know anything about what happened to the pig," Rhodes said.

"That's right. Nobody I know had anything to do with it, if that's what you're thinking."

Maybe Dalton was telling the truth. Maybe not.

"You're not planning to leave town, are you?" Rhodes asked.

"No, sir," Dalton said. "If you don't think the Herndons will get me, I'll stay right here."

"What about your name?"

"I'll fix that. I'll talk to Mr. Allison. He'll understand. I'll keep right on doing my job for him if you don't put me in jail."

"I'm not going to put you in jail," Rhodes said. "Not yet, anyway. Don't do any more hog hunting, though. You understand?"

"I sure do. I don't want to hunt any hogs for a while. Maybe never."

"That's what Fowler said last night. He was kind of trigger-happy, wasn't he."

"I don't know what you mean, Sheriff," Dalton said, but Rhodes thought he knew, all right.

"He's told you everything you've asked, Sheriff," Lawless said. "Are you going to arrest him? If you aren't, then cut him loose."

Rhodes thought it over. There was no reason to hold Dalton at the moment, so he said, "He can go."

"Thanks, Sheriff," Dalton said. "I'm a solid citizen. Always have been. You watch and see."

"I'll be watching, all right," Rhodes said. "You can count on it."

As it turned out, Dalton wasn't the only one who'd been cut loose. When Rhodes returned to the outer office, Hack said, "The Eccles boys are back on the street."

"Back on the county roads is more like

247

it," Lawton said.

"What happened?" Rhodes asked.

"It was your college pal that did it," Hack said.

"My college pal?"

"The goofy one," Lawton said.

"Seepy Benton," Rhodes said.

"That's the one. He went their bail. Said to tell you to give him a call. Jennifer Loam wants you to call her, too. Wants an update on the murders."

"What about Ruth?"

"She's on her way in," Hack said. "She'll tell you all about that Dalton fella."

"Garver is Dalton," Rhodes said.

"Huh?"

"Later. I have work to do."

Rhodes sat at his desk. He didn't plan to call Loam or Benton at the moment. He started to write up his interview with Dalton. He had the recorder to refresh his memory, but he didn't really need it.

Ruth came in after about ten minutes. She told Rhodes that she'd looked on the computer in her car and found out about William Dale Dalton from Ozark, Arkansas.

"He disappeared about three years ago," she said. "He went squirrel hunting and never came back. His wife said he might have been killed in the woods. That's about all I could find. I guess they're still looking for him. Is he around here?"

Rhodes told her about Ed Garver, who was really Willie Dalton. Hack listened in.

"Well, well," Ruth said. "It's easy enough to live under a false identity if you work at it. Remember that case in Florida, Pompano Beach, I think? A man robbed a 7-Eleven, got caught, then escaped from prison, and lived free for thirty years or so under a name he got from a stolen driver's license."

"I read the story in the paper," Rhodes said.

"Garver didn't make it thirty years, I guess. You want me to check up on his story to see if he's telling the truth?"

"Absolutely," Rhodes said.

"If he is, what are we going to do about it?"

"Nothing," Rhodes said. "He doesn't want to go back, and I'm not going to make him. I don't want to be responsible for what might happen."

"We have to let his family know he's alive," Ruth said. "They're suffering."

Rhodes didn't think so, but he said, "I'll talk to him in a day or two about it. I'll see to it that he lets them know." Rhodes didn't have any idea how he was going to do that, but he'd figure it out later. "Right now, he's still a suspect in the killings. Did you happen to turn up any connection between him and Baty?"

"Nothing like that. No connection to those bank robberies, either, if that's what you're thinking."

"That doesn't mean that there wasn't one. Keep digging around and see if you can find anything else."

"I'll try," Ruth said. "Will you be around?"

"I have some people to see," Rhodes said, "but I'll check back later."

"You're leaving me here with those two?" Ruth asked, looking around at Hack and Lawton.

"Best-looking two men in town," Hack said. "You know you like it."

"There you go," Rhodes said, and he left her there.

Bob Lindsey, the station manager of KCLR — "the Mighty K-Clear," as its slogan had it — was in his office when Rhodes showed up. He had short gray hair cut in a military flattop. He wasn't the only man in town who favored that style, though none of them had been around when it was first popular.

The office was in one of the few downtown buildings still in decent condition. Most of the others hadn't been kept up over the years, and at least half of them were deserted. The windows were cracked and dirty, and the old awnings sagged.

Across the street, the new offices of Randy Lawless glistened white in the sun. Lawless had bought half a city block after some of the old buildings had been demolished, and he'd built what Rhodes referred to as the Lawj Mahal. It was by far the most impressive building in the old downtown, mainly because it was the only new building there.

"You must never get tired of looking at that place," Rhodes said to Lindsey, who could see the Lawj Mahal from his office window.

"I don't even think about it anymore, Sheriff, but I'll bet you didn't come by to discuss the local architecture."

Lindsey was tall and thin and looked like a former college basketball player who'd been on a diet. He seemed a little nervous to have Rhodes in his office.

"No, architecture wasn't what I had in mind," Rhodes said.

"Have a seat, then, and tell me what you're here for."

Rhodes sat in an upholstered wing chair that looked about a hundred years old. Nearly everything in Lindsey's office looked old, as if it might have been a part of the building's original furnishings. The rolltop desk pushed up against the wall to Rhodes's right was new, though. Either that or it had been well cared for.

Lindsey sat in the swivel desk chair and turned to face Rhodes.

"I want to talk to you about Milton Munday," Rhodes said.

Lindsey brushed a hand across his flattop. "Look, Sheriff, I know Munday steps on a lot of toes, including yours, but I have him on a tight leash. There's a line I won't let him cross. You don't have to worry about that."

"I'm not worried, and I'm all for freedom of speech. Munday can say whatever he wants to say."

"Oh." Lindsey relaxed a bit. "What about him, then?"

"I was wondering how you went about hiring a talk show host. Do you advertise for one? Do you put out the word informally? Do you have tryouts? That kind of thing."

Lindsey relaxed even more and leaned back in the chair. It had a tight spring and didn't tip over with him.

"It's a funny thing about that," he said. "I wasn't even thinking about having a talk show again. Red Rogers was good, and he got us some good ratings, but after he, you know, got killed, I couldn't really work up any interest in trying a talk show again."

Rhodes did know. Rogers had been murdered, and Rhodes had solved the case.

"You did try again, though," Rhodes said.

"Yes. I got a letter from Milton Munday. A package, actually. It had an audition disc in it. I suspect he sent them out to a lot of stations, but most of the station managers don't bother to listen to an unsolicited disc. I'm not sure why I did, to tell you the truth."

"You must have liked what you heard."

"I did. It was better than I'd expected. A good bit better. You've heard Munday, I'm sure."

Rhodes nodded.

"Then you know why I was interested," Lindsey said. "He has a fine radio voice, and while he's not polished, he's very good at getting his point across. So I had him come in for a tryout."

"Come in from where?" Rhodes asked.

"I don't remember. He'd worked at some little station somewhere, though."

"You didn't do a background check? Find out why he'd left his last job?"

Rhodes found it hard to believe that anyone got hired these days without someone doing at least a cursory Internet check on him. Maybe a small-town station could afford not to worry about who was hired, but Rhodes couldn't see it that way. It didn't bother Lindsey, however.

"I didn't need to check on him," Lindsey said. "He was good, and we hadn't had a talk show for a while. I thought I'd let him try it for two weeks and see what happened. Turned out very well for both him and the station, so I kept him on."

"You didn't check with the station where he'd been before to find out why he'd left?"

"He told me he was just looking for a new challenge in a different location."

"It had been his lifelong dream to be a talk show host in Clearview, Texas?"

"Look," Lindsey said, "I told you he'd probably applied in a lot of different places. He just happened to wind up here, and he was a good fit for us. I didn't see any reason to worry about him."

Rhodes thought that was a poor business practice, but he didn't mention it. He said, "Is Milton Munday his real name?"

"No. It's just his air name. He's probably had others."

"So who do you make the paychecks to?"

"Ralph King."

"That's not a bad name for a radio personality," Rhodes said. "Ralph, King of the Airwaves."

"We don't talk much about the airwaves these days," Lindsey said.

"I guess not. You're sure King is his real name? Something doesn't sound right about it."

"He has a Social Security number," Lindsey said.

As if that proved anything. Willie Dalton could tell Lindsey a thing or two about how easy it was to get a fake ID.

Rhodes stood up. "I guess that's all I wanted to know," he said. "I appreciate your taking time to talk to me."

Lindsey stood, too, and stuck out his hand. Rhodes shook it.

"I don't know what you were looking for," Lindsey said, "but I get the feeling I wasn't much help."

"I don't know what I was looking for, either," Rhodes said. "Maybe I'll figure it out."

Lindsey grinned. "Good luck," he said.

CHAPTER 20

Just as Rhodes got in the county car, the radio crackled. Hack came on to let him know that Buddy had located Rapper.

"Least he thinks he has. He heard from a fella in Obert that someone's holed up at the Boynton place. You ever been out that way?"

"I can find it," Rhodes said. "It's just outside the town, isn't it?"

"That's right. County Road 118. Buddy's on the way out there, and he says he'll meet you where 117 dead-ends into 118. It'll take him about fifteen minutes."

"All right. You get in touch with Ruth and have her run a check on Milton Munday. Also known as Ralph King. See if she can find out anything."

"You got it in for him?"

"No, but I want to know more about him. He seems a little anxious to me. Maybe he's mixed up in this Baty mess somehow."

"You never know, I guess," Hack said. "You headin' out to Obert now?"

"You know how Buddy is. Sometimes he gets over eager. You tell him not to do a single thing until I get out there to Obert. I'm going to stop off at Seepy Benton's house on the way if he's home. I want to have a word with him."

"Don't hurt him," Hack said. "He didn't know any better than to bail out those Eccles cousins."

"I'll be gentle," Rhodes said.

Benton's Saturn was parked in the driveway by his house. One of the Eccles pickups, the red one, was parked beside it. Rhodes pulled in behind them and stopped. When he got out of his car, he heard Benton talking to someone in the backyard, so he went on around without being invited.

Benton, Lance, and Hugh were sitting in lawn chairs, drinking Dr Pepper from cans. Rhodes supposed Lance and Hugh were admiring the Golden Rectangle while Benton explained the mathematics of it to them.

Bruce lay at the foot of Lance's chair. Rhodes had the feeling that Bruce would understand as much about the Golden Rectangle's mathematical intricacies as anybody there other than Benton.

Or maybe not. Maybe Lance and Hugh were better at math than Rhodes thought. Whatever they were discussing, Rhodes hoped they'd offer him a Dr Pepper. He'd missed lunch again, and he thought a Dr Pepper would perk him up a little.

Bruce raised his head and saw Rhodes. He gave a friendly bark, lowered his head, and closed his eyes. His behavior had certainly changed for the better since Benton had adopted him.

"Good afternoon, Sheriff," Benton said. "We were just talking about you."

"I'll bet," Rhodes said.

Lance and Hugh eyed him and didn't say anything. He got the impression that they'd rather have had a couple of beers than the Dr Peppers.

Benton stood up. "Want a Dr Pepper, Sheriff?"

"I can't stay long," Rhodes said. Benton started to sit back down. "I can take it with me, though."

"I'll get you one," Benton said.

He went into the house, leaving Rhodes alone with Lance, Hugh, and the dog. Only the dog seemed friendly.

"How's it feel to be back in the free world?" Rhodes asked.

"Better'n that jail," Hugh said. "That

258

Milton Munday let us down."

"Naw, he didn't," Lance said. "He mentioned us. That's why Dr. Benton came and set us free."

"Didn't say anything about us getting the tar beat out of us," Hugh said. "We might have to file suit against you and the county, Sheriff. No hard feelin's. Just want to see justice done."

"I understand," Rhodes said. "It might be hard to find a lawyer, though."

"Never can tell," Hugh said.

Benton came back out with a can of Dr Pepper with a paper towel wrapped around the lower half. He handed the can to Rhodes. The can felt cold even through the paper towel, which was slightly wet. Rhodes popped the top and took a sip. The Dr Pepper was colder than the can, and it felt good going down.

"I guess you wonder why I bailed those two out," Benton said. "I asked for you to call so I could explain."

"I was passing by," Rhodes said, "so I thought I'd stop in instead of calling."

"I'm glad you did." Benton glanced over his shoulder at the Eccles cousins. "They aren't as bad as they seem."

"They're bad enough," Rhodes said.

"We can hear you," Hugh said. "We're not

259

all that bad. Bruce likes us."

Hearing his name, the dog looked up again, and Hugh rubbed his head.

"See?" Benton said. "They've promised they'll stay out of trouble from now on."

"Except for suing me and the county?"

"I was just joking," Hugh said, more for Benton's benefit than Rhodes's.

"Sure you were," Rhodes said. "The question is, are you going to tell me what happened the other night while you were hunting?"

"Nothing happened," Lance said.

"I know better than that," Rhodes said. He drank a little Dr Pepper. "I know somebody showed up and there was some shooting. I hear you hunters didn't start it but that somebody shot back. I wonder who did that."

"I ain't sayin' it happened like that," Hugh told him, "but even if it did, we didn't do any shootin'. Ain't that right, Lance?"

"That's sure enough right, Hugh."

"Then who did?" Rhodes asked.

"We couldn't tell," Lance said. "We were too scared of all them hogs that got stirred up, not to mention bullets flyin' all around. Hugh and me, we jumped into a little patch of yaupon bushes and stayed there till things calmed down. Then we got out of there. So did everybody else."

That was pretty much the same story that Dalton had told, and Rhodes was beginning to think it might have been close to the truth. It still didn't help him with the murder of Baty. Any one of them could have done it, though he couldn't think why they would have.

"You didn't see who was shooting?" he asked. "You didn't see anybody else there?"

"Nobody was there," Hugh said. "Not that we saw. We figure that whoever started shootin' must've been as scared as we were. They got out of there, too."

"You think it might have been the Chandlers?"

"They don't like us much," Hugh said. "They don't like any hunters much, from what I've heard, and I'd like to say it was them that did the shootin'. Get 'em in trouble, maybe get 'em arrested. I can't say that, though. Me and Lance, we've turned over a new leaf. We're law-abidin' citizens, and we cannot tell a lie." He raised a hand as if pledging. "We didn't see nobody, so we can't say who might've been there."

"You must've heard about the Chandlers' pig," Rhodes said.

"The one somebody cut up?" Lance asked. "Yeah, we heard about that. Doesn't have anything to do with us."

"What about the other hunters? They ever mention it?"

"Sure, they mentioned it. People talk about weird stuff like that. We all wondered about it. You don't think we had anything to do with it, I hope."

"We cannot tell a lie," Hugh reminded Rhodes. "We didn't do it, and we don't know who did."

Rhodes knew he wasn't going to get any more from them, so he thanked Benton for the Dr Pepper and started to leave.

"I'll walk you to your car," Benton said.

When they got around the house out of sight of the cousins, Rhodes said, "Are you sure you want to be responsible for those two?"

"They're all right," Benton said. "They like Bruce, and he likes them. They check on him all the time. They just got mad at you and got carried away."

"You're probably right, but if they get in any trouble, I'm coming to look for you."

"I'm easy to find," Benton said.

"I know," Rhodes said. He took a last swallow of the Dr Pepper and handed Benton the empty can. "Thanks for the drink."

"My pleasure, Sheriff."

"You be sure to recycle that can."

"I always recycle," Benton said.

It took Rhodes about five minutes to drive to the place where he was to meet Buddy. He was glad to see that Buddy's cruiser was pulled off onto the side of the road, about halfway in the drainage ditch, and that Buddy was standing beside the car, waiting. Buddy was a good lawman, but he was impulsive, and sometimes he got a little ahead of himself.

Rhodes parked his car nose to nose with Buddy's and got out.

"Hey, Sheriff," Buddy said, "you ready to go after that Rapper fella?"

"He has his sidekick with him," Rhodes said.

"Nellie." Buddy fondled the handle of his service revolver. "I remember him."

"We don't want to kill them," Rhodes said. "Just talk to them."

"Seems to me they don't like talking much. They shoot first and ask questions later."

Buddy talked like that now and then. Rhodes overlooked it.

"Rapper's probably hurt," Rhodes said. "Might even need a doctor."

"Won't matter. Those two are mean as

snakes."

"We'll see. Where are they?"

"You know where the Boynton place is?"

"It's not far," Rhodes said, looking over Buddy's shoulder. "Right over that hill and around the curve."

"You got it. You turn in at the gate there, and there's an old house back off the road about a hundred yards. Nobody's lived there for fifteen or twenty years. That's where Rapper is, I heard."

"How'd you hear it?"

"I asked around a little in Obert. You know that barbershop they got there?"

Rhodes knew the barbershop, all right.

"There's a new barber there now," he said.

"Yeah. Name's Swanson. He's my wife's third cousin. You know that?"

"No," Rhodes said. "I didn't know that."

Buddy looked pleased to have come up with something Rhodes didn't know.

"Well, he is. Anyway, I asked him if there was any funny goings-on around town. Barbers hear about everything that happens, pretty much, and he told me that one of his customers had seen some lights out at the Boynton place. Said they'd heard some noises, too. Motorcycles, maybe."

"Sounds like Rapper, all right," Rhodes said. "Let's have a look."

"How'll we do it?"

"You go ahead and open the gate. Leave your car by the road and ride up to the house with me."

"Gotcha," Buddy said.

He got in his car, backed up the hill a short distance until he came to a wide place, and turned around. Rhodes followed him over the hill and down the other side to the barbed-wire gate to the Boynton place. Buddy opened the door and got in the car with Rhodes.

"You think they've heard us yet?" Buddy asked.

"I don't know." Rhodes saw no movement or lights. "They might not even be there."

"Maybe not. You see any motorcycles?"

"No sign of them," Rhodes said. It was getting late, and the light was tricky as the sun started down behind a bank of clouds. "They'd be hidden if they're there. Behind the house, most likely."

"Maybe Rapper's already gone," Buddy said. "He knows you always get the best of him."

"His brother's dead," Rhodes said, "and he's not happy about it. I don't think he'll leave for a while."

"You know where his brother's to be buried?"

Rhodes hadn't called Ballinger to ask. He hadn't even thought about it.

"I haven't heard anything," Rhodes said. "You ready to see what we can see?"

"I was born ready," Buddy said.

Rhodes overlooked that, too. He started the car and drove up the narrow dirt road toward the abandoned house, which could have used a coat of paint and a new roof. A few new windows wouldn't have hurt, either. If Rapper and Nellie were there, they didn't have deluxe accommodations. That wouldn't have bothered them, however. They'd stayed in worse places when visiting the county in the past.

When he was about halfway to the house, Rhodes stopped the car.

"Sure is quiet," Buddy said.

Rhodes resisted the urge to say, "Too quiet."

"How are we gonna play it?" Buddy asked.

Rhodes had to think it over. They couldn't sneak up on the place because it was out in the open except for a few high weeds here and there, and Rapper had probably heard the car anyway.

"I'll give them a shout," Rhodes said. "You stay in the car."

"You sure?" Buddy asked.

"I'm sure."

Rhodes got out and opened the trunk of the car and got out a blue and white bull-horn. He held it by the pistol-grip handle and pulled the trigger.

"Hello, the house," he said. "This is Sheriff Rhodes. Come out on the porch and let's talk."

Nobody came out on the porch. Rhodes didn't blame them. The porch looked pretty rickety from where he stood.

"I know your brother's dead, Rapper, but it's not doing you any good to go around assaulting people who didn't have anything to do with killing him. You're going to wind up in jail and not even get to go to his funeral."

Rhodes thought he saw movement behind one of the broken windows, but he couldn't be certain.

"Nellie, is Rapper all right? If he needs a doctor, we can see that he gets one."

Rhodes heard the squeal of hinges that hadn't been oiled in a generation as the front door swung inward. Rapper hobbled out onto the precarious porch.

"I won't be going to the funeral," he said. "You don't have to worry about that. I got a sister who'll claim the body and see that it's taken care of."

Rhodes had never thought of Rapper as

having a brother, much less a sister. Rapper had always seemed to be the kind of person who springs up out of nowhere, and it was hard for Rhodes to imagine him as a child, playing with his brother and sister just like any other kid.

"You know who killed my brother, Sheriff?" Rapper yelled.

"Not yet," Rhodes said into the bullhorn. "I'm going to find out, though."

"What happens when you do?"

"I'll arrest him and put him in jail."

"Yeah," Rapper said. "That's about what I thought. I like my idea better."

"I saw your idea in action last night," Rhodes said. "I didn't think much of it."

"What you think doesn't matter. It gave me some satisfaction."

"You weren't even after the right man."

"How the hell would you know? My sources're as good as yours. Better, probably."

Rhodes didn't feel like arguing the point. Rapper might even be right about his sources. He'd found out about the hunters and even located the hunt. He didn't seem to know about the other people involved, though.

"My deputy and I are going to have to arrest you and Nellie for the assault last night," Rhodes said. "We'll come on up to the house now. Tell Nellie to come outside, and both of you keep your hands where we can see them."

Rapper laughed. "I always did say you had a good sense of humor, Sheriff."

He turned and went back inside the house.

"What now, Sheriff?" Buddy asked.

"Now we wait for a minute or two," Rhodes told him. "See what happens."

It didn't take even that long.

Rapper must have walked straight through the house and out the back door. The motorcycles rumbled and rattled what was left of the glass in the windows.

"They're gonna get away, Sheriff," Buddy said. "We can't let 'em do that."

Rhodes didn't know how to stop them. If they went the back way across country, the county car couldn't follow.

"Come on, Sheriff," Buddy said. He jumped out of the car, drew his sidearm, and ran toward the house. "We can get 'em before the bikes are warmed up."

"Stop, Buddy!" Rhodes said, but the deputy didn't hear him over the roar of the bikes echoing off the back of the house and into the trees.

Or maybe Buddy did hear and chose to ignore the order. He'd acted too hastily more than once in the past, and he always seemed to be trying to prove how tough he was. Rhodes thought he'd watched too many Dirty Harry movies.

Rhodes got in the car and went after him. When he caught up, Buddy was almost to the house, going full speed down the right rut of the track. Rhodes couldn't pass him, so he honked the horn. That just made Buddy speed up, as if he thought Rhodes would run over him if he didn't.

Rhodes stopped the car and got out. "Buddy! Come on back here."

Buddy reached the house and flattened himself against the front wall. As he eased himself along, Rhodes caught up with him. Both of them heard the motorcycles leaving.

Buddy started to throw himself around the corner, and Rhodes knew he'd start firing his pistol when he did. Rhodes grabbed the deputy's arm.

"Stand still," he said.

This time Buddy couldn't pretend not to hear him, so he stopped.

"They'll get away," he said.

"I wouldn't let that bother me," Rhodes said.

"Why not?"

"Because," Rhodes said, "they always come back."

CHAPTER 21

"Ralph King is Milton Munday's real name," Ruth said. "Believe it or not."

Rhodes decided he might as well believe it, though he'd thought it might be a fake. He didn't know why.

"King Ralph," Ruth said when she saw Rhodes's skeptical look. "It was a movie a long time ago. I saw it on TV once."

"John Goodman," Rhodes said. "Now I remember."

"That's right," Ruth said.

"Never heard of it," Hack said. "What about you, Lawton?"

"If it didn't have the Three Stooges in it, I didn't watch it."

Rhodes had come back to the jail. He'd sent Buddy back on patrol with strict orders to call for backup if he so much as thought he saw or heard a motorcycle.

"You know me, Sheriff," Buddy had said.

"I do," Rhodes answered. "That's why I worry."

Rhodes wasn't really worried about Buddy now, however. He was too interested in hearing what Ruth had found out about Munday.

"He was at a station in Louisiana," she said. "Up in Shreveport."

"Little bigger market than Clearview," Rhodes said.

"There was trouble, though," Ruth said. "He had to leave."

Rhodes wasn't surprised. "What kind of trouble?"

"Wife trouble."

Rhodes looked at Hack and Lawton, both of whom wore bland, innocent looks. They might have been innocent, but even if they were, Rhodes blamed them for Ruth's making him draw out the story.

"What kind of wife trouble?"

"It wasn't his wife. It was the station manager's wife. I found a couple of stories about it in the archives of the local paper. Not on the front page, but hidden away. The station manager caught his wife out with Munday at some kind of club. There was what the paper called an altercation. Munday left the station, and he wound up here."

That explained something Rhodes had wondered about. If people knew about Munday's troubles, they wouldn't be so eager to hire him, and Rhodes was sure the station manager had let people know. He might even have engaged in a little black-balling, so it was no wonder that Munday had taken a job in a small market like Clear-view. He might not have been able to get anything else.

Still, Shreveport wasn't far from Arkansas, which seemed to be the connection in all that was happening. Rhodes couldn't write him off. It wouldn't hurt to talk to him.

"I checked on Garver's story, too," Ruth said. "He was telling the truth, or something like it."

"How much like it?" Rhodes asked.

"Enough. You know how eyewitnesses are."

Rhodes knew more than he wanted to about that. Eyewitnesses were notoriously unreliable. One person would swear that one thing happened, while someone else at the same scene would swear just the opposite.

"You mean his wife might have a slightly different version," Rhodes said.

"Right, but it's basically the same story. More or less."

"I'm still not ready to rule him out," Rhodes said. "I doubt that Rapper is, either."

"You think Rapper's gonna cause any more trouble?" Hack asked.

"Sure he is," Rhodes said. "He's not satisfied. He hasn't killed anybody yet."

As he said it, he remembered that Rapper hadn't tried to kill anybody, just injure them. He must have been saving the killing part until he was sure of who the guilty party was. Either that, or he was content to beat people up. Fowler had gotten away, so it would be his turn next.

As he thought about that, Rhodes realized that he hadn't given enough consideration to Fowler and Winston as suspects in the murders. He'd seen them both at the end of the chase on the night Rapinski was killed, but he'd lost sight of both of them in the woods before they reached the bayed animal. Either one of them could have been separated from the others long enough to have killed the bounty hunter. Rhodes had concentrated on Garver because he was so obviously out of sight of everyone, and that had been a mistake.

"Duke's on tonight, right?" Rhodes asked.

"That's right," Hack said.

"Tell him to keep an eye on Fowler's

place. Rapper might turn up there. Tell him I'll see him later on."

"Gotcha," Hack said.

"Ruth, you check up on Arvid Fowler."

"Hold on," Lawton said. "Arvid's lived around here for a long time. You don't think he's done anything wrong, do you?"

Lawton was right. Arvid had been in Clearview for at least fifteen years, but he'd kept pretty much to himself. Other than the hog hunters, he wasn't involved with anybody else in the community as far as Rhodes knew.

Fowler had his own electrical business, and he was known to be good at what he did. Good enough for Ivy to call him when there was a problem with the air conditioner. He didn't have a fancy house or drive a new pickup. If he was wealthy from some source of ill-gotten gains, there wasn't any evidence of it in the way he lived.

Or was there? Fowler and his wife took several vacations a year, sometimes for a couple of weeks. Could he have done that on what he charged for electrical work? Considering his rates, it was possible.

"Ivy says he overcharged us for some work on our air conditioner," Rhodes said.

"Get a rope," Hack said.

"I don't think we need to go that far,"

Rhodes said.

"Ivy might."

"I doubt it."

"She can be mighty tough," Lawton said, "but I guess you know all about that."

"I know enough," Rhodes said. "Ruth, while you're at it, check on Len Winston, too. Short for Leonard."

"Nothin' wrong with Len," Lawton said. "I've known him since he was a kid. You must really be outta leads when you go after somebody like Len."

"I'm not out of leads," Rhodes said. "I'm just being sure I don't overlook anything."

"He's outta leads," Hack said to Lawton. "Next thing you know he'll be gettin' testy with us. He always gets testy when he's outta leads."

Rhodes glanced at Ruth, who seemed to be enjoying the banter far too much, but he resolved not to get testy.

Then Jennifer Loam came in.

"Sheriff's got a bunch of leads," Hack said before she could speak. "Ask him if you don't believe me."

"I was wondering about that," Jennifer said. "You haven't been in touch with me, Sheriff, and I've called here several times."

"I told him you did," Hack said. "He would've called you back, but he's been busy runnin' down all those leads."

"I've been doing a little background work," Jennifer said, ignoring Hack. "I thought you might like to know what I've found out."

"Every little bit helps," Rhodes said.

"It's a little bit, all right, but I was wondering where Gary Baty stayed while he was in town. I checked the motels, and he didn't stay in any of them."

"We checked, too," Rhodes said. "The way he turned up here and the little petty thefts now and then more or less indicated he was coming into town and then leaving again. I don't think he wanted to hang around. He might have known he was in danger."

"So you do have some leads," Jennifer said.

"Just like I told you," Hack said. "A whole bunch of leads."

"Not leads," Rhodes said. "Just ideas and speculations. Right now, that's all I have."

"Do you have anything you can act on?"

"I'm waiting for more information," Rhodes said, without admitting that she'd just given him another idea for something to check on. It was something he'd do himself as soon as she left.

"You're not holding out on me, are you?" Jennifer asked. "I don't want Milton Munday to scoop me."

They all had a little laugh at that, though Rhodes didn't laugh as much as Hack and Lawton.

Jennifer said a few words to Ruth, and then she was gone.

"You really ought not to mislead the press," Hack said.

"I wasn't misleading anybody," Rhodes said. "Maybe I do have some leads."

"Humpf," Hack said.

He started to work on his own computer, which he used mainly for writing up reports. This time, he went into the complaints received by the department. Sure enough, there was an interesting correspondence. Maybe it meant nothing. Maybe it did. He'd wait on some more reports before he decided.

He wished there was some way he could check on Arvid Fowler's vacations and see if they matched up with the times of the bank robberies. He needed the information on the robberies first, so he asked Ruth to get that for him.

"Where you goin'?" Hack asked as Rhodes started to leave. "Gonna run down some of those leads?"

"No," Rhodes said. "I'm going home and eat supper."

■ ■ ■ ■

Rhodes had missed lunch again, so he thought he deserved a night out. Ivy was willing, so they went to Max's Place for barbecue. Seepy Benton had a gig performing at the restaurant on some nights, playing guitar and singing his own compositions, and sure enough, this was one of those nights, according to a computer-printed notice on the door.

"How lucky can we get," Rhodes said.

"What do you mean?" Ivy asked.

Rhodes didn't get a chance to answer because Max Schwartz came over to greet them as they entered. Schwartz had a music store as well as the barbecue restaurant, but neither one of them was doing well, or so Rhodes had heard. Rhodes wondered if Schwartz would be able to keep them going.

"Things are looking up," Schwartz said when Rhodes asked him how business was. "Benton's been packing them in. I think his students like to come hear him sing."

Rhodes looked across the dining area. He did see a few young people in the sparse crowd. He also saw the Eccles cousins. It was nice of them to support Benton. After all, he'd gone their bail.

Schwartz led Rhodes and Ivy to a table and gave them a menu. He'd bought the building after the death of a man named Jerry Kergan, and since it wasn't set up for cafeteria-style dining like a lot of barbecue restaurants, he'd decided to go for a more upscale approach.

"The sauce is the key," he'd once told Rhodes. "The meat matters, but the sauce has to be good or nobody's coming back a second time."

Rhodes liked the sauce, which Schwartz had concocted himself from a now-secret recipe, but the brisket was lean and tender and sliced thin. It was so good it didn't even need the sauce, though Rhodes never turned it down.

"I think I'll have the ribs tonight," Ivy said. "With all the fixings."

"The brisket dinner for me," Rhodes said. After all the vegetarian meals he'd had lately, he could use some beef. He handed Schwartz the menu. "Why isn't Benton sing-ing?"

"It's his break. He's right over there."

Rhodes hadn't noticed, but Benton was sitting at a table in a corner, and there was someone with him. Ruth Grady. Rhodes had seen them together before, and he

281

couldn't quite grasp the fact that Ruth would be interested in Benton, though he knew why Benton might be fascinated with Ruth. She was in law enforcement, after all, and Benton fancied himself a sort of unofficial deputy. The fact that she was smart, young, and cute might have had something to do with it, too.

"I wonder if it would be wrong to talk business with Ruth," Rhodes said after Schwartz left their table.

"Yes," Ivy said. "She's busy."

Rhodes had known she'd say that. He didn't know why he'd even bothered to ask. He unrolled the cloth napkin beside his plate and arranged his silverware. He glanced over at the Eccles cousins, but they weren't looking his way.

A waiter brought glasses of ice water to the table, and Rhodes took a sip. The ice cubes bumped against his teeth. When he set the glass down, Benton was standing at the table.

"I've been thinking, Sheriff," he said, after greeting Rhodes and Ivy.

"Always a dangerous thing for you to do," Rhodes said, and Ivy kicked his ankle under the table.

"It's about that movie *Avatar,*" Benton said. "Have you seen it?"

Rhodes didn't have any idea what the movie had to do with anything, but it didn't matter since he hadn't seen it and wasn't likely to. From what he'd heard, it wasn't the kind of film that would look good on a TV set, and he preferred lower-budget movies anyway.

"Haven't seen it," he said. "What have you been thinking?"

"Well, the word *Na'vi* used in the film is also the Hebrew word for 'prophet.' Its literal meaning is 'mouthpiece,' which is how people thought of the prophet in ancient times. He was an avatar of God's voice. And *Eywah,* the name of the deity on Pandora, is an alternate pronunciation of the Hebrew *Yahweh.* Did you know there are no vowels in Hebrew?"

Rhodes admitted that he hadn't known that.

"I did," Ivy said, and Benton nodded his approval.

"Since there aren't any vowels," he said, "you can take the same spelling for *Yahweh* and pronounce it as *Eywah* or *Yaywah,* which happens to be the most sacred name for God in the Cherokee language. Only their priests were allowed to pronounce it, just as only the Hebrew priests were allowed to pronounce the name of their God."

Rhodes looked over to where Ruth was sitting, waiting for Benton to return. She grinned and shrugged.

"I'm sure there's a good reason you're telling me this," Rhodes said to Benton.

"Not really," Benton said, "except that sometimes you can find spirituality in strange places." He nodded toward the Eccles cousins, who were eating ribs and laughing at the same time. "Even Lance and Hugh have a spiritual side, and I think you'll come to realize that they didn't mean you any harm yesterday."

"Don't count on it," Rhodes said.

"I'm a math teacher," Benton said. "I count on everything. It's been great to see the two of you. I hope you'll stay for my show."

Rhodes didn't say anything, but Ivy said, "We'll be here for a while."

"Good," Benton said. "I'll dedicate a song to you. How about 'Ghost Riders in the Sky'?"

"I thought you sang songs you wrote yourself," Rhodes said.

"I usually do, but my version of that one's pretty popular on YouTube. At least twenty-five people have looked at it. You should check it out."

Rhodes tried not to look incredulous.

"You're on YouTube?"

"Isn't everybody?" Benton asked.

He walked back to his table, and Rhodes said to Ivy, "Twenty-five?"

"Maybe he meant twenty-five thousand," Ivy said.

"No, I'm pretty sure he meant twenty-five," Rhodes said.

"He's a little odd, isn't he?"

"A little?"

"Just a little, and he's a very smart man. You should listen to him."

"That's what he tells me," Rhodes said.

Their food came then, and Rhodes forgot about Benton as he dug in. The sauce was tangy and sweet, and Rhodes was about half finished with the meal when Benton started his program. He strummed his guitar, tapped the microphone with his index finger, and announced that his first number would be "Ghost Riders in the Sky," dedicated to Sheriff Dan Rhodes.

"He's not going to make anybody forget Gene Autry," Rhodes said, as Benton started to sing.

"Much less Riders in the Sky," Ivy said. "The group, I mean, not the song." She paused. "Do you think the Eccles cousins are spiritual?"

Rhodes looked over at the two men, who

both seemed to be listening intently to the song. Their apparent absorption didn't change his opinion of them.

"Not in the least," he said.

CHAPTER 22

Rhodes dropped Ivy at home after they'd eaten and listened to a couple of songs by Seepy Benton. Then he drove out toward Arvid Fowler's place, thinking all the way about spirituality and the Eccles cousins. It hadn't been too long since Rhodes had experienced something strange with some turtles, something he'd never mentioned to Benton and never would. It had been close enough to a mystical experience to baffle Rhodes, however, so maybe Benton had a point about Lance and Hugh. Not that Rhodes would ever admit it.

While they were driving home from Max's Place, Rhodes had told Ivy about Arvid Fowler's vacations and asked if she had any thoughts about how to find out when Fowler had left town.

As usual, Ivy had come up with a good idea. "I can just call Bennie Fowler and ask her. I'll tell her that you and I are thinking about taking some time off, and we'd like to know where she and Arvid went."

Rhodes had said he didn't know how that would help.

"I'll tell them that we'd like to know the best time of year to go to those places."

That would work, Rhodes thought. Even if the Fowlers hadn't gone where they said they'd be going, Bennie would give away the times when they'd left town. The times might not be exact, but they'd be close enough to give Rhodes something to work with.

He got Hack on the radio and asked where Duke was.

"He just checked in about five minutes ago. He was about to drive by Fowler's again. He says it's been clear the last couple of times."

Rhodes looked at the green glow of the dashboard clock. It was three minutes past eight. Rhodes didn't think Rapper would do anything so early in the evening, and maybe he wouldn't do anything at all. It didn't hurt to be careful, however.

Fowler lived out toward Milsby, just outside the Clearview city limits. Beside his house he had a little shop building made of sheet metal where he did minor electrical repairs and stored parts. There were other houses nearby, but in the back there were open fields. It would be simple for Rapper to find a way to get to the house or the shop without being seen. He'd be heard, of course, if he rode his motorcycle, but Rapper was sneakier than that. Rhodes knew he'd figure out a way to get there without being detected if he wanted to get at Fowler.

Rhodes saw the red taillights of a car just ahead of him. It was Duke's county car, so Rhodes popped his flasher. Duke pulled over. Rhodes parked behind him and got out.

"I swear I wasn't speeding," Duke said as Rhodes approached.

It was an old joke, but Rhodes smiled anyway. Duke Pearson was an experienced cop who'd come back to Clearview so his wife could care for her mother, who had some form of dementia. He'd been looking for a job, and his experience made him a perfect fit for the sheriff's department.

"How's your wife's mother?" Rhodes asked.

"About as well as can be expected. Callie's helping out with her tonight."

Callie was Callie Swan, a local woman who sat with the sick or helped out around the house or did whatever needed to be done. She was a good person to know.

"Seen anything around Fowler's house?"

"It's all quiet as far as I can tell the couple of times I've been by. Haven't heard or seen anything unusual."

"Let's drive past and take a look," Rhodes said. "I'll ride with you."

He got in on the passenger side, and Duke drove down the road past Fowler's house. A light glowed in one of the rooms, and Rhodes caught a glimpse of a TV screen through the window. Everything seemed normal, but Rhodes thought it wasn't quite right. It took him a second to figure out why.

"Where's Fowler's pickup?" he asked.

"It was parked by his shop the last time I drove by," Duke said.

"Go back and stop," Rhodes said.

Pearson turned the car around as soon as he could and drove back to the house. Rhodes got out of the car, went to the door, and knocked.

Bennie Fowler answered the knock. She was a short woman, not more than five feet tall. She wore a faded blue robe and blue bunny slippers. Rhodes hadn't seen any bunny slippers in years.

"Sheriff Rhodes," she said. "What brings you out here?"

"I'm looking for Arvid. Is he home?"

"No, he got an emergency call. Somebody

in Milsby's heating system went out, and they needed it fixed. Had to have it done right now, they said. It's supposed to get cold tonight, and they didn't want to be without heat. Arvid told them it would cost them double if he made a trip at night, but they said they'd pay."

"Who's this *they?*"

"I can't remember the name. Arvid took the call, and he might not have mentioned the name to me. It's the second house on the left on County Road 265, though. I remember Arvid saying that."

"I'll look for him there," Rhodes said.

"Your wife called about your trip," Bennie said. "I didn't know you ever took a vacation."

"We're going to try," Rhodes said.

He thanked her for her help and jogged back to the car. He had a feeling that Arvid was in for a surprise when he got to the house.

"That's Wex Mallory's house," Duke said when Rhodes told him the story. "Wex's in the hospital in Dallas with heart trouble, and his wife's staying up there till he can come home. She let me know so I could take a look at the house now and then. There's nobody there."

"It's a setup for sure," Rhodes said. "You

go on ahead. I'll follow you there."

"Siren?"

"No siren. We need to be quiet and careful. Stop about a hundred yards from the house."

Rhodes went back to his own car and followed Duke's taillights down the road. They made a couple of turns and passed a house where lights showed in the windows. Mallory's house wasn't much farther down the road.

The pale moon was past the full now. It hung big in the sky, giving enough light to throw shadows on the ground. Duke pulled over to the side of the road, and Rhodes did the same. Both men got out of their cars. Rhodes had his shotgun.

"Better get yours," Rhodes said. "If Rapper's there, you might need it."

Pearson got the shotgun, and the two of them jogged toward the house. When they got closer, Rhodes saw Fowler's pickup in the dirt driveway. There were no lights anywhere.

Motorcycle engines roared to life and echoed off the back wall of the house. Rhodes began to run. Pearson tried to keep up but fell behind as Rhodes turned into the driveway.

When Rhodes was almost to the pickup,

Rapper and Nellie came booming around the corner of the house. They weren't wearing helmets tonight. They probably hadn't thought they'd meet up with the sheriff.

When they saw Rhodes, Rapper yelled something to Nellie. Rhodes couldn't hear what it was, but Nellie must have. The motorcycles swerved, and both of them headed straight for Rhodes. He jumped aside, pressing himself against the door of the pickup and wishing that he hadn't eaten so much barbecue. Rapper went by him before he could make any defensive moves, but as Nellie passed, Rhodes made a quick jab with the shotgun. He hit Nellie in the upper arm.

Nellie wasn't knocked off his motorcycle, but he was knocked off balance. The bike tipped and swerved wildly, first to the right and then to the left as Nellie tried to get control.

Rapper made a wide, curving turn, nearly running over Duke in the process. The deputy dived to the ground and rolled over as Rapper headed back toward Rhodes.

Rhodes opened the pickup door and jumped inside, aiming the shotgun out the window.

Rapper turned again, moving across the front yard. Nellie had his bike back under control, and both he and Rapper rode straight across the yard, parallel to the county road.

Duke was back on his feet, but there was nothing he could do other than try to shoot them or watch them ride away. He let them ride.

Rhodes got out of the pickup, and Duke walked up the driveway to meet him as Rapper and Nellie came to a fence and cut back toward the road. The front yard wasn't fenced, so they got to the road easily. They zipped along it, turned at the corner, and disappeared from sight.

"Those two are real pieces of work," Duke said. "Are we going after them?"

"We'd never catch them," Rhodes said. "Let's see if we can find Fowler."

The electrician wasn't hard to find. He lay not far from the pickup near the entrance to a detached garage that held an old Massey Ferguson tractor of faded red instead of a car.

Rhodes knelt down and felt for a pulse in Fowler's neck. He found it beating steadily and strong. Duke turned on his flashlight and put the beam on Fowler's face. There was a bruise under his left eye and a deep scratch on his cheek.

"They didn't give him much of a chance,

did they?" Duke asked.

"Probably slugged him a couple of times as soon as he got out of the pickup," Rhodes said. "He's lucky we got here when we did."

Rhodes stood up, wondering if he should call the EMTs yet again. While he was considering it, Fowler groaned and moved around.

"Careful there," Duke said.

The deputy bent down and helped Fowler sit up. Fowler put a hand to his head and said, "What the hell happened to me?"

"You got hit," Rhodes said. "You don't remember?"

"I remember getting out of the truck. Some guy came up to me, and I thought he was gonna tell me about the heater problem. That's about it."

"He must've hit you right about then," Duke said.

"If he did, I don't remember it. My head hurts like hell, though."

Rhodes told Duke to go get his cruiser. When he was on his way, Rhodes turned to Fowler.

"Duke will take you to the ER so you can get checked out. He'll drop you off, and you can have your wife pick you up. Better lock up your truck."

Fowler didn't argue. "Who hit me?"

"A guy who thinks you might've killed his brother. You didn't kill him, did you?"

"I don't even know what you're talking about." Fowler held up a hand to Rhodes. "I want to stand up."

Rhodes wasn't so sure that was a good idea, but he helped Fowler to his feet. Then he helped him walk the three steps to his pickup so he could brace himself against the hood.

"Who does the son of a bitch who hit me think I killed?" Fowler asked.

"Hoss Rapinski."

"The bounty hunter? Why would I kill him? I didn't even know him."

"He was looking for somebody involved in some bank robberies up in Arkansas," Rhodes said. "You ever take a vacation in Arkansas?"

"Bennie and I went one fall. Looked at the leaves."

"That's it?"

"You think I'm a bank robber? Lord a'mighty, Sheriff. I make enough money fixing heaters and air conditioners and such. I don't need to rob banks."

Ivy would agree, Rhodes thought.

The headlights from Duke's cruiser threw long shadows as he turned into the driveway.

"I think I can manage for myself," Fowler said.

"Best you don't try," Rhodes said, and Fowler didn't argue.

Duke stopped the county car, and Rhodes got Fowler into the front seat. He seemed to be feeling okay, but it wouldn't hurt him to get checked out. Rhodes got in the back, and Duke drove him to his own car.

"How does it feel in the perp seat?" Duke asked.

"Almost like home," Rhodes said.

On his way back to town, Rhodes wondered about Rapper. Would he be satisfied now, or would he hang around and see what other damage he could do? It was hard to say. Rapper was never predictable.

Rhodes also wondered how badly Rapper's leg had been hurt when he fell from the motorcycle the night before. If it was the same leg Rhodes had sunk the hay hook in, it had to be mighty sore.

One thing Rhodes had to say for Rapper, the guy could take punishment. He might be finished with his business in Blacklin County for the time being, but he'd be back. Rhodes wasn't looking forward to that.

CHAPTER 23

Rhodes thought he'd stop by the jail on his way home and see if Ruth had left any notes about Fowler and Winston for him. He'd have asked her at Max's Place, but he knew Ivy was right about talking business with one of his deputies who was having dinner with a friend, even if the friend was Seepy Benton, who thought that the Eccles cousins had a spiritual side.

Hack and Lawton were glad to see Rhodes come in. They must have been bored, and it perked them up to know that they'd have Rhodes to pick on for a few minutes.

"Duke called in," Hack said. "He took Arvid Fowler to the ER. Told us all about what happened tonight, too."

The implication was that since Hack and Lawton already knew what had happened with Fowler, Rhodes couldn't torment them by holding back information. A further implication was that the two of them knew something that Rhodes should be told but that Rhodes would have to drag it out of them.

He didn't really feel like playing around, but he knew it was best to humor them. So he said, "Did anything happen tonight? Anything I need to hear about, I mean."

"Could be," Lawton said.

He might have said more, but Hack silenced him with a look.

"Wasn't anything that happened," Hack said. "Just got a phone call, that's all."

"A phone call," Rhodes said.

"Yep." Hack looked at Lawton. "Phone call."

"Somebody need help?" Rhodes asked.

"In a manner of speakin'," Lawton said.

"No such thing," Hack said. "Friendly call, that's what it was."

"Who called?" Rhodes asked, hoping to cut things short.

"Sheriff McDade."

McDade was sheriff of the neighboring county. Rhodes wondered what he'd be calling about. He also wondered how long it would take him to get the answer from Hack and Lawton.

"Look," Rhodes said, "it's late, and I want to go home. Why don't you just tell me what McDade called about."

"Steak," Lawton said.

Rhodes thought about the stolen rib eyes. "Did our steak thief get out and get to his county?"

"Not those steaks," Hack said, and then Rhodes remembered something else.

A couple of weeks ago, one of McDade's deputies had arrested a burglary suspect, and in the course of the interrogation that followed, the deputy had discovered that the man had also committed a series of similar burglaries in Blacklin County. Rhodes had remarked at the time that he ought to buy the deputy a steak dinner, and Hack had relayed the information to McDade. It had been a joke, and Rhodes had thought that would be the end of it. Maybe he'd been wrong.

"Did McDade say his deputy was coming here so I could buy him a steak?" Rhodes asked. "I guess I could take him to the Round-Up."

The Round-Up was a specialty restaurant, but not in the way that Max's Place was. The Round-Up served nothing but beef. If you insisted, you could get vegetables, potatoes being the most popular, but you didn't dare ask for chicken.

"Him?" Lawton asked, and Hack wheeled his chair around.

300

Lawton looked up at the ceiling and whistled something that might have been a tune. If it was, Rhodes didn't recognize it.

"That was sexist of me," Rhodes said. "I apologize."

"Sex ain't got nothin' to do with it," Hack said.

"What does, then?"

"Numbers," Hack said.

Rhodes thought of Seepy Benton. Numbers were his life. Rhodes, on the other hand, would rather not do any calculating he wasn't required to do.

"What numbers?" he asked.

"Eight," Hack said.

Rhodes was lost now. He had no idea how they'd arrived at the number eight. He felt as if he'd stumbled into some bizarre episode of *Sesame Street*.

"Eight," Rhodes said.

"Eight," Hack said. "Or maybe nine. McDade's not a hundred percent sure."

"Of what?"

"Of whether it's eight or nine."

Rhodes was convinced that if he fired both Hack and Lawton at that very instant, nobody would blame him. No arbitration board would ask him to reinstate them, no jury in the world would side with them if they took the matter to court.

Rhodes, however, chose forbearance. It wasn't an easy choice, but he made it.

"Eight or nine what?" Rhodes asked.

"Steaks," Lawton said, earning himself a hard look from Hack.

"Nobody can eat that many steaks," Rhodes said.

"It's not one person," Hack said, relenting. "It's eight."

"Or nine," Lawton said.

"Or nine," Hack said.

Rhodes thought he was catching on at last. "McDade says I owe him eight or nine steaks."

"Not him," Hack said. "See, it wasn't him that cracked that burglary case."

"I know that," Rhodes said.

"He's gettin' testy," Lawton said. "I told you when he didn't find out who killed those fellas in the woods he'd get testy."

"I'm the one who told *you* that," Hack said.

Lawton looked stubborn. "I don't think so."

"Maybe you're right," Hack said. "I can't remember."

"It was me. You said —"

"Never mind who said what," Rhodes said, "and I'm not testy. I just want to know what's going on here."

"You're gettin' testy," Lawton said. "That's what's goin' on."

Rhodes looked from Hack to Lawton and then back at Hack.

"Tell me about the eight steaks," he said. "Or nine," he added before Hack could get it out.

Hack grinned. "That's what I been tryin' to do. The thing is that it wasn't just one person that broke that burglary case. It was eight or nine of 'em workin' together. So McDade figures you need to treat all of 'em to a big steak dinner. Seems like the fair thing."

"Fair to McDade, maybe," Rhodes said. "Not to my pocketbook. If he calls back, you can tell him I changed my mind, but I'll give everybody involved a stick of gum."

"You sure you can afford it?"

"Not on what the county pays me," Rhodes said. "I'll dig into my savings for it."

With that, he sat down at his desk and checked to see what kind of information Ruth had left for him. It wasn't much. Arvid Fowler had no criminal record of any kind, unless you counted his overcharge on the repair of Rhodes's air conditioner, but Ruth didn't mention that. Winston, as far as Ruth could determine, had lived all his life within a twenty-mile radius of Clearview and had never been out of the state. He hardly ever left the county, and while he'd gotten a couple of speeding tickets, that was the extent of his criminal past.

Some of Rhodes's suspects had been eliminated but not all of them. He had a few ideas, but he'd have to do some more digging to find out if he was on the right track. He preferred to let Ruth do the computer research, but since she wasn't there, he'd give it a try.

He turned to the computer, but before he could get logged on, the phone rang. Hack answered, talked into the receiver for a minute, than turned to Rhodes.

"You want to pick up line one?" he asked. "It's Commissioner Burns."

Rhodes was tempted to say that no, he didn't want to pick up line one, but Lawton would just have said he was being testy. So he picked up.

"Sheriff," Burns said, "I called you at home, but your wife said you were working. I suppose that's commendable."

"I'd have to agree," Rhodes said.

"I'm sure you would. Anyway, I'm glad I caught you. I'm not calling to check on your work habits, though. I wanted to let you know that I'll be a guest tomorrow on

304

Milton Munday's program."

It wasn't a good sign that Burns thought Rhodes needed a warning.

"You didn't have to tell me that," Rhodes said.

"I know I didn't, but I thought you might want to hear what I have to say."

Rhodes wasn't enthusiastic. "I'll try to remember to tune in."

"We'll be talking about the hog problem."

"I see," Rhodes said, though he didn't see at all.

"And my solutions to it."

Rhodes began to catch on. "Bow hunters."

"That's right. I think it's something that would work."

So they were back to that again. "Did you ask the Chandlers what they thought about it?"

"No. I checked. They're not registered to vote."

Nobody could say that Burns wasn't a practical man.

"Did you talk to anybody else? Any of the other commissioners?"

"I did, and I talked to the county judge, too."

The county judge presided over the commissioners' meetings. Rhodes had been friends with the previous judge, but he'd retired and been replaced in the last election by Gene Brent, a retired attorney who'd specialized in wills and financial planning. Rhodes hadn't worked with him enough to know him very well yet.

"Did you happen to mention that you thought my deputies would make good hunting guides?"

"I told you already," Burns said. "It just makes sense to use them. Gives the whole thing the air of authority. Lets the farmers and ranchers know the county government cares about them and the losses those hogs are causing."

What Burns cared about was the votes, but it wouldn't be a good idea to say so.

"What did Brent say about that idea?" Rhodes asked.

"It's something we'll be talking more about."

It was something Rhodes would be talking to Brent about, too.

"It might not be a good idea to go into anything like that on the air before you've cleared it with the judge," Rhodes said. "And then there's the overtime pay."

Burns brushed that off. "We'll work that problem out. Munday thinks the story will make good radio. It might influence people to think about it in the right way."

Or the wrong way, depending on your point of view, Rhodes thought. He told Burns he'd listen to the show and hung up.

"Sounds like you and Mikey don't agree on everything," Hack said.

"We never do," Rhodes told him. "Every now and then he tells me something helpful."

"That's good," Lawton said. "The commissioners ought to support their local sheriff."

"I didn't say he supported me. Just that he was helpful. I don't think he intends to be. It just works out that way now and then."

"You oughta go along with him on that hog thing," Hack said. "Get rid of one more hog a day, and you'd do some good even if you never can get all of 'em."

"You think I want Buddy out there guiding hunters?"

"Well, maybe not. He has better things to do."

"We all do," Rhodes said.

"Maybe if you'd bought that M-16 when Burns wanted you to, you could go out and hunt 'em yourself," Lawton said. "That's what Sage Barton would do. Wipe out a whole herd in about five seconds."

Rhodes didn't want to talk about Sage Barton.

307

"I'm going home now. It's past my bed-time."

"You gonna leave the computer on?" Hack asked.

"I've heard that's okay," Rhodes said.

"Some say it ain't."

Rhodes turned off the computer and made his escape.

"I'm glad to see you aren't muddy or bloody for a change," Ivy said when Rhodes got home.

"I've turned over a new leaf," Rhodes said. "No more mud and blood."

Yancey yipped his approval of the new leaf. Rhodes reached down to pat him, but Yancey took off at a run.

"Where's he going?" Rhodes asked.

"The kitchen," Ivy said. "He's found out that sometimes Sam's so asleep that he can sneak up on him."

Rhodes thought that might be interesting. "What happens when he sneaks up on him?"

"Sam wakes up."

"And then?"

"And then Yancey runs away. He thinks it's a game."

Rhodes heard a sharp yip from the kitchen, and Yancey came streaking back. He skidded on the floor as he turned the corner, and then he fled into another room to hide.

"How long has that been going on?" Rhodes asked.

"Most of the afternoon. They both seem to enjoy it."

"It takes so little to make them happy," Rhodes said.

"Right. They remind me of someone I know."

"You know what would make me happy?"

"I can think of a thing or two that might work."

"Why don't we find out, then," Rhodes said.

"Follow me," Ivy said, and Rhodes did.

Chapter 24

Milton Munday was really laying it on.

"Do you really think the town of Clearview is in danger of being overrun by wild hogs?" he asked.

Mikey Burns really did. "I think it's entirely possible. They're moving closer to town all the time, and they're getting bolder, causing more and more damage. The next thing you know, they'll be rooting up flower beds along the streets at night."

"And who knows what might come after that," Munday said, making Rhodes think of some old black-and-white horror movie of the kind they used to show on late-night TV, a town terrorized by giant feral hogs with tusks two feet long and hooves shod with iron. Rhodes hoped nobody else thought like that. Things were bad enough already.

"They've caused two deaths that we know about," Munday said. "A man named Baty died first, and then a famous bounty hunter named Hoss Rapinski."

Fugitive recovery agent, Rhodes thought, and the hogs didn't kill either one of them, not that Munday would let a little thing like the facts bother him.

Neither would Burns. "That's absolutely right, Milton, and who knows what they'll do when they get to town. Our citizens would be endangered. If we only had some plan in place to stop them, it would be different."

"Folks," Munday said, "our guest today is County Commissioner Mikey Burns, and he has a plan to stop the devastation that's tearing our county apart. What's the plan, sir?"

Rhodes couldn't take it anymore. He turned off the radio.

"It was just getting interesting," Ivy said. "I'd like to hear the plan."

"No, you wouldn't," Rhodes said. "It's a bad plan."

"You know what it is?"

"I know, and it's bad."

"If you say so."

Rhodes told her the plan.

"You were right," Ivy said. "It's a bad plan."

"That's what I told Burns, but he wouldn't

listen to me."

"He'll be sorry," Ivy said.

"Is that sarcasm?"

"Not a bit. I'm just agreeing with you."

Rhodes wasn't convinced, but he let it ride. It was time for him to get to the jail.

"What about those two dead men?" Ivy asked. "Have you figured out who killed them?"

"I'm still working on it," Rhodes said.

Ruth Grady wasn't there when Rhodes arrived at the jail, but Hack and Lawton were already in midmorning form.

"You hear Milton Munday today?" Hack asked when Rhodes came in.

"He never listens to that show," Lawton said, "not even when the commissioner's on."

"He told the commish he'd listen," Hack said. "On the phone last night."

"I listened to some of it," Rhodes told them.

"How much?"

"Enough."

"You hear the part where Milton Munday said that law enforcement in this county left a lot to be desired?"

"I must have missed that. Burns stood up for me, though, right?"

Hack and Lawton got a good guffaw from that.

"He kind of mealymouthed around," Hack said after he'd stopped laughing. "He must think you have a few fans around the county."

"Besides me and Hack, that is," Lawton said. "Seems to us like you got a pretty good record."

"I knew I could count on you," Rhodes said.

"You want us to call in and tell Munday you've cracked the case?" Hack asked.

"Not today," Rhodes said. He turned to the computer. "Maybe tomorrow."

Ruth Grady came in a bit later while Rhodes was doing some paperwork. He asked if she'd gotten a report back on the blood in Baty's car.

"I got it late yesterday," she said. "Baty didn't kill anybody. It was animal blood. He might be a deer hunter, or maybe the owner of the car is."

"So it was deer blood?"

"They didn't say that. They're still working on that. They'll let us know."

"Okay. I want you to keep an eye out for Rapper and Nellie today. I don't know if they've done all the damage they intend to do."

"I'll watch for them, but they don't show up a lot during the daytime, do they?"

"With those two," Rhodes said, "you never know."

"Did you hear the show?" Mikey Burns asked.

Rhodes had started to tell Hack to lie to Burns and say the sheriff was out on an investigation, but he'd changed his mind and taken the call.

"Some of it," Rhodes said.

"I thought it went pretty well. We got quite a few calls of support for the bow-hunting idea."

That wasn't good news, but Rhodes wasn't too worried about it. Once the other commissioners and the county judge found out that it would cost them quite a bit of money, they'd veto the idea. Besides, "quite a few" might mean two. Or even one.

"Munday had a great idea, didn't he?" Burns asked.

"I must have missed that part."

"He's going out to interview the Chandlers tomorrow. He's going to get them to talk about their animal shelter and see if they can justify saving any feral hogs."

"That does sound interesting," Rhodes said, thinking that Munday was just trying to stir up trouble. "What does he think he can accomplish?"

"He wants to start a dialogue with the community about my idea, and he thinks the Chandlers' would be the best place to get it going." Then Burns got to the important part. "I'll be there, too."

Rhodes could tell that Burns had gotten the radio bug. He liked being on the air and having people all over the county listening to him.

"Remote broadcasts don't always work out," Rhodes said.

"Munday's a pro, and the station's got a good engineer to set it all up. I'm not worried about it. There's one other thing."

It seemed to Rhodes that there was always one other thing. He asked what it was.

"We thought it would be a good idea if you were there, too."

Rhodes wondered why they thought that would be a good idea. He could think of only one reason. It would give Munday and Burns a chance to put him on the spot about both the hog hunting and the murders.

"What's in it for me?" he asked.

Burns seemed surprised that Rhodes

would ask. "Why, ah, you'd . . . get some good publicity. Sure enough. That's it. People would hear their sheriff tell them what a good job he's doing, how he's protecting the county and seeing that they're safe in their homes. Dialogue. You know the kind of thing."

Rhodes knew, all right. He knew that Burns and Munday didn't plan to give him a chance to brag on himself. He'd be lucky to get a word in.

"I'll do it," Rhodes said.

"You will?" Burns asked. "I mean, that's great. I'll tell Milton. He'll be tickled."

"I'm sure he will," Rhodes said.

The rest of the day went about as days usually did. There were a couple of minor traffic incidents, a dispute over a welding machine that escalated into a fistfight, a domestic dispute in which a woman brandished a knife at her husband, a little problem with public intoxication.

The only thing involving animals was a call from a woman named Janie Miles, who said there was a fuzzy black dog in her front yard, and it wouldn't leave.

"She says it's not her dog," Hack told Rhodes. "She says she wants to get rid of it, but she doesn't want it hurt."

"Tell her the animal control officer's on the way," Rhodes said.

Hack talked into the phone, then turned to Rhodes again.

"She wants to know if the animal control officer has a gun."

"Tell her he's not going to shoot the dog. Nobody is. Boyd's just going to pick it up and take it to the pound."

Hack told her.

"She wants to know what happens to dogs at the pound."

"The people there take care of them and try to find them a home."

"What if nobody wants them?"

"Maybe that won't happen," Rhodes said.

Hack talked some more.

"She wants you to come over there," Hack said.

"It's Alton Boyd's job."

"She heard Milton Munday's show today, and she thinks everybody in the county wants to kill all the animals that are roaming around loose."

Rhodes could see how she might have gotten that idea.

"Tell her I'll come," he said. "Then call Alton and tell him to meet me there. I'm not adopting any more dogs, though."

"I'll tell her," Hack said.

■ ■ ■ ■

The dog was fuzzy and black, all right. That was as close as Rhodes could come to identifying its breed. It could have used a bath.

"Someone threw it out on me," Janie said. She was about sixty, with gray hair and a wide, pleasant face. "I don't know why people do things like that."

Rhodes didn't know, either. He and Alton Boyd looked the dog over. Boyd took his unlighted cigar from his mouth and said, "I don't think he's going to hurt anybody."

"Why not?" Janie said.

" 'Cause he's just about blind. He's probably lost and afraid."

"Oh, the poor thing."

The dog wagged its tail.

"He's hungry, too, I'll bet," Boyd said. "He looks fairly good, but he ought to see a vet."

"Will the pound get a vet to look at him?"

"Eventually," Rhodes said.

He felt sorry for the dog, but he was sure Ivy would kill him if he took it home.

"My husband always liked dogs," Janie said. Rhodes could tell she was having a change of heart already. "We had one right up until he died last year. My husband, I mean. He's the one who died last year, not the dog. The dog died a year or so before that. I've been kind of lonesome ever since. Since my husband died, I mean."

"This is a good dog," Boyd said. "He just needs somebody to take care of him. He'd need some looking after, but he'd be good company for somebody."

Janie looked at the dog. "You think I could take care of him?"

"Sure you could. He'd be a lot better off with somebody who'd do that than he would in the pound."

"What if he didn't like me?"

Boyd reached down and rubbed the dog's head. The dog's tail wagged furiously.

"He likes ever'body," Boyd said. "Come on over here."

Janie walked over, and when Boyd encouraged her, she leaned over and patted the dog's head. His tail wagged again.

Janie looked up at Boyd. "I'm going to name him Henry," she said. "That was my husband's name. You think he'd mind? My husband, I mean. Not the dog."

"I think he'd be proud," Boyd said. "You want me to take him to the vet for you and get him checked out? Dr. Slick could call you when Henry's ready to come home."

"That would be just fine," Janie said.

Boyd went to his truck and got a light rope that he tied around Henry's neck.

"You follow me, Henry," Boyd said.

He started toward his truck, giving a little tug on the rope. Henry followed right along. So did Rhodes.

"You're really good," Rhodes said. "I'm glad the county hired you."

Boyd grinned at the compliment, the cigar right in the middle of his mouth.

"You mean good with people or good with animals?"

"Both," Rhodes said. "I wish we could find some way to take care of the wild hogs the way you took care of Henry here."

Hearing his new name, Henry wagged his tail.

"Ain't gonna happen," Boyd said. "I don't like killing animals, either, but there's a big difference in Henry and in those hogs. Henry's not hurtin' anybody or anything. The hogs're overrunnin' the county, just like Milton Munday says they are."

Another Milton Munday fan.

"We can trap some of 'em," Boyd went on, "and we can hope some of 'em move on, but if they do, they'll just move on to other counties. We can kill a few, but there's too many of 'em. I don't know what we're gonna do about 'em, but I'm pretty danged sure we can't hunt 'em all down."

"Not even with bows?" Rhodes asked.

Boyd helped Henry into a cage in back of the van and closed the cage door. Henry didn't seem to mind.

"That's the silliest thing I ever heard of," Boyd said.

Rhodes was glad he agreed. "How'd you like to be on the radio?"

"You mean like on Milton Munday's show?"

"Not *like* Munday's show. That's the one you'd be on."

"That'd be fun," Boyd said. "I'd like it a lot. How you gonna get me on?"

"The broadcast tomorrow's going to be a remote from the Chandlers' animal shelter. You be at the jail at six thirty, and I'll pick you up."

"Hot dog," Boyd said.

CHAPTER 25

In addition to Boyd, Rhodes invited a couple of other guests to go with him to the Chandlers' animal shelter. Ruth Grady was at the jail at the appointed time, and she had Ed Garver with her.

"Did he give you any trouble?" Rhodes asked.

It was a cool morning, and Rhodes was wearing a light windbreaker, but there was plenty of sunshine, or there would be when the sun was well up. There was no wind at all. Rhodes and Ruth stood well away from the cars so that Garver, who was still in Ruth's cruiser, couldn't hear them talking.

"No trouble at all," Ruth said. "He's happy to be on the radio and talk about hog hunting."

Everybody wanted to be a star.

"Good," Rhodes said. "I wouldn't want him to start anything."

"You don't have to worry about that. He

knows what's what."

Alton Boyd drove up in his van.

"What about Alton?" Ruth asked. "Did you tell him anything?"

"No. He's just going along to tell everybody what a bad idea it is to let a bunch of bow hunters loose in the woods with deputies to guide them."

"What's the matter with Mikey Burns, anyway?" Ruth asked. "Doesn't he know that we have real jobs to do?"

"He's just trying to score some political points," Rhodes said. "He knows the bow hunting wouldn't help, but he thinks it would look good to the voters."

"I'm surprised he isn't lobbying for hunters to come in and shoot from helicopters."

"I'm pretty sure he knows that wouldn't go over."

"You are? I think there are people who'd like for it to happen. Milton Munday for one."

"Maybe we won't have to worry about him for much longer," Rhodes said.

"We can hope."

"Hope what?" Alton Boyd asked as he joined them.

"Hope we all sound good on the radio," Rhodes said. "Are you ready to go?"

"You bet. I turned on the radio when I left home, and I told Donna Lou not to turn it off till the Milton Munday show was over."

Donna Lou was Boyd's wife. She was as good with animals as Boyd was and liked them just as much.

"You mean she's not a Milton Munday fan?" Rhodes asked.

"She'd rather watch TV," Boyd said, "but I told her I was gonna be on the air. She wouldn't want to miss out on that."

"I don't blame her," Rhodes said. "We might as well get on out there. We don't want them to start without us."

"We sure don't," Boyd said. "I never been on the radio before."

Garver got out of Ruth's cruiser and walked over. He looked anxious rather than eager.

"What are we waiting for?" he asked.

"Not a thing," Rhodes said. "Let's go."

The setup at the Chandlers' place was simple enough. The KCLR van that carried the sound equipment was parked at one end of the circular drive in front of the house. Mikey Burns's red Solstice was parked behind the van. Rhodes stopped behind the

Solstice, and Ruth Grady was right behind him.

A table was set up at the side of the van, and an awning stretched from the top of the van to shade it. The side of the van was open, and Rhodes could see the broadcasting equipment inside with the sound man. Burns and Munday sat at the table. Wireless microphones and earphones were in front of them, along with a couple of notebooks and a digital clock with large numbers. The earphones were the old-fashioned kind that covered the ears.

Janice Chandler sat beside Burns, and Andy was next to her. Janice didn't have on a bonnet, and Rhodes got a good look at her. She wasn't wearing any makeup, and she didn't look young this time. She looked twice Andy's age, and maybe she was.

Everybody had a mug of coffee, but nobody was drinking any. They must have been nervous about going on the air.

Burns and Munday looked a little surprised when Rhodes and Boyd walked up, with Ruth and Garver close behind.

"What's going on, Sheriff?" Munday asked. "I didn't know you were bringing a posse."

Ah, that quick radio wit. Rhodes was impressed.

"I thought these people might have some-thing to contribute," Rhodes said. "Alton Boyd's our animal control officer, Ruth Grady's a deputy, and Ed Garver's a hog hunter, so they all fit right into your topic for today."

Munday didn't look convinced. "We don't have enough mics for everybody. We'll have to swap around."

"That won't be a problem, will it?"

"I guess not," Munday said. He gave Burns an accusing look. "You should've told me about this."

Burns pleaded ignorance and shifted the blame where it belonged. "Sheriff Rhodes neglected to tell me that he was bringing anybody with him."

"I didn't think it mattered," Rhodes said. "I just wanted to be sure we had the subject covered. Is there coffee for everybody?"

"We have some in the van," Munday said.

"I don't drink it myself," Rhodes said. "Anybody want a cup?"

Nobody did, or at least nobody admitted it.

"How long before the program starts?" Boyd asked.

"We still have a few minutes," Munday said after a glance at the digital clock. "Let me tell you how I'll handle things. Commissioner Burns will be first. I'll ask him about the hog situation, and after he fills us in, I'll move to the Chandlers. When they have their say, I'll do some commentary. After that, we'll get to you and your friends, Sheriff. How does that sound?"

"Sounds all right to me," Rhodes said. "This is a dialogue, right?"

"Right," Munday said. "We want everyone to have a say."

"So we'll have time to respond to your commentary."

"That depends." Munday patted a notebook. "We have commercials to do, and we don't want to make any of the sponsors unhappy."

Burns laughed. No one else did.

"This isn't a solemn occasion," Munday said. "We're here to have fun."

"I'm sure we will," Rhodes said. "Well, some of us will. How about it, Alton?"

"You bet. I'm ready to get on the air."

Munday got some kind of signal from the man in the van, and he put on his headphones. Burns followed suit. The man in the van started a countdown.

Rhodes hadn't noticed a little bar that sat on the front of the table, but he did when it flashed red letters that read ON THE AIR.

"Good morning, Blacklin County," Munday said. "Welcome to the first hour of the Milton Munday show, coming to you live from Janice and Andy Chandler's animal shelter. We're brought to you today by your friends and neighbors at Tacker Auto Supply, Wagner's Feed and Seed, and Billy Lee's pharmacy."

With that, Munday launched into a pitch for auto supplies that featured the folksy personal approach. Munday himself had been in the store only a couple of days ago, he said, in dire need of a new alternator for his car.

"And do you know what? Good old Doug Tacker himself was there, and he not only sold me the alternator but he told me where to take my car to get the alternator put on. I swear, folks, you just can't go wrong if you visit Doug when you need any kind of auto parts. Why, he's got it all, and more."

Munday went on in that vein for so long that Rhodes wasn't sure there'd be any time for the guests, but after a while Munday stopped his praise of Doug Tacker and said, "Our first guest today is Commissioner Mikey Burns, the man who keeps the trees trimmed, the ditches clean, and the county roads fit to travel. He's going to tell us about a big problem in this county, one we've talked about on this program before." He lowered his voice. "Wild hogs." His voice returned to its normal tone. "Is there anything we can do about this menace, Commissioner Burns?"

Burns talked about the menace, with, Rhodes thought, some exaggeration. Make that a lot of exaggeration.

"Is there anything that we can do?" Munday asked, and Burns told about his wonderful plan.

Rhodes tuned him out. He watched the Chandlers, who sat there with tight-lipped disapproval, waiting their turn. They had to wait quite a while because after Burns finished, Munday got started on the miracles of modern medicine that were wrought daily at Billy Lee's pharmacy, which Munday had also visited only a couple of days earlier right after his stop at the auto parts store. No wonder the sponsors, not to mention the KCLR station manager, loved him.

When he was talking, Burns handed the mic to Janice Chandler. He didn't offer her the headphones, so Rhodes supposed she could do without them.

Munday finished his spiel and introduced Janice.

"Here's a woman who's come into Blacklin County and spent a fortune on a big spread in the country," Munday said. "Her name's Janice Chandler, and she's taking care of animals that don't have anybody else to help them. That's good, right? Everybody loves cats and dogs. They're cute, and they're cuddly, and dogs are a man's best friend. Cats are a little snooty, but they keep us company and make us feel good.

"It's not just dogs and cats out here at the Chandlers' shelter, though. It's bigger animals, too. Like hogs. Wild hogs. They're not cute, and they're not cuddly. You've heard Commissioner Burns's take on them, but Ms. Chandler feels differently about those hogs. If they're wounded, and if she can get to them, she'll help them. She's even protective of the ones running loose all around us. Ms. Chandler, how can you justify such a thing?"

Ms. Chandler didn't look pleased at the question. "I thought we were going to talk about the good work my son and I are doing here, not about feral hogs."

"The hogs are part of the work, aren't they? Or maybe you don't regard your work with them as being good. It's something my listeners would like to know about."

Andy stood up and loomed. His size made it easy for him. Rhodes took a step toward him, but he wasn't needed. Janice raised a hand, and Andy sat back down.

"All right, Milton," Janice said. Her voice was calm and level. "This is how it is. We care about animals here, and we care *for* animals here. It doesn't matter to us what kind of animals come here or are brought here. We take care of them. We don't have any prejudices. Does that answer your question?"

"You have a fine accepting attitude," Munday said, "but why save animals that other folks here in the county regard as a menace to society?"

Rhodes remembered a movie from a long time ago. He wondered if Munday had seen it. Probably not.

"The hogs have as much right to live as any other animal," Janice said.

"Commissioner Burns might not agree with that."

"That's his right."

"We have to break for a commercial now," Munday said, "but we'll be right back and hear how Sheriff Dan Rhodes feels about this issue."

Munday took off his headphones and laid them on the table. Burns followed his lead. Rhodes assumed that the commercial this time was prerecorded. He didn't know how long it would run, so he went over and took

Janice's place in the chair.

"I'm leaving," she said as she stood up. "Let's go, Andy."

"You should wait," Rhodes said. "You might be interested in my opinion."

"I don't think so."

"At least give me a chance."

Janice looked at Andy, who shrugged.

"All right. We'll stay, but I think we were ambushed."

She glared at Munday, who gave her a complacent smile in return.

Munday got some kind of signal from the man in the trailer and put his headphones back on. Rhodes took the pair that Burns had used, hoping that the commissioner didn't have any infectious ear problems.

"We're back, friends," Munday said, "and before I talk to the High Sheriff, I want to say a good word on behalf of my good buddy Wash Walker over there at Walker's Feed and Seed. I know he's listening right now because he always has the radio at the store tuned to KCLR when I stop by, and he goes in early every day so he can be ready and waiting if someone needs a sack of feed before going to work."

There was more in that vein, but Rhodes had stopped listening. He was thinking about what he was going to say if Munday asked him the right questions. He was counting on Munday's doing it. After all, Munday had ambushed Janice Chandler in a way, so he was just as likely to ambush Rhodes.

Or try to.

"You be sure to see Wash for all your feed and seed needs," Munday said in concluding his commercial. "Now, as I promised you, our next guest is Sheriff Dan Rhodes. You probably know that Sheriff Rhodes is investigating a couple of murders that are tied directly to the wild hogs in Blacklin County, and now we're going to find out why the killer is still on the loose. How about it, Sheriff?"

Rhodes grinned. He'd known he could count on Munday.

"How about what?" he asked.

"How about the killer that's roaming the county? Why haven't you put him behind bars? When are you going to make Blacklin County a safe place to live in again?"

Rhodes couldn't resist having a little fun with Munday. He tried to sound puzzled by the questions. "You mean if I catch the killer, the hogs won't be a menace anymore?"

"No, Sheriff, that's not it. The hogs will still be a menace."

"To society?" Rhodes asked.

Munday looked at Rhodes as if he might have begun to regret having invited him on the show.

"To all of us," Munday said. "As is the killer that's hiding who knows where. What are you doing about that?"

"I'll tell you the truth," Rhodes said. "I don't think the killer is hiding."

"You don't? Where is he, then?"

"He's closer than you think."

"If you know where he is, Sheriff, why don't you let us in on the secret?"

"All right," Rhodes said. "I will. Do we have time before the next commercial?"

"Don't worry about the commercial. Everybody will rest easier if they know the killer's been caught."

"I didn't say he's been caught. I said he's closer than you think."

"How close?" Munday asked.

"Close enough," Rhodes said. He looked at Ed Garver. "He's right here with us."

Chapter 26

Munday looked stunned. His mouth opened, but no words came out.

Garver didn't look happy, but he walked over to Rhodes, who stood up and handed him the mic.

Since Munday wasn't using his mic and appeared to be speechless, Rhodes took it from the host's hand.

"What's going on here?" Mikey Burns asked. "Are you saying that Ed Garver's the killer?"

"In case you didn't hear that," Rhodes said to the radio audience, "Commissioner Burns just asked if the next guest was the killer. The guest he's talking about is Ed Garver, who works for our good friend Trey Allison at Allison's Plumbing. If you have a stopped-up drain or a broken pipe, give old Trey a call. He'll get somebody right out to solve your problem."

Everyone was looking at Rhodes. He

grinned, thinking he might be able to get his own talk show if things kept on going well.

Munday wasn't grinning. He stood up and grabbed at the mic, but Rhodes backed away.

"Ed Garver," Rhodes said, "isn't a killer, but I think he can identify the killer. Ed got separated from some other hunters the other night when Hoss Rapinski was shot, and Ed got a look at the shooter. He's here today to tell us who that shooter was. Isn't that right, Ed?"

Garver looked nervous and unhappy. It was clear that he didn't want to say anything, and he didn't.

"Ed?" Rhodes prompted. "You did see the suspect, didn't you?"

Garver nodded.

"The listeners can't see you nod, Ed. You'll have to speak up."

Garver cleared his throat and said something, but nobody could understand it. Before Rhodes could ask him again to speak, Munday made another grab for the mic. He wasn't successful, so he left Rhodes and headed for Garver.

Things were beginning to go bad. Rhodes had thought it would be simple enough for Garver to play his part, but he hadn't counted on mic fright. Since Garver hadn't seen the killer at all, Rhodes had thought that the threat of a revelation would make the killer confess. It worked in old movies, but it wasn't working on radio.

Garver cleared his throat. "That's him," he said, and he pointed at Andy Chandler.

"They can't see you pointing at Andy Chandler, Ed," Rhodes said.

At this point, Ruth was supposed to take over and arrest Chandler on suspicion of murder.

It didn't work out exactly like that.

Munday lunged at Rhodes and wrenched the mic away from him.

Andy Chandler grabbed his mother and shoved her into Ruth. Janice and Ruth fell in a tangle, and Andy sprinted around the radio van. Rhodes started after him. Janice, though she was hampered by Ruth, stuck out a foot and tried to trip him.

Rhodes stumbled, got his balance, and kept going. He thought he could hear Munday screaming into the mic, describing the action as if he were doing play-by-play at a football game.

Andy was headed for the house, and Rhodes figured he was going after some firepower. In reruns of *Perry Mason* that Rhodes had seen, the guilty party always jumped up in the courtroom when Mason pointed him out, and Lieutenant Tragg grabbed him. Simple as that. Rhodes wished that he'd been lucky the way Perry Mason was. Maybe he should have stationed himself closer to Chandler. He hadn't counted on Janice's interference, which was yet another rookie blunder.

The reasoning that had led Rhodes to Andy was simple enough, and Rhodes should have figured out that Janice was also involved. Two people come from nowhere with a lot of money, and nobody questions them when they say it's from an inheritance. They seem like civic-minded people, interested in good things and in the improvement of the community, but, as Burns had told Rhodes, they hadn't registered to vote. Could they have been worried that registering would have somehow led to something that revealed their past? Rhodes didn't know. They seemed like such nice people. Certainly nobody would suspect their money came from bank robberies.

Nobody but Gary Baty, and he knew the truth. He'd somehow discovered that his old partner had located in Blacklin County. Rhodes was sure that Baty was the one who'd slaughtered Baby the hog and put the bloody body parts at the Chandlers' place. The convenience store thefts had occurred when Baby's remains turned up, according to the crime reports Rhodes had checked, and, sure enough, traces of animal blood were in Baty's car. Rhodes figured the hog butchering had been done just to let Andy know that Baty had the goods on him. The Chandlers must not have realized at first that Baty was the hog killer, or they'd never have called Rhodes. When Baty revealed himself to them, he no doubt tried a bit of extortion. He'd met Andy, and they'd been headed to the Chandler place when Rhodes started chasing them. They'd abandoned the car because of the accident, and when they'd gotten into the woods, Andy had decided to get rid of Baty once and for all.

Andy and his mother had turned up in the woods both times there had been a death. Rhodes was pretty sure Andy had called Janice on a cell phone and had her meet him in the woods after Baty was killed.

Rhodes figured that Hoss Rapinski had talked to Andy the afternoon before his own murder. Rapinski couldn't have been sure Andy was the bank robber he was after, but he must have hinted something. He'd also made the mistake of telling Andy he'd be hog hunting. So much for Rapinski. His own rookie mistake had been a lot more costly than the ones Rhodes had made.

Things might not have happened exactly the way Rhodes had them figured, but Rhodes was certain his reconstruction was close to the truth. Andy had confirmed it by running.

Rhodes didn't know the extent of Janice's involvement, but he knew that Ruth was taking care of that end of things. He hoped Munday thought it made for good radio. A murder suspect on the run. Too bad it wasn't on television.

It wouldn't be much good for radio or TV, either, if Rhodes didn't catch Andy Chandler. Chandler had nearly reached the house, and Rhodes wasn't far behind. Rhodes had ditched his little .32 for the occasion and was carrying a .38 Police Special in a leather holster at the small of his back. It had been concealed by the windbreaker that he wore. Most law enforcement officers had given up revolvers for automatics with more firepower, but Rhodes was a traditionalist.

He didn't want to try to pull the pistol out while he was running, and he didn't want to stop running. So he yelled at Andy instead.

"Chandler! Stop and talk to me. We can

work this out."

Rhodes didn't mention that he'd already worked it out, and he was quite surprised when Andy stopped.

He was even more surprised when Andy proved that he, too, was carrying a pistol. Not a revolver, though. Rhodes didn't know where the gun had been, but it was in Andy's hand now. Rhodes dived to his left, off the asphalt driveway and onto the grass. He hit and rolled just as he heard the crack of the pistol. When he stopped rolling, he came to his knees with his own gun in his hand, but Andy had gone behind the house.

Rhodes holstered the revolver and went after him.

He didn't see Andy anywhere, but the animals were excited. Dogs barked. Hogs grunted. Horses whinnied. Cows bawled.

There was a large barn near the back of the animal pens. The barn door was open, and Rhodes went in that direction. He hadn't gone far when he heard a noise above the racket the animals made. It was the sound of an engine starting.

A big gray Toyota pickup erupted from the barn and bore down on Rhodes, who didn't have time to draw and shoot. He jumped out of the way, and as the pickup went by him, he reached out and grabbed

341

the tailgate. He was jerked off his feet and his arms nearly popped out of their sockets, but he held on.

It was quite an accomplishment, and it would be a lot more impressive if he managed to get himself into the bed before his arms separated from his body. As it was, he had all he could do to hang on. The toes of his shoes bounced in the dirt as the pickup pulled him along.

Rhodes knew that a good movie stuntman would be in the pickup bed in seconds. It was too bad he wasn't a stuntman.

After a few seconds, Rhodes realized that Chandler wasn't going back toward the radio van or the road. He seemed to be headed for the woods. Rhodes didn't know if that was good or bad. It was definitely bad if he couldn't get into the bed, because he knew he couldn't hang on much longer.

Rhodes tightened his grip on the tailgate and tried to swing his legs to the right. He didn't get them far enough to do much good the first time, but he was encouraged enough to try again. This time he succeeded in getting his heels onto the wide bumper that Andy had installed on the back of the pickup. With his feet braced on the bumper, Rhodes could push himself up enough to hook his arms over the tailgate. When he'd done that, he hauled himself over the top of the tailgate and into the bed. He lay on his back and tried to let his breathing get back to something resembling normal while he bounced around. He hoped Andy didn't know he was there. If he did, all he had to do was stop the truck and shoot Rhodes, who couldn't do a thing to stop him. His arms felt like boiled noodles.

The pistol dug into Rhodes's back, and his head bonged on the metal bed every time the pickup went over a bump, which was every time the wheels turned.

It wasn't easy, but Rhodes tried to think. Andy was going to bypass Ruth, which was probably a smart move for him, but to get across to the road, he'd have to go through the woods. Rhodes didn't see how a pickup could get through, but Andy might know a route that Rhodes wasn't aware of.

Rhodes got to his knees and reached behind his back for the pistol.

Andy made a sharp turn, and Rhodes fell over on his side. He slid and bumped his head, but he held on to the pistol.

Andy drove into the trees. Bare branches lashed the pickup. The tips skreeked along the side, scoring the paint. Rhodes stayed down to avoid being slapped in the face by the branches.

When they came to a clearing, Rhodes tried again to get up. He almost made it, but there was a hole in the ground that Andy must not have seen, and the pickup's front right wheel went into it.

The bumper of the pickup slapped the ground, and the bed whipped right, throwing Rhodes out. He landed hard and rolled over a couple of times before coming to a stop against the trunk of an elm tree. He spit out some dirt and pushed himself into a sitting position as quickly as he could. The pickup sat twenty feet away with the bumper dug into the dirt. Andy was gone.

Rhodes didn't know if Andy had seen him. He did know that the air bag in the truck had been disabled. Too bad that wasn't a felony.

Using the tree trunk to push against, Rhodes stood up. He didn't think he had any broken bones, just bruises and scratches. He couldn't hear anything other than the hissing of the radiator or a broken hose. Rhodes looked around to see if he could tell which way Andy had gone. No clues. Rhodes started in the direction of the county road. He limped a little at first, but by the time he crossed the clearing, he was jogging pretty well. He kept his pistol in his hand.

He wasn't far into the woods, and the ground was rutted and churned. Hogs had been there, rooting for acorns. That was no surprise, but what bothered Rhodes, aside from the difficulty of walking, much less jogging, was that the earth was freshly turned. The hogs had passed that way not long before. They rambled at night and went into hiding during the day. Nobody hunted them in daylight.

Rhodes thought he heard Andy thrashing through the trees ahead of him. Andy wasn't trying to keep quiet, so it was likely he didn't know Rhodes was after him. Rhodes hoped to catch up with him and take him by surprise.

Unfortunately, the hogs surprised Andy first. Rhodes had just caught sight of him through the trees when Andy stumbled into an area of fallen branches that some of the sows had taken for nesting with their young. The sows didn't take at all well to being disturbed, especially with the little ones nearby. Rhodes heard the grunting and then the squealing.

Andy skirted the place where the sows congregated, but the noise of the sows aroused some of the boars. Rhodes drew his pistol, even though it wouldn't be much protection against a feral hog. He didn't think Andy's automatic would be any better.

Andy heard the hogs and started to run. Most of the hogs stayed where they were, but not all of them. Rhodes heard a boar snort, and then it came crashing through the trees after Andy.

Rhodes stood still. He didn't see any point in attracting attention to himself. He hadn't started this, and as far as he was concerned, Andy's problems were his own.

Hogs didn't see too well, and since Rhodes had been a good distance behind Andy, he didn't think the boar had spotted him. If it had, it wasn't interested. It didn't even glance in his direction.

Andy was moving faster than Rhodes would've thought he could, dodging trees and jumping over fallen limbs. Within seconds he was out of sight. Rhodes followed at a slower pace, moving away from where the sows nested and being as quiet as he could. Let sleeping hogs lie, that was his new motto.

Even though he was going slowly, Rhodes caught up with the hog. He heard it before he saw it. Besides the snorting and grunting, there was another noise, almost like a hammer hitting a board.

Rhodes picked his way, being careful to

look as far ahead as he could. After he'd gone about fifty yards, he saw the big hog ramming the trunk of a tree. Not far above the hog, Andy sat on a limb. He had one arm wrapped around the trunk of the tree, and he held the automatic in the other hand. Rhodes started to yell at him and tell him that if he shot the hog, he'd only make it mad, but it was too late for that.

Andy pulled the trigger. Either because the hog shook the tree or because Andy was nervous, he missed.

Worse, he fell out of the tree.

Even worse, he landed on the hog.

Rhodes didn't know who was more surprised, Andy or the hog, which stood frozen for a second with Andy draped over its back. Then it bucked like a bronco, throwing Andy into the air. Andy did a flip and landed flat on his back. Rhodes heard something crack, but he thought it was a stick and not Andy's back. The pistol lay a few feet away from Andy, but he didn't make any move to get it. Rhodes didn't think he *could* move.

The hog could move, though. It pawed the ground and glared at Andy with beady black eyes.

Andy still didn't move. Rhodes didn't think that would save him. Being motionless hadn't saved Rhodes a few years before when he'd been the victim of an enraged hog.

It worked for Andy, however. The hog watched him for a full minute without moving. Then it turned and headed back in Rhodes's direction. Rhodes moved behind a tree and stood as motionless as he could. The hog took no notice of him.

When Rhodes was sure the hog was gone, he rounded the tree, expecting to see Andy still lying there, but Andy was gone.

The pistol was gone, too.

CHAPTER 27

Rhodes wasn't resentful that Andy's playing possum had kept him safe from the hog, but he wished the trick had worked for him. It didn't seem fair.

Andy no longer tried to keep quiet. Rhodes could hear him blundering along through the trees. Rhodes heard something else, too: a siren.

Rhodes started jogging again in an attempt to catch up to Andy. It didn't take him long. Andy had been hurt when he fell on the hog or when the hog had thrown him, and he was limping badly.

The siren sound got louder, and Rhodes saw Ruth's county car through the trees. She had pulled into the field, anticipating that Andy would drive the truck out and try to get to the road. She stopped the car and got out.

Andy saw her, too, and as he limped out of the trees, he fired his pistol. Rhodes heard the shot. He saw the bullet dimple the car door, but he didn't hear the sound.

Ruth wasn't in much danger. She had crouched behind the front of the car so the engine would protect her from bullets. Rhodes knew she wouldn't fire back at Andy, because she didn't know where Rhodes was and wouldn't take a chance of hitting him by accident. Considering that he was in the line of fire, Rhodes was glad she was being careful.

Andy pulled the trigger again, and another bullet hit the cruiser. Mikey Burns and the other commissioners weren't going to like that. Ruth took a quick glance over the hood of the car and ducked back down.

Andy stayed where he was for the moment. He couldn't go forward with Ruth blocking his way, and the hogs were behind him in the woods. So was Rhodes, who still wasn't sure if Andy knew he was there. Andy knew, though, and he must have decided that he had a better chance against Rhodes and the hogs than against Ruth. He was a bank robber, after all, and it takes a certain amount of nerve to go into a bank lobby and demand that the teller hand over the money, even if you have a gun and the teller doesn't.

When Andy made his decision, he didn't

waste any time. He turned back to the woods and started to run. Rhodes stepped out from behind a tree.

"Stop right there, Andy. We have you covered from two sides."

Andy wasn't impressed. He didn't stop running, not even when he raised his pistol and started to shoot.

Rhodes wasn't too worried about being shot. Hitting a target is hard enough for someone who's standing still. Hitting something while running on unlevel ground is next to impossible. Andy might get lucky, but the odds weren't in his favor.

"Stop where you are, Andy," Rhodes said.

Andy wasn't listening. He didn't stop. A bullet hit a tree about five yards from Rhodes, and chunks of bark flew off the trunk.

Rhodes didn't want to shoot Andy, but it looked as if he didn't have much choice. He checked on Ruth. She was still hidden behind the car. Rhodes raised his pistol.

Andy stumbled. His arms windmilled as he tried to regain his balance, but he couldn't. He continued to run, leaning farther and farther forward. After a couple of steps, he was almost parallel to the ground. He stretched his arms in front of him and landed facedown. The pistol went off, but the bullet didn't come anywhere near Rhodes, who ran out of the trees and kicked the gun out of Andy's hand.

Andy tried to get up.

"Not a good idea," Rhodes said. "Just lie there still and quiet for a while."

Rhodes looked toward the county car. Ruth was already on her way over. She had her handcuffs ready.

"Hands behind your back," Rhodes said to Andy, who complied without bothering to argue.

"Did you shoot him?" Ruth asked as she walked up.

"No," Rhodes said. "He fell. Cuff him."

"Glad to," Ruth said, and she did.

Andy wasn't the only one who was cuffed. When they got back to the KCLR van, Rhodes saw that Janice Chandler also had a pair of cuffs on and was sitting in a chair. Buddy watched her, his hand only a few inches from the butt of his .38. Like Rhodes, Buddy was a traditionalist.

"How'd Buddy get here so fast?" Rhodes asked Ruth before they got out of the county car. Andy was safely stashed in the backseat.

"He was listening to the radio show," Ruth said. "When he heard what was going on, he drove out here. Got here just in time, too."

"He didn't try to shoot anybody, did he?"

"No, but he did ask Ms. Chandler if she felt lucky."

"He loves that line," Rhodes said. "I take it she didn't feel lucky."

"No. I was pretty much in control by then anyway. Buddy cuffed her, and I went to look for you."

"You were just in time, like Buddy. How about Alton?"

"He was great. He's the one who pulled Ms. Chandler off me just before Buddy got here."

They got out of the car. Milton Munday waved them over.

"Here they are now, folks, Sheriff Dan Rhodes and his courageous deputy Ruth Grady. They've captured the killer, and I can see him sitting in the backseat of their car right now. He appears to be very subdued. Maybe we can get the sheriff to say a few words for us. How about it, Sheriff?"

He stuck the microphone out at Rhodes, who walked up to it and said, "Just doing our job."

Munday pulled the mic back. "How about that, folks. Just doing their job and keeping Blacklin County safe. We can be proud that we have a fighting sheriff like Dan Rhodes and deputies like Ruth Grady to watch our backs."

Rhodes was amazed at how suddenly his reputation had turned around. He looked at Mikey Burns, who was shaking his head in agreement with Munday. Then he looked at Buddy, who looked a little miffed.

Rhodes gestured for the mic, and Munday handed it to him.

"Let's not forget Buddy, here. He's another of the county's fine deputies. In fact, you could say that he's the Dirty Harry of Blacklin County, and without him we'd never have subdued one of the Chandlers. Take a bow, Buddy?"

Buddy, grinning like a schoolboy, took a bow. It probably didn't even occur to him that no one could see him. As soon as he completed the bow, he turned back to Janice Chandler, watchful and serious as ever.

"Then there's Alton Boyd," Rhodes said. "He's the county's animal control officer, but he helped control a different kind of animal today. Thanks, Alton."

Boyd smiled and waved. Rhodes didn't know who he was waving to, but maybe Alton had somebody in mind.

"Finally, let's not forget Ed Garver," Rhodes said.

Garver was beside Burns, and Burns stuck out a hand for Garver to shake. Rhodes wished they were on TV.

"It was Ed Garver's testimony that helped us bring this whole thing off," Rhodes said. "Remember, Ed works at Allison's Plumbing, and they can take care of all your plumbing needs. Give them a call, and maybe Ed Garver will show up at your house to help you out."

"Are you getting a kickback?" Ruth whispered.

Rhodes grinned and handed the mic back to Munday. The broadcast went on for a while after that, but Rhodes and the deputies didn't stick around to hear the rest. Ruth and Rhodes drove back to town in her cruiser with Andy, and Buddy took Alton Boyd back with Janice stashed in the rear seat. There was no room for Garver, so he stayed until Mikey Burns could give him a ride back to town.

Rhodes thought it would take a while to get confessions from the Chandlers, but he hoped to play them off against each other and find out the whole story that way. It worked out pretty much like that, and as it turned out, things had happened just about the way Rhodes had it figured. There was one surprise, however. Rhodes had been right about Baty and Andy having been on the way to the Chandler place when he started chasing them, and he'd been right about Andy calling Janice. It was Janice, though, who'd brought the pistol to the woods, and she was the one who'd killed Baty. Or at least that was Andy's story. Janice said it was all a lie, which was fine by Rhodes. He'd go on letting them implicate each other until they got tired of it and he got the whole story.

That is, he would if Randy Lawless didn't stop him. The Chandlers had refused to say a word after they had a lawyer, and of course they'd gone for the best in the county. Rhodes wasn't worried. Lawless had never come out ahead of him yet, and he hadn't been successful in keeping the Chandlers quiet so far.

Jennifer Loam was a bit annoyed with Rhodes for using the radio show to stage the capture. She told him he was contributing to the downfall of newspapers, but she was only kidding. Or so Rhodes hoped. He promised her an exclusive interview as soon as the Chandlers confessed, and that was pretty much it, except for one thing.

The phone call came two days after the Chandlers were arrested. Hack answered, listened, and looked at Rhodes.

"This is for you. I don't know who it is. Line two. You want to take it?"

Rhodes picked up the phone. "This is Sheriff Rhodes."

"Yeah. This is Lenny Rapinski."

Rhodes knew the voice immediately. Hack had known, too, no matter what he'd said, and he grinned widely. Rhodes knew why. *Lenny?*

"Hoss's brother," Rapper said, as if Rhodes might not know.

"What can I do for you, Lenny?" Rhodes asked.

"I hear you got the guy who killed my brother."

"You heard right."

"That's good. I give you credit."

"Thanks," Rhodes said.

"That doesn't mean anything's changed between you and me, though."

"I never thought it did."

"You messed up my leg again. It got infected. I can't hardly walk on it now."

"I'm sorry to hear that."

"Yeah, I bet you are."

"Thinking it over, though, I believe you're the one who hurt your leg, not me."

"It was your fault."

"I don't see it that way."

Rapper didn't say anything.

"Seems like you get hurt every time you come to Blacklin County," Rhodes said. "Might be best if you stayed away from now on. Sooner or later, I'm going to get you in jail on a charge that will stick. Like some of the assault charges you accumulated on your last trip."

"I wouldn't count on it. Anyway, I just wanted to say you did good, and I appreciate it. That's as far as it goes."

"You're lucky you didn't hurt anybody more seriously."

Rapper didn't answer. He'd already ended the call.

"Who was it?" Hack asked.

"You know who it was."

"Rapper. He's a sharp one. Never gives anything away."

"I wouldn't say that. Now we know his real name."

"You gonna run a check on him?"

"Sure, but I doubt it'll do any good. He's lived off the grid for so long that he might not even have a record as Lenny Rapinski."

"Prob'ly not. You think he'll be back?"

Rhodes rapped his knuckles on the top of the desk.

"I think we can count on that," he said.

The employees of Thorndike Press hope you have enjoyed this Large Print book. All our Thorndike, Wheeler, and Kennebec Large Print titles are designed for easy reading, and all our books are made to last. Other Thorndike Press Large Print books are available at your library, through selected bookstores, or directly from us.

For information about titles, please call:
   (800) 223-1244

or visit our Web site at:
   http://gale.cengage.com/thorndike

To share your comments, please write:
   Publisher
   Thorndike Press
   10 Water St., Suite 310
   Waterville, ME 04901